CREEP

ER BOOKS BY RON G. HOLLAND

Get Out of Debt and Into the Money

Talk and Grow Rich

Turbo Success

Escape From Where I Am

Disciple of Mammon *

* Is written under the pen name of John T. Foster. It is the sequel to The Creep, and is due to be published in the near future. Look out for it in all good bookstores.

THE
CREEP

JOHN T. FOSTER

EUREKA PUBLISHING GROUP

This paperback edition first published in 1994 by
Eureka Publishing Group
BCM Box 8061
London WC1N 3XX

A CIP catalogue record for this book is available
from the British Library

ISBN 1 871040 02 7

Edited by Richard Glyn Jones
Jacket design by Trevor Webb
Printed and bound by Cox and Wyman, Reading

10 9 8 7 6 5 4 3 2

this book is dedicated to Anita, the only girl I ever really loved

PREFACE

Each year, over 24,000 people in America are murdered. But that figure never accounts for serial killers like Bishman.

Many serial killers victims are never found and are often just listed as missing persons.

Bishman is the man nobody would notice, but everyone should fear. He doesn't need a reason to kill. Perhaps that's why, when Bishman walks into the consulting room of the world's leading hypnotherapist, Bill Harvey - and the reader - can't help but want to know more.

In the true tradition of *The Silence of the Lambs* what unfolds is a full blooded account of a cold blooded killer, driven by the insatiable need to take everything life has to offer - and then take life itself.

But if you're expecting a cosy ending with justice prevailing, forget it. Life - and death - are never quite that simple.

WARNING: *The Creep* contains scenes of explicit sex and violence that some readers may find too strong.

ONE

It was late evening. The sun had gone down, but it was still plenty warm. Bishman found himself walking along the embankment of the Charles River. He was humming a variety of tunes, as was his way. This particular evening, he was going through some Beach Boys' and Beatles' hits. Over and over again.

A solitary jogger padded past. All the others had quit hours before. Like the sailboats moored on the other side of the river at the Yacht Club, they had all quit. A few bats dived and swerved in the heavy evening air, snatching up insects with unerring precision.

Bishman found a bench fifty yards up from the Harvard Bridge and sat down. A guy was already sitting there. He was probably taking in the solitude but that didn't concern Bishman, who took out a cigarette and offered the guy one.

"Smoke?"

"Yeah, sure," replied the stranger.

"It's good here," said Bishman, "I'm just passing through on my way to Detroit," nodding toward the other side of the river, he continued; "I never knew Harvard over there was one big campus. You from round here?" Bishman lit his cigarette. The stranger had already lit his.

"Yeah. I go to MIT. I'm studying metallurgy, of all things."

"What's metallurgy? Sounds exciting," plied Bishman.

"Not really, it's the study of metals. We have to know all the metals - what elements make them up, strengths, weaknesses - all that sort of thing. It's more complicated than you think. There's some amazing metals out there these days. Incredible uses as well."

The stranger deliberately crushed the cigarette with his foot before it was finished.

"I was sitting here yesterday," began Bishman, "and a guy told me all about the markings on the bridge. A lot of people probably wonder what they are." Bishman took a deep breath of fresh air and continued smoking.

"Yeah, I've seen them. I've often wondered. There's one in the middle that reads *Halfway to Hell*," said the student, giving Bishman a quizzical look.

"Apparently one of the guys from a fraternity rolled all the way across the bridge to measure it. Each roll was a 'Smoot' - his name was Smoot, obviously. His friends marked it out, 40-Smoots, 50-Smoots and so on. The half-way point they called *Halfway to Hell*. At the end it's marked *364.4 Smoots and one ear*. The one I like best is 69-Smoots - that's called *Heaven*!"

2

The two of them roared with laughter. It wasn't that funny, but laughing was their way of saying, *I like talking to you. Let's talk some more.'*

"D'you smoke? I mean as in *smoke*?" Bishman tapped his trouser pocket, as if to signal he had something there - a joint maybe.

"Yeah, sure. What ya got?"

"A little Sinsemilla. Really good shit."

Bishman took out a crumpled joint and lit it. He took a long toke and passed it onto the guy, who took one himself.

"Let's walk," said Bishman, "I'd hate someone to come up behind us and tell us we're doing something illegal!" Bishman laughed and eased away. Without hesitation, the student followed.

The Charles River was like glass. The only ripples were caused by eight or nine ducks who were just treading water. A green bottle was lazily bobbing up and down. In the half light, a continuous stream of car lights flowed over the nearby bridge, their engines combining to create a constant monotonic drone.

They walked maybe two or three hundred yards from the bridge and sat on the embankment. Apart from the two of them, it was deserted. They smoked the joint and talked quietly.

Bishman calmly walked to the water's edge and picked up a large solid granite boulder. The guy appeared to know what was going to happen next but he didn't move. Bishman walked towards him and brought the boulder crashing down on his head. He was killed instantly. The boulder crushed the skull, releasing a mass of blood, grayish fluid, splintered bone and cartilage.

It was like a gazelle being run to ground by a lioness on the Serengeti Plains of Tanzania, submitting when it knew its time for death had come.

He's stone dead, thought Bishman as he carefully rolled the rock out into the water, scarcely making a splash. He dragged the body to the water's edge and left it there. Blood seeped into the river turning the surrounding water brown in the slowly ebbing light. Bishman picked up a pebble and skimmed it across the water. It bounced three times. He missed the bottle.

The victim was Charlie Stranberg, a twenty-three year old student from Boise, Idaho.

Detective Superintendent Howard Mainwarring wiped the sweat from his brow with a not-so-clean linen handkerchief. He was beginning to get frustrated, the traffic was slow, the heat unbearable, he almost slipped into a trance. What stopped him was the sounds of bugles, drums, trumpets and cymbals.

The changing of the guard at Buckingham Palace was in full swing as his black cab swung somewhat erratically into The Mall and headed down towards Whitehall.

Mainwarring was relishing the pomp and pageantry, and was wondering how the guards put up with the heat under their busbies.

4

He was also congratulating himself that he had persuaded Stan Barron, the supersleuth and forensic psychologist, not to join the FBI's Behavioural Science Unit in the States, but to stay in England with him, and help solve the serial killings that had taken place over the last five years.

Furthermore, he was looking forward to briefing Detective Sergeants Martinson and Flackman at New Scotland Yard, two key players, in his seventy-strong team.

TWO

When you see car chases like Steve McQueen's in *Bullitt* and the one with Gene Hackman in *The French Connection* it's thrilling, but there are people who drive like that in Britain, on a regular basis, without even realizing what they're doing, without even being filmed. Make McQueen and Hackman look like a coupl'a kids on the dodgems at the county fair.

Multi-millionaire Bill Harvey, world renowned hypnotherapist, was peering out of his immaculate white Pontiac Firebird Trans-Am, embellished with a blue firebird decal on the hood, and blue racing stripe. It was parked on Westminster Bridge, overlooking the River Thames and the Victoria Embankment. Big Ben stood glistening in the early morning sun, monumental and majestic. This was to be the Trans-Am's last airing before he left for the States.

Harvey tried to get a cartridge into the tape-deck, but something had jammed.

There was a mobile vendor selling burgers and coffee on the bridge, and every now

6

and then cars would pull in. Harvey looked at his attractive passenger and said "It's a shame they don't sell pretzels or bagels like they do in the States. You can't beat it you know, bagels with cream cheese and lox." Harvey finally got the tape deck to work.

"You can't wait to get back out there, can you? I bet you've got a woman lined up already." Ginny whined in a pleasant, teasing sort of way.

"I haven't, and I've told you: I'll be busy." Harvey switched on the ignition and turned up the tape deck volume-loud. The song was *Be-Bop-a-Lula*, the singer was Gene Vincent.

A car pulled out from behind the Trans-Am and cut in close. It was a red XJS V12 Jaguar. The guy looked at Harvey and scowled. He gassed it hard and turned left at the lights, past the Houses of Parliament and went hurtling down Millbank. Harvey was immediately in hot pursuit - 90 mph and still accelerating.

The guy in the XJS knew what he was doing. This was a fast car and one very quick and skilful driver. The race was on and they very quickly followed the contour of the river.

He braked hard, and threw the Jaguar around the particularly tight left hand corner and over Chelsea Bridge at 100 mph, asking for trouble. Bill Harvey was with him all the way.

Harvey drifted the American muscle car round the roundabout at 75 mph plus, rear end chopping and hopping and trying to get away from him. He straightened out and could feel his pulse

7

begin to race. Within seconds he was up again to something over 90 mph.

Suddenly, to Harvey's horror, less than a hundred yards in front of him was an idiot pulling out of a side turning. The car just kept coming out into the middle of the road with another car right behind it, on a tow rope - a steel rope...*Fuck!*

Harvey had a slow-motion vision of hitting the tow-wire and pulling one of the cars into his right-hand side and the other car into his left, making a steel sandwich, his beloved Trans-Am being the filling. Harvey felt his heart in his mouth.

He hit the brakes, *hard*, and screeched to a halt. Tires smoking, he actually stopped on the steel tow rope...they were intact, but the XJS was getting away again.

The road was completely blocked, two cars across the road with a tow-rope stretched tightly between them.

Harvey sat. Ginny gawked, her mouth wedged open. Eight doors opened from the two cars and four Road Rats got out of each car. Road Rats are the Hell's Angels' opposition, except they drive around in cars----well, wrecks actually. They wear colors and carry around live rats, stuffed in their pockets and in their hair.

Each of the eight now converging on Harvey and Ginny carried a baseball bat, with nails driven through the business end. A formidable weapon. Disaster for tires, no good at all for bodywork, and they'd do your head in pretty bad, too. Indeed Mungo, their leader, had just finished serving his penance to society in Wormwood Scrubs for throwing a nun, that he had just raped, off the top of the Novotel Hotel in Hammersmith.

Harvey slammed the Firebird into reverse for twenty yards, braked, cogged into low and hit the gas. The Road Rats thought he was coming straight for them, the more quick-witted of them diving over the trunk of their car for cover, but at the last moment Harvey shot up onto the sidewalk, just missing a lamp-post and a road sign, before swerving back onto the road and hitting the gas.

Harvey built up speed fast: seventy, eighty, *Shit! Cyclist!* Down to 50 mph, up to 90 mph again. Queenstown Road has lots of tight bends in it. *Ooops!* He was all over the show, drifting, skidding, wheels spinning, tires smoking, jabbing at the steering wheel, *Be-Bop-a-Lula* still going flat chat. But the big Jaguar had disappeared. *Shit!*

Acting on some kind of hunch, Harvey swung down a side-road that opened out into a huge commercial vehicle park. Being Saturday it was completely empty, all except for one bright and shiny red XJS, parked right in the middle.

For twenty seconds Harvey paused on the perimeter of the vehicle park, pointing directly at the XJS. He cogged into low and left it there, held his left foot on the brake and revved the big seven and a half litre V8 flat chat with his right until it reached six thousand revs, then released his foot from the brake and all hell broke loose. The tires spun like catherine wheels, propelling Harvey directly towards the stationary XJS like an Exocet missile.

Harvey kept his foot to the floor, never faltering, not even for a fraction of a second. A twitch of the steering wheel at the very last moment and he shot past the XJS, missing it by a millimeter and then started making dozens of tiny jabs at the power steering, coaxing the big car into a deliberately provoked slide.

The Firebird began to drift around, Harvey's foot still flat on the floor, tires belching out smoke. The G-forces exerted were enough to slow the car down to the correct speed, so Harvey didn't have to lift his foot from the gas pedal when making the slide. He executed a perfect circle with a huge radius, completely under control and headed back towards the Jaguar. This time he passed it on the other side, again missing it by a millimeter.

Wheels still spinning, tires still belching smoke with bits of rubber flying in all directions, Harvey jabbed continuously at the power steering again, gently coaxing the big car into another complete drift, using only the G-forces to slow the vehicle down. Second circle complete, he was now back on the rubber tracks he'd made at the start.

He pulled up right next to the XJS, in a perfectly controlled skid. He had laid a perfect figure-of-eight in molten rubber. It looked good, too: perfect proportions. The smell of burnt rubber pervaded the atmosphere, tire smoke hung in the still, crisp morning air.

Harvey switched off the endless loop tape of Gene Vincent, got out and walked over to the Jaguar where the driver was just getting out. Jimmy Holmes was an old friend of Harvey's. He was going to be responsible for looking after Harvey's car collection while he was in the States setting up new franchisees.

They had an almighty chuckle about Harvey's antics, tied up a few loose ends, and went to get breakfast. They settled on the Hotel Russell. Harvey and Jimmy Holmes ate heartily. Ginny just nibbled.

Max Hatfield, Harvey's business manager, greeted him at Los Angeles International Airport on his first day back in the States. Within the next two weeks Harvey well and truly settled into Pinewood, the magnificent fifteen-bedroom, two-pool, ex-Charlie Chaplin mansion in Beverly Hills. Harvey knew the Los Angeles area pretty good. He'd never actually lived in Beverly Hills before, but he had lived in Santa Monica on and off and he sure knew a lot of people.

America was a tremendous challenge. Harvey was happy to be the figure-head of the International Organisation of Hypnotherapy, although he didn't want anything to do with the actual day-to-day running of the business or the one-on-one hypnotherapy. He saw himself in the same role as Colonel Sanders of Kentucky Fried Chicken fame. Merely a figurehead. Hey, why not?

Before Harvey left England he'd already decided that he wanted his office away from his home. He'd been tied to the International Organization Of Hypnotherapy headquarters in England for many years. He wasn't going to make *that* mistake again. The comprehensive I.O.H. headquarters were in Springfield, Missouri, not far from Max's thousand-acre ranch, but he had Max set him up an office in Pasadena. Small and efficient: just a reception area that doubled as the secretary's office and Harvey's consultancy room. Not that he intended doing any hypnotherapy.

Things were working out like a military operation, just as Harvey had visualized before he left England. Jai, his personal assistant, was there to greet him as he arrived.

"I know this is your first morning in, sir, but there are some messages for you. Max Hatfield has called a number of times from Springfield. Nothing important, he wants to know if you've settled in and if there's anything he can do for you. Here are the other messages. I've also had a string of telephone calls from a Mr. Bob Bishman who says he wants to see you about *personal problems*. I tried to explain that you weren't taking on private clients, but he keeps calling. What should I do?"

"Put him onto Max directly. He'll fix him up with a hypnotherapist in the L.A. area. What else?"

12

"That's all, sir. Would you like some coffee?"

"Yes I'd love some: black, no sugar and please call me Bill. We went over this at the interview, I won't tell you again. Bill - right?"

"Right sir. I mean Bill." Jai did that on purpose and gave a little flip of her leg as she walked out of the door, as secretaries sometimes do to humor and tease their bosses. Harvey loved it. *Simple things, right.*

THREE

Once a week Harvey flew his Lear jet to the I.O.H. headquarters in Springfield, Missouri to work with new franchisees. Everything Harvey did was covered in numerous books, videos and audio cassette programs that all the franchisees had bought as part of their package. The in-house hypnotherapists also did all the lectures and seminars that Harvey did. But nothing, not a single thing, could measure up to a performance by the master of hypnotherapy, the maestro himself, Bill Harvey.

"Give clients time to assimilate what you have told them," said Harvey as he loosened his loud Disney-imaged tie.

"Let me give you an example. If I said to you *first kiss*, then stopped to pause, you'd immediately conjure up images of your first kiss. You'd go into great detail, in your imagination, about the time, place, person, perfume, your feelings. Not because I said two words, *first kiss* but because I paused and allowed you time to assimilate the information. If I said *first kiss* and kept right on talking, I'd have you thinking about the next subject. Giving people time to *assimilate* what you have just told them is crucial."

"It allows you to mentally transport your client from where they are now to where you want them to be."

Harvey deliberately allowed *them* time to *assimilate* what he had just told them.

"Bill, you remember about two weeks back I told you about a Mr. Bob Bishman calling a number of times? Well, I did put him onto Max as you suggested but he's here right now, in the waiting-room. He says he won't go until he speaks to you. He's extremely insistent."

"OK Jai, bring him in." Harvey put down the phone, and thought. He really didn't want to take on private clients in America. He'd done years of practice and was feeling drained. But he knew persistent behavior when he saw it and he knew that if he refused to see this Mr. Bob Bishman that wouldn't be the end of it.

Jai knocked on the office door and entered.

"Mr. Harvey, this is Mr. Bishman whom I told you about." Jai showed Bishman into the wainscoted consultancy room.

"Is there anything else I can get you? Coffee perhaps?"

"No it's all right Jai, we'll fix our own coffees, thanks. Please hold all calls, no

interruptions whatsoever. You know what to do."
Jai smiled and left without saying anything.

"Make yourself comfortable. What can I
do to help?" Harvey motioned Bishman to pull up
a chair to the extravagant Australian Walnut desk
where he was sitting and they shook hands over it.

Harvey found himself looking at a man
five feet seven inches tall and what you would call
broad-shouldered and trim. He had a carefully
clipped moustache, short brownish hair and the
coldest expression you've ever seen. Sort of
intense. He wore brown corduroy trousers, a light
blue sweatshirt and sneakers. He looked
nondescript, an ordinary guy. He was smoking.

"Can I call you Dr. Bill? I know from
what I've read in all the magazines that everyone
does. I need your help." Bishman was not
backward in coming forward.

"Well, I must tell you, as you probably
know already, I'm not really in the States to take
on private clients. I'm here to make sure the
training programs for our franchisees are in place
and working properly, that sort of thing. All
somewhat boring really. I even have a business
manager, Max Hatfield, who does all the day-to-
day running of the business and sells the
franchises."

Harvey got up and filled two mugs with
coffee from the hissing Cona machine. "Cream,
sugar?"

"Yeah, cream and four sugars. Thanks."
Bishman took the coffee and lit another cigarette.
Harvey pushed a heavy glass ashtray towards him.

16

"Yes I know that - I've already spoken with Max - but what I have is something a little different. I know I need help and I also know you're the only one who can help me."

"How do you know that?" Harvey said in amazement. He was trying to elicit a response.

"Well I've read some of your articles in various magazines, and lots of the things you write about and do for druggies and alkies, like me, make a lot of sense. I've done a lot'a bad things to a lot'a people. You know, really bad. I've done a lot of Mario's bananas and cannibal's resin, speed, LSD and booze. Huh. Boogaloo. I've been in and out of detox, mental institutions, I've had electric shock treatments and a frontal lobotomy. I've had all sorts of medication. I was well fucked up, but I'm all right now. All I have now are these terrible depressions, headaches and nightmares, but I know you can cure me with your hypnotherapy treatment. I need a check-up from the neck-up."

"You've certainly been through a lot. Can I call you Bob? You're going to call me Dr. Bill, right. Tell me a little more about yourself and I'll see what I can do. Why don't you start at the beginning."

"How long have I got?" Bishman was serious. He finished his coffee and lit up again.

"I don't know about you, but I've got the rest of my life!" Harvey smiled. He knew he was already in the thick of it, but there was something about this guy that he liked. He could tell that his new client had been through a lot and perhaps had a highly intriguing story to tell. Harvey was a connoisseur of human nature and

17

couldn't resist the out of the ordinary. Such is the thirst for knowledge.

"The first time I ever took a drink was when I was fourteen years old and I drank a complete bottle of gin, chug-a-lug." He demonstrated by holding an imaginary bottle up to his mouth, tipping his head back and holding it there.

"I passed out for three days. My sister kept an eye on me. She told me my eyes rolled around in my head and I snored loudly and just slept for three whole days. Since that day, the one drink I've never been able to touch is gin, although I drink everything else. Gin makes me violently sick the minute I touch it.

"We used to drink and smoke dope and pop pills all day, every day. That was when I was fourteen, I'm now thirty-eight. We used to take bottles of liquor and beer up to the farmer's field at the back of my place and ride the pigs. We'd be as drunk as skunks and try to hang on to the fuckers for as long as we could. We used to get covered in shit and stuff but we just didn't care.

"One day we got hold of this kid and held him up by his ankles to shake him down for money, for booze. He only had a couple of bucks on him so we took him over to the laundromat and put him in the spin dryer for about ten minutes. When we let him out he was all red in the face and crying. He ran like hell." Bishman didn't smile or laugh. He just kept deadpan, his eyes bugging out of his head, those cold light blue eyes. Death eyes.

"One day we asked this bitch to give us money for booze, but she gave us a hard time. We

18

gave *her* a hard time. We slashed her tires and kept leaving dead rats on the back seat of her car and in her glove compartment. Harder than you'd think to slash the tires of a car. They're really tough. You need a bayonet. We'd take it in turns to phone her up and say her son was dead and leave messages on her answering machine to freak her out."

Bishman sat expressionless. Smoking, talking, talking, smoking. The ashtray filled up. The room was clear of smoke - luckily the air conditioning worked extremely well.

"Do you know what a serial killer is? Well I know quite a bit about serial killers. In fact I know there's the body of a five-year-old boy buried in a clump of trees not two miles from here...so I'm told.

"I'm not talking about the Hillside Strangler or Mack the Knife or The Boston Strangler, Henry Lee Lucas, Benny the Axe Man, or Melvin the Monster. I'm not talking about the ones you've heard of, the jerks who get caught. I'm talking about the professional serial killers who operate in the States today.

"All this stuff you read about in the newspapers is bullshit. It would frighten you, if you knew the truth. The newspapers will tell you, at any one time there are about one hundred and seventy serial killers on the loose and on an average they may kill about twenty or thirty people over a period of years. There are the jerks that get caught, like the Black Panther, Son of Sam, Peter the Pervert, John Wayné Gacy, The Goat Man - he only killed kids - Theodore Bundy, and the Driller Killer.

"The real serial killers don't get caught and they operate on a simple basis. There's a figure-of-eight loop that goes across America. New York to Los Angeles with about thirty-eight States in between. Texas is the heart of the figure of-eight-loop. That's why Texas has the highest murder rate in America. They start there and end there. It gets double whammy, if you like.

"The serious killer keeps on the loop and doesn't stop. He's on the move continually and I can assure you there are about fifty of these guys on the circuit, and they have killed over a thousand people each, say over a period or ten or fifteen years. They don't get caught because they know the rules of the game. I'll tell you what the rules are. Yeah, Boogaloo."

Harvey finished his coffee, although it was cold. He was deep in thought, taking it all in. He knew this guy was for real. He was intrigued and wondered where it would all end. A shiver went down his spine.

"First one is, don't get caught, but that's my joke." Bishman wasn't laughing, his ice-blue eyes just bugged out of his head like chapel hat pegs. Other than that he remained completely expressionless. He lit a cigarette from the butt of the last one. Harvey felt another cold shiver go down his spine.

"Another thing of course is that the statistics the police and press release are wildly out. Out of the twenty-five thousand people murdered in America every year they say only about five thousand go unsolved, which is bullshit. The reason it's bullshit is they don't include the files on the missing persons. Most of the serial killers' victims will never be found because they're buried under rocks and earth, six feet underground. So the real figure stands at about ten thousand murders a year unsolved. Instead of being listed as murder victims they're listed as missing persons, which throws the true unsolved murder figures right out.

"The serial killer is hard to track because he doesn't have an M.O. Every murder's different. He could be hiding in a closet in someone's home, waiting underneath someone's car or in the back of it. He might meet a hitchhiker, or come across someone on a river embankment or train carriage. He takes advantage of each situation as it arises and uses whatever weapons are to hand.

"The other thing is that men get raped all the time, just as much as women, but they hardly ever report it. The victim could be walking through a park and two guys, even one guy, jumps him and fucks him up the poop chute. Many times a serial killer will rape both female and male victims, whether they're dead or alive.

"The rules of the game are simple. The first one is that once you've killed someone you put the miles in. That's the biggest secret of all. Doesn't matter what a cop has as evidence, if you're a hundred miles away or better still thousands of miles away, what good are a few pubic hairs, skin samples from under a victim's finger nails, semen, blood or even fingerprints? It's a joke.

"The second thing is, if you steal something, make sure it's small and disposable.

Things like watches, rings, jewelry, antique pens, cash - they're OK, obviously. All things that can be thrown out of a car window and all things that the fences will pay you cash for; ten cents on the dollar, no questions asked. If the items are thrown out, then they're nothing to do with you. Don't ever get caught with anything that connects you to the scene of a crime. Many times I would even dump my sneakers and put on another pair so there was no dust or dirt from the crime scene. Sneakers cost about five bucks these days or you can pick them up at the Salvation Army for free.

"The last thing is, use safe parking techniques all the time, whether you own or borrow cars, even if you steal them.

"These jerks who get caught, they've got subconscious death wishes. They *want* to get caught. That's why they operate within a hundred-mile radius of where they live, they deliberately leave clues to alert the cops and show how big they are. They're too stupid to put the miles in. *Assholes*!

"The other thing that's obvious is, the serial killer never carries weapons. He uses weapons, but he never carries them, so he's never caught with anything that links him to a crime. There are weapons everywhere. Every job you do, every break-in has weapons, every household has a gun somewhere. At the very least they have kitchen knives or screwdrivers and hammers in the garage.

"When you're on the street there are weapons all around you can use. Iron bars, debris, two-by-fours, trash-can lids, rope, wire, bottles.

22

And when that runs out you have your bare hands, which are favored by a lot of serial killers anyway, boogaloo. *You always have your hands, you never leave home without them. Boogaloo.*"

He bugged his eyes and stared coldly. He was as cold as a witch's tit.

"There's killing in cold blood, and there's killing in hot blood. Serial killers always kill in cold blood. They have time to think and plan and are always prepared to put the distance in. Fights break out and weapons are flashed and people get killed in the heat of an argument. That's killing in hot blood. No plan. They're not prepared to leave the scene of the crime and they get caught."

Bishman picked up his coffee mug with more force than was necessary, he thought it was full, when in fact it was empty. The cup went right up in the air. Harvey noticed and topped up the coffees.

"As *you* know, making money takes power, but the ultimate power is taking lives in a controlled and orderly manner, as and when you please. Ask John F. Kennedy. He'd tell you the exact same thing, if he could. The ultimate power lies in a small cylinder, about one and a half inches long and half an inch in diameter. It's called a bullet." Bishman sat there for a moment without moving, as though he was stuck, then he reached out for a cigarette, which he lit with a bent paper match.

"Coming back to safe parking techniques, you were saying...?" Harvey raised his eyebrows, as if in questioning.

23

"Oh yeah, I lost my train of thought. It's obvious really, but so many people get caught because they park their car in the wrong spot. You have to look out areas to see where your car will fit in, where your car looks the same as others and you won't stick out like a sore thumb. Important if you're doing a burglary or abduction in a well-to-do neighborhood.

"It's best to park your car well away from where you actually commit the crime, then walk back to your car in your black track suit which you shed on the way back to the car. The last thing you lose are your sneakers. You can drop these in a trash can as you drive away. The other thing is, always park with the car facing outwards, just in case you have to make a quick getaway. Never use angle parking where you'd have to reverse into a busy main road.

"OK, it's all common sense, but you've got to remember most serial killers get caught by accident, doing the most stupid things.

"I used to spend hours laying on my bed fantasizing all sort of things. Rape, murder, sex, what it was like to have a baby. That's an interesting one. If you've wondered what it would be like for a guy to have a baby, imagine swallowing a grapefruit...whole. I'd fantasize ripping women, shooting and just about every sexual fantasy you can think of. I'd lay there for hours. In actual fact I've carried out most of my fantasies.

"The first time I decided to go out and kill someone I put a .357 Magnum and a shovel in the trunk of my beat-up Mustang and I drove around looking for a hitchhiker. I drove around for a complete summer and I never saw a soul. The thing was, every time I drove around a rotary or went around a corner quickly the gun and shovel would slide from one side of the trunk to the other and frighten the shit out of me."

Bishman stopped. Behind those cold, death eyes, Harvey could see the recall process going on. But just as suddenly, the memory bank switched tack:

"The more you drink, the more you need to keep up the buzz. You know? In the end we were drinking pints of vodka, whiskey, rum, beer, anything we could get our hands on. Except I never touched gin, I couldn't, I told you that.

"The more we got into booze and drugs the more we needed to keep the buzz going. I was out of it most of the time. In the end I thought I could actually see lice under my skin and ended up back in detox. There wasn't anything there really, it was all in my mind, but I'm OK now. Yeah boogaloo.

"The same started happening with sex. In the end straight sex with girls was no good. After a booze session one night, I woke up in the morning in a strange room and was getting the most fantastic head I'd ever had. I looked up and it was a *guy* going down on me! After that I went right off females and we started fucking each other.

"The first time I ever fucked a guy up the ass, I pulled out and had a tomato skin on my helmet. Tomatoes don't digest too good that's why you always see tomatoes growing near sewage

25

works, because the seeds and skins go straight through you."

Harvey interrupted Bishmans train of thought. "Bob, do you want to tell me about when you were a kid, even before you chug-a-lugged the bottle of gin. Tell me about the years before that. Is that on? More coffee?" Harvey moved over to the Cona machine that had stopped hissing and was now emanating an aromatic smell of fresh-brewed coffee.

"Yeah, cream, five sugars. Yeah I'll tell you about Mommy fuckin' dearest. I used to get beaten with a belt and stripped and thrown in the coal cellar, all the normal stuff, I've had it all happen to me. Fucked me up. But I'm all right now. My father fucked my ass when I was seven and I fucked my sister when I was about twelve. Incest is best. The game the whole family can play, right! Keep it in the family, right?

"My father used to work at the docks as a stevedore. He was always drunk and beat on my mother. My sister went through hell, she O.D'd way back. My mother used to give us enemas. My mother never held me, that I remember. Never once held me, touched me or told me she loved me. Ever! Mommy fuckin' dearest! You've heard that expression, right? Boogaloo." Bishman sat and stared emotionless. No tears, no love, no feeling, no nothing. Just ice-blue eyes bugging out like a monster.

"Bob, anytime you want to stop, or not talk about something you just let me know. No problem. I know you've been through a lot." Harvey held his coffee mug to warm his hands and

26

his spirit, and was thinking, *at the age of thirty-eight, a study of hate.*

"Bob, you've got an interesting story to tell. You've been through enough for ten lifetimes. I think I *can* help you. I know you don't have money, and that's OK, I have plenty of money. What I don't have is much free time, and as you know I didn't intend to take on private clients. Hypnotic regression can take quite a time and it'll be draining for both of us.

"I'll make a deal with you. You show up at the appointments when I set them, wherever I set them, and we'll start work. You can meet me here, say, on Wednesdays, but I don't like using the office all that much. I hate being tied to one place. Not only that, most of the work I do is done in here." Harvey tapped his head. "If you're up for meeting me in Santa Monica or Venice or the Hollywood Hills, we can work together. Don't tell *anyone* what we do or talk about and don't come to sessions drunk or doped up. Do we have a deal?"

"It's a deal. Boogaloo." Bishman bugged his eyes and stretched forth his hand.

"First meeting here, next Wednesday morning at nine."

"I'll be here. I want to know when you're actually going to hypnotize me," quizzed Bishman.

"You were hypnotized the minute you walked into my office and shook my hand." Harvey smiled as he opened the door and Bishman walked out into a blast of hot air and Californian sunshine.

27

Mainwarring slumped back in his easy chair; he felt like shit. He stared out of the bay window of his country retreat. His head was spinning, he knew he'd drunk too much, but he was having a thinking, drinking session, so it didn't count.

His thoughts were not all that clear, but if anything, he did know what he was *trying* to accomplish.

He wanted clues, hunches, missing links, patterns. He had his team working in harmony, now he wanted this serial killer caught.

It was a great achievement that Scotland Yard and the Behavioural Science Unit at Quantico in Virginia were working so closely together. That was all down to Mainwarring's charisma and the way he deliberately created rapports with people who counted, on both sides of the Atlantic.

Mainwarring wondered if his colleagues would think he was level-headed because burgundy was dribbling from both sides of his mouth. He smiled at his own humour. He knew what he had to do. He had to go to the bathroom and sick up.

However, it was easier to stumble out the front door. He only just made it, and to finish the job off, he jammed two fat fingers down his throat and made sure he completely cleared himself out of the offending liquid. As he closed the front door, he wondered if the birds would eat all the big bits.

Then he noticed all the red wine vomit down the front of his white shirt. It looked as though he'd been shot. He not only felt like shit, he looked like shit. He never made it to the bedroom, he slept on the couch.

The caterers had been at it all day and so had the florists. Harvey's party, that Max Hatfield had organised, promised to be one elaborate affair.

By 8:30 in the evening Pinewoods' extensive drive was already full of exotic cars; more were pulling up every minute. Cabs pulled in every thirty seconds and dropped celebrities off. It was like rush hour in Manhattan.

There were stars and starlets, actors and actresses and professionals from all walks of life. Dentists from Newport Beach, lawyers from Burbank, judges from Pasadena, doctors from Glendale, businessmen from Huntington Beach and captains of industry from all over the States.

Max Hatfield made himself busy. He diplomatically waltzed Harvey around and shared him out amongst the franchisees and well-wishers. He was extremely clever the way he did it. As soon as he saw Harvey getting bogged down, he would drag him away, making the excuse that he'd bring him back. Of course he never did.

Guests were dressed in suits and evening gowns, others in slacks and sneakers - markedly informal. It was a mixed bunch. Wannabees walked in and out looking for prey.

Judging by the laughter and buzz, there were probably quite a few successes.

Every now and then Harvey and Hatfield would get a few moments to talk shop: who had bought a franchise and who was thinking about buying a franchise, who a certain party was, and the size of so and so's tits. But the banter never lasted long.

Most of the guests would end up being clients. *That's* what they'd been invited for.

One girl in particular kept catching Harvey's eye. She was in her early thirties, willowy, five eight and wearing classic black high-heel shoes and a long black evening gown. She had wonderful long blonde hair that went half way down her back. She seemed to be enjoying herself and was always smiling. Harvey managed to catch her eye a few times, but there was always a distance between them, bridged by guests, tables, waiters or piles of food.

Of course, no party for the world renowned hypnotherapist would have been complete without a bit of stage hypnotism and throughout the evening Harvey made people's eyes stick together, had other's bodies locked in chairs, made others forget their names - and a few more risqué things as well.

Eventually, both he and the willowy blonde were free and Harvey saw his opportunity. "Here, let me do that." He took the gin bottle and poured. He noticed her finger-nails, perfectly shaped, not too long, but finished with exquisite pink nail-varnish.

"What would you like with that?" He could smell the perfume. *Serendipity*.

"Tonic, plenty of ice." She noticed *his* finger nails, perfectly manicured.

"You've probably gathered I'm Bill Harvey. I'm so pleased you came." He passed over the drink, and couldn't help but notice her cleavage. Full breasts, perfectly tanned, and what a smile.

"I love your accent," she said, staring straight into Harvey eyes. "You're from London, right? I've had a good look around the house, Max told me to. Once Charlie Chaplin's, I'm told. I'm glad I came along." She looked confident, relaxed, radiant.

Harvey smiled "Yes, that's right. One of the bedrooms is laid out with all sorts of memorabilia. A real-estate salesman's ploy I reckon." He laughed.

"I saw that room, but there were others I liked better and I loved the pools." She took a sip of G&T.

"How long have you known Max Hatfield?" He studied her long blonde hair and her eyes. He couldn't take his eyes off her. He also kept coming back to her cleavage, although he tried not to.

"We go back ages. We went to Venice High together, and we've been good friends ever since. Speak of the devil." As she looked up, she saw Max was trying to get Harvey's attention.

"Bill I'm sorry to break up the party, but you know how it is, I've got the guy over there who bought a licence for St. Louis and he'd like a quick word. He's well up to speed." Hatfield tugged on Harvey, who reluctantly agreed to follow. He looked back over his shoulder, the blonde girl lifted her glass as if to toast him. "I'll be back soon, please excuse me," he said. This time he meant it.

When Bill Harvey got into his stride he was unstoppable. The party was now in full swing, and Max Hatfield had introduced him to everyone who was anyone. He'd even managed to exchange a few more words with the delectable blonde girl in the black evening gown. He called her *the rose amongst the thorns*, although he still hadn't got her name.

Harvey had a plan. He was going to do a little court-holding. He sat in the middle of the large living-room, in front of a polished teak coffee-table which had his props: a bottle of tomato sauce, salt and pepper shakers and, of course, a glass of pink champagne garnished with strawberries.

He started his party piece by doing the odd 'hic' and telling everyone that he was hungry. Guests were rolling around laughing already. He made apologies for being a drunk host, but explained that was part of life. They loved it. He spotted the blonde bombshell out of the corner of his eye and played the part especially for her.

More guests gathered around. When he sensed he had enough people watching he proceeded to cover the fingers of his left hand with tomato sauce. He then added salt and pepper to his first finger, in just the right quantity, and started to eat it. He put the finger in his mouth and munched on it. He made all the facial expressions and crunching movements, swallowed, bit and chewed some more. He rolled his eyes and crunched up a tough bit of bone. When he took his hand away from his mouth the finger had gone and he proceeded to pepper and salt the next one.

He did this four times, making an elaborate show of biting and munching, crunching and swallowing, carefully adding the condiments to get the flavor just right each time. By the time he had finished, all you could see were four bloody knuckles, his fingers being carefully tucked on the inside of his hand.

He washed each finger down with large gulps of pink champagne. The whole illusion looked superlatively realistic and even if you'd been only slightly tipsy you wouldn't have taken much convincing that Harvey had actually eaten his four fingers. If you'd had a joint or some coke you would *know* Harvey had eaten his fingers.

The party piece accomplished what he wanted. He had the beautiful blonde's attention, *well and truly*. He caught a gust of her perfume again: Serendipity. He noticed the long slit in her evening gown and saw her beautiful long evenly-tanned thighs. He noticed the white pearl necklace and the tiny pearl ear-rings. More than anything he noticed her cleavage and her breasts.

"That was wonderful, you'll have to teach me how to do that some time, I've never seen anything quite so funny. And I thought you were such a serious person." The beautiful slim vision stopped talking. She knew something about timing too.

"I'm sorry about what happened earlier. Max has been dragging me away all evening. It won't happen again, I promise. He's under a lot of pressure trying to make the party a success. I'm so sorry, I didn't even get your phone number, I mean your name - or your phone number for that matter." Harvey laughed. It was a genuine Freudian slip.

Harvey picked up his champagne glass as if to toast and the blonde vision replied: "My name is Anita, Anita Broughton. You can have my telephone number later. I don't think it's quite appropriate that I give it to you right now, not at this precise second." She smiled and Harvey noticed how straight and pearly white her teeth were.

They chatted away and amazingly enough no-one disturbed them. Harvey introduced Anita to pink champagne with strawberries. She was the easiest convert he'd ever made.

Eventually the evening wound down and the time came for Anita to depart. Harvey gave Anita a quick kiss on the side of her cheek, she slipped him a business card that read *Horwitz Solomon Investment Trust*. Her home phone number was pencilled on the back. She'd drawn a tiny heart over the 'i' in Anita.

FOUR

Harvey made a point of getting stuck straight into work when he arrived at I.O.H. headquarters in Springfield. There were always franchisees ready to listen and learn, and sometimes Harvey carried out impromptu sessions with them. This was one of them, at 11:30 on the night he arrived:

"The collection of fees is highly important. As you know, I.O.H. has already created over thirty millionaires in Europe. I believe the States offers an *even greater* opportunity.

"We know that we have a fabulous service to offer society. Industry alone loses billions of dollars every year through alcohol abuse and its associated problems of absenteeism, industrial accidents, mistakes, insurance claims, lethargy, wasted products, bad boardroom decisions and lack of morale in the work place. Soon companies will be employing us to cure their staff from smoking and business and industry will do everything it can to protect itself from passive smoking liability claims.

"Many of our clients, as you know, pay us huge fees to keep their employees on track. At the moment, thanks to the efforts of our franchisees, hundreds of Europe's top companies are our clients. All we have to do is keep doing more of the same, here in the States."

A week after their first meeting Bishman arrived at the duly-appointed hour of 9:am, ready and willing for his first session of hypnotic regression with Dr. Bill. He didn't know what to expect but he was willing to do whatever it took to get rid of his headaches and depressions. Jai showed him into Dr. Bill's office and Harvey immediately started his monologue:

"I want to explain a little about hypnotic regression, Bob, so that we get the best from our sessions. To get maximum benefit you do not necessarily have to go into a deep trance. You can go into whatever state of consciousness suits you at any particular time.

"When I regress you, don't try to recall specific events. Just let the images and feelings and emotions come to you. The events may or may not unfold in chronological order. They may come piecemeal or in complete sequences. Don't worry or try to control the scenario. Ultimately a story will unfold, but it may not come about as you anticipate. Don't worry about that, we'll unravel it at a later date. That's what I'm here for, to give you feedback and to put all the pieces together.

"You'll find your subconscious mind may want to tell you lots of little details about various things and not even bother to give you any information about other events. This is the beauty of the subconscious mind.

"You'll be living these past events as though they are happening right now. We'll see as we progress whether you want to talk them out as we go or talk about them later. Either way is fine. Don't try to find out what's giving you headaches or making you depressed. Just do the sessions, live out the past experiences. The solution to the problem will come once the subconscious has divulged everything it wants to. The solution will make itself apparent to you when the time is right.

"You must remember that every time you go into hypnosis it will get easier and easier, and you'll find you will be able to go into an altered state anywhere, any place.

"You can go into a relaxed state any time you like now, as shallow or as deep a trance as you like, whatever is comfortable to you and if you like you can start at the beginning or wherever is appropriate for you."

Bishman slipped into a deep hypnotic state. His eyes darted around accessing information from his gory past. Harvey was listening attentively and was armed with a tape recorder and note pad, ready to script:

Bishman started in the post office, a slip went over the counter. The official handed Bishman a package. These were the books Bishman had been waiting for. He ripped the package open on the way home, like a tiger clawing the meat from a zebra. The books fell out in a heap on the sidewalk and Bishman gloated over them: *How to Keep a Severed Head Alive, How to Perform Cunnilingus, Don't Get Mad - Get Even!, Talk and Grow Rich, Street Fighting,* and *Grotesque and Deformed Human Beings.*

Over the next few days the books were studied. *Talk and Grow Rich* suggested that you need a list of goals and to fill it in right now. He did:

1 - Annual income of $500,000. I own a $10,000,000 castle in the woods, on its own twenty-acre estate, fully furnished, fire places, eight bedrooms, huge games room, indoor pool.

2 - I own a fully loaded Lincoln Continental Mark 5 that is fire-engine-red. I also own a powder-blue Porsche 911.

3 - I own a motor home that is fully equipped and fully furnished.

4 - I have close relationships, in which sexual activity is both fantastic and very important, with Jimmy Franklin, Brian Pearlstein, Michael Passalaqua, (now in Little League), David Stone, Martin Silver, Chris Macrea and John Bruce (none of these acting violently towards me, none of these attempting suicide, none of these informing the authorities, their parents or any other person).

5 - *I am Head Director of non-governmental youth activities for various housing projects.*

6 - *I successfully complete a human services course in a reputable college for psychology.*

7 - *I have tremendous personal charm and charisma which attracts dozens of physically gorgeous young males 13 to 18, for relationships and sexual purposes.*

8 - *I own a mansion by the water which has 22 bedrooms, boat deck, fantastic grounds that include own zoo, firing range and gun collection.*

9 - *I am a billionaire.*

10 - *My penis is eight inches in length when erect as well as being proportionately as long when in the soft state. Penis sexually functionable at all times. Penis and the rest of me in exceptionally good health.*

11 - *I'm the top winner in the next Irish Sweepstakes.*

12 - *I have love, sobriety, energy, wit, serenity, happiness, joy, understanding.*

13 - *I own a .357 Magnum handgun, a .45 Colt automatic and a Kalashnikov assault rifle.*

Bishman's eyes stopped moving, his face was flushed, he stopped talking. He was breathing deeply and sweating profusely, his skin tone was an ashen grey. Suddenly the flood gates opened again and the tormented past poured out afresh, Harvey scripted as fast as he could, with his cassette recorder as a back-up:

Bishman was walking down Dana, in Somerville, a predominantly Catholic neighborhood in a Boston suburb, when a guy came up to him and asked him what he thought.

"I've never seen so many crucifixes and effigies of Christ. Everyone seems to have one in their front yard." Bishman was transfixed by the array of religious artefacts.

"You see that one there, where Jesus is in a cave surround? We call that Jesus on a half-shell. Get it? Clam on a half-shell, Jesus on a half-shell." They both laughed.

Bishman was staring at the swastikas graffitied all over the effigies of Christ in one particular front yard. His mind raced back to when he was at school and he'd painted swastikas all over the roof of the guy's house who owned the local bowling alley, because he wouldn't allow Bishman in there with booze. He was caught because one of the school teachers remembered Bishman always carried around a lucky swastika, mounted on a disc of mother of pearl, set in a gold wishbone. Bishman used to have it under his lapel along with a skull and crossbones and hundreds of pins and fish hooks.

God help you if you grabbed Bishman by the lapel. This is what had happened to the teacher. Got his fingers shredded by all the pins and fish hooks, and when he turned the lapel back he found the swastika.

When the news broke about the roof getting painted with swastikas, the teacher put two and two together and came up with Bishman. Bishman learnt a valuable lesson that day, about carrying things around with him and a pattern slowly started to gel.

Bishman was thinking, *a swastika is a beat-up cross,* when his mind tracked back to Somerville:

"Where's there a place to eat around here?" Bishman asked, looking around.

"There's Arthur Treacher's Fish and Chips at the top of the road."

"You springing?" said Bishman, giving an encouraging smile.

"Why not?" said the guy as they walked casually down Dana, toward Arthur Treacher's.

The smell of fried food was nauseating and Bishman wanted to eat and get out as quickly as possible and get on with the action he had in mind. Neither did he want to be seen too long with his next victim. But, as they were eating, Bishman heard police cars constantly patrolling the area, up and down, round and about. The sirens never seemed to stop. A voice popped into Bishman's head: *Not tonight old buddy. Not tonight.*

Harvey made many notes to enable him to give valuable feedback to Bishman. He listed various facts about personality disorders and neurosis and finished off by writing: *I have a <u>professional</u> duty to help this guy as much as I can, <u>within</u> my God given powers.*

Martinson and Flackman glanced at each other as Detective Superintendent Mainwarring continued, "This weekend I'm go to get some silence, stillness and solitude, up in the Lake District. A few bottles of burgundy. You'll see, I'll come up with a few Eurekas! Damned if I won't"

FIVE

Venice is not recreated anywhere else in the world. It is its own place. It has a magic and a quality all of its own: seedy, exotic, weird, wonderful, whacky and hot. Venice is California dreamin' at its best.

The beach is long and sandy and, this day, like almost every other day, there were a lot of evenly tanned, lithe bodies roller skating up and down the promenade.

There were people jogging backwards, roller skating backwards and people riding bicycles backwards and others on skate boards. Yes, they were going backwards too. In a world of excess, people have to do something out of the norm. In Venice, anything goes.

A guy skated past, full beard on one side of his face, clean shaven on the other. A black guy followed him, with a Bronx attaché case on his shoulder blaring away so loud you could have probably heard it in the Bronx. A juggler tempted fate by juggling three chainsaws. He finally made it. Then he started them up, each of its tiny two-stroke motors revving away like a swarm of bees. He managed to do it without dropping them. You don't get too many chances. The crowd put in lots of money, bills only, no small change, to show their affluence and appreciation.

Arm in arm, Harvey and Anita strolled over to Scallywags Bar. "I know the guy here," she said. "He'll let us take a pitcher away with us." Anita took out her crocodile-skin pocket book.

She gave Harvey the pitcher and carried the frosted glasses herself. Harvey was already carrying a hamper. "Are we nearly there or what? This is heavy, the beer's spilling and I'm starving." He laughed and sipped the ice cold Budweiser directly from the top of the pitcher.

"We've arrived," said Anita; "Maybe we can grab a little shade under that awning over there. They won't mind if we grab these chairs either." Anita pulled two plastic chairs up to a table that belonged to one of the coffee bars.

She started to lay out a feast of a picnic. First the heart-shaped paper plates, then the heart-shaped napkins. She put another paper plate on the table with heart-shaped sandwiches. Harvey was getting the idea.

He took a long draught of beer, licked his lips and suppressed a burp: "I love it. Let me guess where you got the idea for all the hearts. I bet you went into the heart room at Pinewood." He put his glass down and licked his lips again.

"I did and I fell in love with it. Do you like this, are you pleased?" She passed him the delicately produced heart-shaped sandwiches.

Harvey loved it. He couldn't take his eyes off Anita either.

Up on the promenade, people gathered. In the middle there were two youngsters, a boy and a girl about twelve or thirteen. Everyone seemed concerned and offered advice. Some were creasing up with laughter, others were calling their friends to take a look. The unfortunate young couple had started kissing and got locked together by the braces on their teeth. A guy went passed doing the moon walk on roller skates. It all happens in Venice.

Another session, another slice of the past. Harvey managed to open the doors on lots of the memories Bishman had tried to suppress.

Like Harvey said, the memories unfolded in no particular order. He was right too in the astonishing detail the subconscious memory retains:

Bishman had already spotted his next victim. A young girl, probably a hooker; then again, maybe not.

It was a warm evening and, although the sun had just gone down, it was still bright. Fishermen had lines out at the end of Santa Monica pier and Bishman was watching them. Suddenly one of the fishermen shouted out with excitement. He had a bite. Something big by all accounts and everyone rushed over to see him land it. In the crowd was Bishman, closely keeping one eye on a pretty young raven-haired girl, in dark blue jeans, a tight fitting sweatshirt complete with designer motif and neat little moccasin shoes.

The angler landed an octopus, about the size of a small football; it took some skill to get the lump up onto the pier without breaking the line. He had disgorged the hook and was about to kick the octopus off the pier, back into the deep blue sea. He hesitated as quite a few vacationers were taking photos. They don't have octopuses back in Boise. *They don't have octopussys there either.* Bishman covered his face. He made sure he didn't appear in any photos.

The fisherman addressed his audience. "Ya all look very carefully, because this is the best bit. When I kick this sucker over the edge, with a little luck, it'll ink." He booted the octopus over the edge of the pier and, sure enough, to the delight of the crowd, particularly those from Boise, it *inked*. The surrounding water was completely discolored by the discharge and the octopus made its escape. While the crowd stood fascinated, Bishman made his move, having already caught the girl's eye.

"The last time I saw anything as good as that was about five years ago, when a guy caught a Stingray. I was in Norfolk, Virginia. He called me over as he was reeling it in and told me to watch carefully as the Stingray came out of the water. Sure enough, as the Stingray came out of the water it gave a live birth. A baby Stingray popped out of it. They carry their babies in pouches, just like kangaroos. If they sense they're in danger they birth them."

Amy loved it. She was bored. All she needed was someone to talk to. Someone who understood and cared. Who should pop into her life? Bob Bishman. Arm in arm they strolled back down the pier like long-lost buddies.

They sat on the beach drinking beers and chatting for a few hours, not far from the pier.

"What worries me is the Zuvians. They're on the way here now and it's the Altinium they're after," said Bishman, sipping his Coors.

"Who are the Zuvians, what's Altinium?" Amy lit two cigarettes, passing one to Bishman.

He knew she'd fall for it. "Zuvians come from Zuvia - it's billions of light years away from here and it's the Altinium they're after. They use it for decorative purposes. They've just got to have it. It's only found in the heart of our automobile engines. Only *they* know what it is and what it looks like.

"When they arrive on the planet Earth they'll stop vehicles dead in their tracks. No matter where they are they'll rip the engines out of them and take out the tiny bit of Altinium and leave the rest of the auto where it stands, just a husk. After a few years there will be millions of husks all over America, indeed all over the world. The Zuvians will just keep going, ripping engines out of cars, just to get to the tiny bit of Altinium. There'll be husks everywhere, the car will become extinct."

"Jeeeezus H. Christ! They must be fuckin' mad, nobody in their right minds would do

47

such a thing." Amy crushed her beer can as if it was a Zuvian's head.

"Well that's exactly what we did to the buffalo, ha ha ha ha." Bishman lay on his back kicking his feet in the air, hooting with laughter. Amy howled too. She'd never heard anything so funny. She lent over and gave him a kiss. They got more beers at the Seven-Eleven and sat under the pier drinking. There was no-one else there, which was unusual. Maybe it was too early.

Bishman laid on his back, by the girl's side. Fifty yards away, the sea was slowly edging up the shore, wearing away the resistance of the sand. Amy lent over, kissed him again, and pulled back a few inches from his face, watching to see Bishman's reaction. His eyes seemed filled with something. Some sort of emotion. For a girl like Amy, that was enough. It was a hell of a lot more than she usually got. She bent down to kiss him again - this time, it would be a longer kiss. His hands reached up to her face, pushed her hair away from her throat...and squeezed.

Amy struggled like crazy, humping, bucking and kicking, trying to free herself from the bug-eyed monster that had been her friend just moments before. He noticed that every time he released his grip she would get more oxygen and struggle harder and when he increased the pressure around her wind-pipe she went limp and stopped struggling. He couldn't help thinking it was like playing bagpipes and he played a game with her neck, increasing the pressure and letting her kick and struggle then cutting off the air supply and making her go all limp. Eventually the game came to an end. She went limp permanently.

Bishman decided to fuck her. He pulled off her dark blue jeans and her white lace panties, but try as hard as he may he couldn't mount her. He tried again and again and couldn't penetrate her. He decided to investigate; Bishman thought *Fucking Robin's on the nest,* as he found the mouse's tail and pulled out a tampon. It was messy, it came out more easily than he anticipated and he got blood all over his hands.

For some reason, he tried to stuff it back up inside her, but couldn't, so he left it draped over her forehead like a bandanna. By this time he'd lost his erection and gave it up as a bad job. *If they're young enough to bleed, they're young enough to butcher. I wish I'd never met the slut in the first place,* thought Bishman as he washed his hands in the sea. He didn't even go off humming.

Bishman stopped talking, but remained motionless in a deep state of relaxation for twenty minutes. Harvey took note: Frequently Bishman would abruptly end his dialogue at what seemed conspicuously like the end of an episode, the snuffing out of a victim's life, which it usually was. Bishman took great delight in the chase and capture, the killing was the anti-climax.

Harvey was developing a love-hate relationship with this guy and he knew it. At times he was fascinated, other times repulsed - even sickened. He felt he had to keep going, as though he was driven.

Unbeknown to Flackman and Martinson, Mainwarring had many methods of generating hunches. He knew he had to create his own breaks, and apart from copious supplies of claret he also went to psychic mediums, tarot card readers, séances, spiritualists and palm readers to enlist help, feedback and stimulus. He also dabbled in satanism and the occult...anything to get into the mind of a serial killer.

Mainwarring had his own private motto: *science and intuition*.

One hundred and thirty-seven franchisees from Chicago had enroled to take the special I.O.H. course at Springfield, that had Harvey as the key speaker. As usual, Max Hatfield stayed in the sidelines. He never tried to compete with the master. He did however, make sure everything ran like clockwork, to alleviate any administrative strain on Harvey.

"You've seen it on the videos and heard it on the audios. It's also a case of reading it over and over again. As with all hypnotherapy you don't *know* a thing until you *know* a thing. The only way you really get to *know* a thing is by using it over and over again - whether you're ready or not." The grey-haired master pushed his spectacles up his nose and mopped his brow with a large, white linen handkerchief.

"Getting back to the cancer cure, the most important part of the exercise, from our stand-point, is taking the client into hypnosis and getting them to visualize *something* attacking the cancer cells and diseased tissue. That *something* is what I want to talk to you about today. To create success you must come at the problem from the viewpoint of your client. Maybe you have a youngster who has a cancer - you get him to visualize playing Pac-Man, gobbling up all the cancer cells as fast as he can go. The more cells he gobbles up, the more points he wins. Kids have fantastic imaginations, your job is to fire your client's imagination with something they, as individuals, can relate to.

"For an older client you may get him to *visualize* the cancer cells are cockroaches and he has to come up with every devious method in the book to kill them off. An older woman may see a white knight on a horse slashing at the cancer cells with a huge diamond-and-ruby-encrusted sword.

"Capture your client's imagination so they can actually *visualize* the devil they are trying to beat. Everyone has this faculty, it's just a question of being trained in how to use it. That's our job. We have the written proof; literally thousands of unsolicited testimonials, that I.O.H. has cured more people of cancer world-wide than any patent drug or medicine. Let's keep up the good work."

51

Harvey met Bishman all over town, up in the hills, the beach and *always* the Pasadena office on Wednesdays.

This particular session took place in the Hollywood Hills. Bishman went into an altered state, submerged himself in memories and allowed his subconscious mind to surface. He quickly started his regression:

The first time Bishman arrived in Manhattan he walked around early in the morning to check out the city that has engines in its blood. You see a side of the naked city at 5:30 in the morning you can't see at any other time. He walked past a store doorway where two immaculately dressed hookers were taking it in turns to go down on a guy. Behind them was a junkie, desperately trying to shoot up - probably struggling to find a vein that was still working.

Another junkie, sitting on the ground, shouted. Startled, the one trying to shoot up swung around and accidentally jabbed the needle straight into his buddy's eye. Blood shot out from the tiny hole for about seven feet in a tiny jet - and spurted all over the two exquisitely beautiful hookers *and* the guy getting the blow job.

Welcome to New York, pal, thought Bishman.

Harvey let Bishman be motionless for the next ninety minutes. He studied his facial expression, which was completely relaxed. He looked almost *angelic*. Harvey made a note about this, alongside seven other pages of observations, including some he'd previously made about paranoia, hypoglycaemia and vitamin deficiency.

After floating around in a sepia haze for about ninety minutes and without prompting from Harvey, Bishman started his dialogue again. More horrific revelations. Still in New York - Harvey quickly picked that up - but surmised this was an account of activity some three years later:

Bishman had made an appointment over on the Lower East Side and, for sentimental reasons, he walked down Bleecker Street in Greenwich Village, although it took him out of his way. Nostalgic thoughts raced through his mind. The last time he was here he'd seen Jimi Hendrix, the legendary guitarist and folk hero, in the back of a stretch limousine and Hendrix was absolutely out of it. There was no one else around, all the windows of the limo were open and Hendrix just sat in the back seat, looking like death warmed over. It was awful. Bishman remembered reading about Hendrix live in concert. He came up on stage and strummed his guitar with the amps turned up on full volume and all the people on the front row ended up with broken ear drums and blood trickling from their ears. Next time Bishman read about Hendrix, he was dead.

It was early evening when Mark Townsend, a.k.a. Bob Bishman, arrived at the apartment, which was dirty and dingy, and not far from a shanty town by Manhattan Bridge Plaza, near Canal Street. The female occupants were a mother of two, who sold either herself or her kids to make a quick buck, and another woman of dubious repute, Diane.

There was no wallpaper on the walls and the floor did not have a carpet. The furniture was sparse and looked as though it had come from the trash. *It had*. The smell of cats; or to be more precise, tom cats' piss, was everywhere. The place reeked of it.

On the table there was leftover food. It looked like it had been there for days. Cockroaches the size of golf balls scoured the place for food. This was the ultimate in squalor. The people living there didn't even notice.

"Tell us again what we've got to do, so Diane can hear it for herself," Linda said lighting a cigarette.

Townsend suppressed a burp. "Like I told you yesterday, I know this guy who wants to set up a new business." He stubbed his cigarette out and lit another with the girl's lighter, hoping the smoke would kill the smell of the cats' piss.

"This guy supplies sexretaries to companies. You and Diane can make a lot of money. Much more than you're making now." Townsend rubbed some ash into his pants.

"All you have to do is turn up at the office addresses that he gives you and wait around. You'll be told who to suck, and who to fuck." Diane was going to say something but took a sip of her TAB instead.

54

"The main thing is to help me get it set up. Once it's set up you'll get paid every day just for making sure girls turn up at the various offices. I don't live in Manhattan so he'll send my money onto me wherever I am. I need someone like you two girls who will be reliable and make sure the deal comes together. The other point is that you two know lots of other working girls, you've got contacts." He stubbed the cigarette out before finishing it. A television was blaring away in another room. Cigarette smoke hung in the room but couldn't kill the reek of cats' piss and the uncleanliness of human habitation.

Townsend lay back in the scruffy armchair and blew a smoke ring, then blew a stream of smoke through it, almost perfectly. "You've already told me that you and the kids turn tricks, too. You've got nothing to lose.

"I want to make sure you all perform and we'll do that tonight and if I'm happy with tonight's performance, I'll meet the two of you tomorrow on 34th Street and Ninth Avenue and I'll introduce you to the guy. He's all right, but he needs reliable girls to make this work. Three weeks' hard work, then you can stop. Just make sure you have got other girls to turn up at the offices." Townsend paused and made himself comfortable.

"I've got it," said Diane excitedly, "We go in as sexretaries, not to type or answer the phone, but to service the johns. That's right isn't it? Gee! What a great idea. Sexretaries! Who came up with that idea?"

55

Townsend lit another cigarette, ignoring the half finished one in the ashtray. "I came up with the idea and persuaded the guy on Ninth Avenue to exploit it. We all get a cut, if we get the project off the ground. That's why I need to try you out, to make sure you all perform." Townsend glanced at the two girls to elicit a response.

"You can use the other bedroom," said Linda, "It's empty now, our last room-mate left yesterday and we haven't found anyone to replace her yet. Who do you want to start with first?" Linda stood up and turned around as if to offer herself.

"I'll start with the kids, then you two can finish me off, one at a time. Have you got a plastic bag I can put all my clothes in? I don't want to get them dirty."

"I'll get the kids ready. Give me a shout when you're done with them, and I'll come in and show you what I do for a living," said Linda pursing her lips and smiling at the same time. As an afterthought she added. "The only plastic bag I've got is one from the supermarket, there ya go, will that do?" She handed Townsend a large plastic bag.

Townsend got up and once again was hit by the ammoniac smell of human sweat and cats' piss, *I'll be fuckin' glad to get outta here*, he thought.

Townsend left there at 5:30 in the morning after having a forty minute shower. He left there satisfied - well satisfied!

Harvey dated and numbered every one of Bishmans sessions. Sooner or later a jigsaw puzzle would form and he would put all the pieces together. He was absolutely sure he hadn't heard the last of *this* story, but for the time being at least, Bishman's mind had hung out the "Do Not Disturb Sign."

The number of Federal Express overnight packages, faxes and information transmitted by modem from the Behavioural Science Unit at Quantico to Mainwarrings office in New Scotland Yard at Whitehall was impressive in volume and content. Some of it was sickening, some revealing, all of it important.

However, it needed sifting, sorting, reading and above everything, it needed assimilating, before handing it over to his dedicated team.

It was time for Detective Superintendent Howard Mainwarring to crack a bottle of claret and burn some midnight oil again.

What was nice, thought Mainwarring, was that Special Agent Dave Wead always enclosed some American stamps for his nine-year-old son, Rolf. Mainwarring always made it a point to reciprocate when he sent packets to Quantico.

Harvey was eminently successful. He dressed in expensive clothes, dark Savile Row suits, Italian leather shoes and what Harvey would call born-again Christian Dior shirts. He also wore gold cufflinks, a gold tie bar, a Rolex Oyster and glittering diamond rings. He looked successful but he always had the top button of his shirt undone or his tie loosened or taken off completely, or something else that would give him a particularly relaxed and approachable demeanor.

Bill Harvey didn't have any academic qualifications. He didn't need them. He had picked up his understanding of psychology from life and he knew his subject inside out and backwards as well. He'd become the world's leading authority in hypnotherapy simply by practising it every day of the week for the last thirty years. He began messing around with hypnosis when he was fifteen, he was now forty-five. You do one thing solidly for thirty years, and by the end, you find you're pretty damn good. Harvey was not just *damn good*, he was *brilliant*.

Harvey was addressing a late evening group at I.O.H. headquarters, Springfield.

"Clients will come to you totally wrapped up in themselves, thinking all the time about *their* problems, behaviors and hang-ups. One of the things you can do, to stop this, is to give them even more to think about. Usually people can only cope with and process seven bits of information at a time.

"The formula is seven, plus or minus two. Give them things to do *outside* their normal realm of activity, and they'll have to spend time working on those and that will distract them from their own problems. The more they do for you, the less time they have to think about their own problems. You can give them all sorts of interesting little projects. Use your imagination. As the Chinese professor said 'Use your noodle.' A lot of ideas will come to your mind as you work with each client."

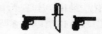

It was Wednesday morning and Bishman met Harvey at the Pasadena office for his regular 9:am. appointment. At hypnotherapy appointments Harvey would immediately take Bishman into an altered state and start work.

That didn't mean to say they never talked to each other on a conscious level. Quite the contrary - many times Harvey met Bishman for a meal (Harvey always picked up the tab) to talk things over and give feedback. But this was a set appointment, so down to hypnotic regression. Bishman searched his mental atlas of far away places and began:

Many times when you're on the road things go wrong, or at least not according to plan. One time Bishman was in Texas and got caught up in a brutal road accident. The truck in which he was a passenger wasn't directly involved and only due to the swift reactions of the driver did they avoid getting entangled in the carnage.

The noise had been horrendous: smashing glass, the noise of steel grinding, twisting, buckling, skidding, scraping and banging along the ground in a shower of sparks. It seemed to go on forever but, in reality, it was all over in seconds.

The truckie pulled, or rather lurched up. The two of them jumped out to see if they could help anyone. Apparently some maniac, a drunk, had somehow got onto the freeway and was driving down it the wrong way, at excessively high speed. He ploughed headlong into oncoming traffic. There was wreckage strewn everywhere.

Bishman was the first to find the body, a woman's. She'd been cleanly decapitated. Bishman wondered what could have caused such a clean cut. He didn't have to look for the head, it was right next to him. It was truly awesome, and he couldn't help staring at it. The eyes were fully open and looking around as if to say, *what's happened, why can't I move?* Her lips were moving but no noise was coming out of them. The eyes kept looking around and eventually their gaze fell on her own body which was about six feet away. Her eyes and lips then started going mental.

Just then, Bishman's buddy arrived, took in the scene, heaved up, then threw his coat over the victim's head. Bishman didn't like to say anything, but he was fascinated by the woman's reaction.

Harvey waited patiently. He had an intuition Bishman would mentally click back in; whether it would be a continuation or another track would be anyone's guess. Without warning, Bishman started again, Harvey was ready *and* willing:

Bishman got lost in Upstate New York or Connecticut. He'll never know exactly where, all he knows is what happened.

He was dropped off out in the middle of nowhere by a severely angry truckie. That didn't happen often, but it did happen. It happens because a truckie gets bored with the conversation or he's as high as a kite or he's paranoid about something or he's a complete asshole. Bishman thought he was probably a combination of all these.

He walked ten, maybe twelve miles in the bitter cold and, despite his heavy jacket, he had to walk briskly to keep warm. The moon was full and the stars were bright and as he walked along, he spotted six falling stars. *Huh, some consolation!*

Bishman heard the noise way before he actually reached it - metallic, droning and constant. The nearer he got, the louder the noise got. Eventually he reached a junction off the main road. By now, the noise was getting painfully loud. A few hundred yards down the junction, he discovered an immense train yard. There must have been at least a hundred trains there, all big diesels, all running their engines to stop them from freezing up. Bishman remembered he'd read that during the war they ran the big tank engines every hour to keep them warm, sometimes they'd have to leave them running all night. If engine oil gets too thick you can never start the cumbersome engines again - especially the enormous diesel engines they use on trains.

A huge pall of oily smoke hung in the air, a powerful, solitary lamp casting grotesquely-shaped shadows over the yard, like a scene from hell. The din was horrendous; the belching of the exhaust, the detonation of the actual firing of individual cylinders and the metallic knocking of engine parts that diesels tend to make, all combined to make one unique, deafening rumble.

But there was no one around. That made the whole thing even more awesome. The moon and one lamp lighting up the place, an ungodly din, and the place was deserted. *Spooky!*

Bishman thought he'd snoop around and find somewhere warm to sleep the night, then push on in the morning. The thought even crossed his mind to go by train, there were enough of them.

"Hey you, fella, what are you up to?" Bishman was taken by surprise. The guy was about six foot two and about two hundred and fifty pounds. Really ugly. If you'd seen him you'd know we'd descended from apes. The security officer summoned Bishman to the office for questioning. Bishman realised the truth was as good a story as any. "You sure you ain't lying to me, fella?" The guard asked in a relaxed and friendly manner.

"No of course I'm not fuckin' lying to you. How the hell do you think I got here, fuckin' parachute?" Bishman took out his cigarettes, lit one and, as an afterthought, passed one over. The guard took the cigarette and lit it with a large table lighter from a desk that was full of paraphernalia.

Bishman rubbed his hands together to warm himself over the electric heater and said, "Anyway, you know what the three biggest lies in the world are?"

"No, go on," said the guard.

"I won't put it in if it hurts, I won't come in your mouth, and the check's in the mail." They both laughed and the guard put on some coffee.

"Yeah, I've heard it before but I can only ever remember two, I always forget the last one."

The guard made coffee in brightly glazed mugs. Bishman added his own milk and eight sugars, which shocked the security officer.

Bishman burped. "Did you hear the one about the old prossie?"

The security officer stirred his coffee and drew deeply on his cigarette.

"No, go on," he said.

"Fucking old prostitute had worn out her pussy and was starting to get complaints from her johns. They complained that her pussy was so big they couldn't feel anything. So she went to her pimp. 'No problem,' he told her. 'All prostitutes wear their pussies out sooner or later. All you have to do is get it rebushed.' The old prossie wanted to know how, so he told her.

"You buy a large leg of ham from the butcher's with a bone that goes right the way through it. Boil it for at least five hours, seven would be better. Then you shove the whole thing up your pussy and pull out the bone. That should do you for another twenty years." Bishman was already laughing before he finished the joke and the guard wasn't far behind him. Tears were trickling down their cheeks.

"More coffee?"

"Yeah, I'll force one," said Bishman, getting out his cigarettes again.

"Is that a .38 Smith and Wesson?" asked Bishman enthusiastically, pointing to the gun in the security guard's hip holster. "We call those Saturday Night Specials where I come from."

"Yeah, it sure is. You know something about guns then?" The guard poured coffee into two cups and pushed one towards Bishman.

"Sure I know a bit. I've owned over a hundred and fifty guns in my time, so they're like second nature to me. Mind if I take a look?"

"Sure, there ya go. Don't fire the fucker though. That's all we need." The guard took the gun from its holster and handed it to Bishman.

Bishman deftly flicked open the chamber, *six bullets,* clicked it back, spun the chamber, satisfied himself he had a perfect working specimen in his hand. The guard watched, fascinated. Here was someone who obviously knew what he was doing. Bishman lined up an imaginary target in the middle distance, his arm extended, his eyes fixing themselves, bugging out with concentration. Slowly, slowly, he brought his arm round, in a 90 degree arc as if he was lining up a moving target, until it was pointing directly above the guard's head. Slowly, carefully, he brought his arm down to chest height.

The guard had only an instant to recognise the danger he was in, his face only briefly flickering with fear, before Bishman let him have six slugs at point blank range, his body jerking like a marionette. He died instantly, a crumpled heap face-up, spilt coffee steaming off his coat. Six neat holes meant that remarkably quickly there was a large pool of incredibly dark red blood. Very quickly too the color drained from his face. He looked like an ugly ghost. *Apelike.*

Bishman bent down and fumbled through his pockets. He knew there had to be a car outside although he hadn't seen it. He found the keys in the pocket in his pants, not the jacket. *Shit! Things are always in the last place you look for them.*

Bishman closed the door behind him and went looking for the car. He found it quickly, it was a fire-engine-red Lincoln Continental. He put the key in the door and opened it. *JEEEEEZUSSS!!!!!!* He got the fright of his life. It was a big German Shepherd, a *Schutzhund Three* attack dog, and as soon as it realized Bishman was not with his master, it went berserk. It jumped out of the car and was all over Bishman before he could close the door. Snapping and biting, growling, frothing, lips curled back, Bishman was getting pinned down. He thought he was going to die. He tried to protect himself but the dog kept tearing at his arms. Flashing its teeth and snapping furiously, this dog was not going to quit. *This is a professionally trained attack dog, no doubt about that,* thought Bishman. *Fuck! I'm gonna die, get killed by a lousy fuckin' dog. No way, José. Boogaloo.*

With the strength and determination of a desperate man, Bishman forced his arm deep into the dog's mouth, jammed it there and grabbed hold of the root of his tongue for good measure. He then sank his teeth into the dog's nose and bit it clean off. You should have heard that dog yelp. It ran off, all the fight had gone out of it. It whimpered, yelped and yowled. Bishman spat out the dog's nose thinking, *pick the bones outta that ya bastard*, spat again to get rid of the blood and the salty taste, and lit a cigarette, holding the smoke in his mouth.

Bishman was in agony. Both his forearms felt like they were on fire. He fired up the Lincoln and drove like hell, spinning its wheels all the way out of the yard and a good fifty yards down the road. He nearly overshot the junction, his adrenalin was pumping so hard.

He looked at his watch, then checked the clock in the car. It was ten minutes to midnight, Saturday night. *Now you know why we call them Saturday Night Specials, pal.* Bishman had gone into the train yard humming *Catch a Falling Star*. He came out humming *You Ain't Nothing But a Hound Dog*.

Bishman drove five hours and ended up in Cranston, Rhode Island where he parked the car and attended to his wounds. Not as bad as he had thought. His heavy jacket had let the teeth through but stopped them tearing his flesh.

Bishman was covered in sweat, his head lolling around and his eyes rolled in their sockets. Harvey did nothing, he was quite used to hypnotic phenomena, he did however neaten up his notes and try to make sense out of the last sessions.

When Bishman eventually came round they were both starving and Harvey took Bishman for a beer and pizza in North Hollywood and eventually they parted company in Wilshire.

"I'll tell you why I'm crying," sobbed the twenty-eight-year-old hooker whose name was Tina, who now lived in a lemony fresh apartment on 52nd Street and First Avenue.

"You know I used to live in that filthy tenement on the Lower East Side. I bumped into Marguerita today. She told me that Diane and Linda and the two kids were murdered the day after I left. I knew that place wasn't safe. I told you that at the time, that's why I had to get the hell out of there. I had a sort of premonition." She tried to hold back the tears, but couldn't.

Marcia lit two cigarettes and gave one to Tina.

"It's terrible. Do you know how they found out about it? Because the cats were leaving bloody footprints everywhere, and the guy who lived on the first floor decided to go upstairs and investigate. They reckon it was a massacre. According to cops they were butchered so badly there was over thirty pints of blood spilt at the scene of the crime. Apparently whoever slaughtered them took a long shower and just walked out. Four of them hacked to death, in a sickening bloodbath and no clues other than the fact the police reckon the guy must have put his clothes in a plastic bag to stop blood being splashed on them." She threw up some bile and the Chinese food that she had eaten earlier, and went to clean herself up.

Howard Mainwarring had a leisurely lunch with Stan Barron in The Bicycle Club in Covent Garden. Not that either of them had time for leisurely lunches - they didn't - but Mainwarring had discovered that Barron also had a penchant for claret and the only way he could get sufficient quality time with Barron was when he 'kidnapped' him for long liquid lunches and got him away from the madding crowds back at Whitehall.

Howard found himself biting his lip when Stan Barron said, "My task is to give you an accurate psychological profile of this individual who has committed dozens of murders - who knows, maybe even hundreds."

He expounded further: "It's like trying to find someone through a fog when the breeze has blown it apart. It's worse than looking for a needle in a haystack. Intuition plays no part in the process, I am no better at guessing than anyone else in the world. It's no mystery to me, we are dealing with psychological science."

Howard Mainwarring was interested to hear that, according to Barron, the Brits were just as good at psychological profiling as the criminal investigative analysts who worked out of the NCAVC at Quantico, the profiling arm of the Behavioural Science Unit.

Copious supplies of claret were consumed before Mainwarring extracted the information he required. Between Dave Wead's colleagues at Quantico and Stan Barron's colleagues in the UK, the psychological profile of the serial killer that had plagued Britain was finally shaping up.

Only time will tell, thought Howard, as he reaffirmed mentally: *Science __and__ intuition*.

SIX

Of course the franchisees at I.O.H., Springfield knew not to expect too many personal appearances from Harvey. This was all part of their franchise agreement. So when the wizard *did* put in an appearance they revelled in it.

Harvey wiped his spectacles, then stroked his full beard. "You must find out what secondary gains your alcoholic client gets from drinking. You do this when you get him to re-create the drunken state. You will find out by careful observation whether the client gets relaxation out of drink, camaraderie or time away from a nagging spouse or an unpleasant domestic or business situation.

"Of course, once you've discovered the secondary gains you must replace them with alternative behaviors that don't cause the problems and bad effects the drinking behaviors have.

"Your clients may very well be alcoholics, but they're not stupid. If you show them alternative behaviors they will usually make the right choice and do what is right for themselves. That all takes place on a subconscious level. Before, they'd never been aware of the options available to them.

"Carry out the procedure to the letter, and your clients will stop alcohol dependency and be able to become social drinkers. They won't access the bad feelings and emotions every time they take a drink, therefore, they will no longer feel the desire to drown their sorrows in booze."

"I don't mind telling you about my work, Bill. It's not that at all. I love what I do, same as you, but the last thing I want is to bore you with tales about investment banking." Anita put her arm through Harvey's as they strolled along Venice Beach. They did this often and loved each other's company. The sand was hot on their bare soles but the waves cooled them down as often as they wished. Twenty teenagers were playing handball and another dozen were surfing. There were sun bathers in deck chairs, and bronzed bodies running and diving into the waves. It was good to be alive. A biplane flew overhead and sign-wrote a message in computerized smoke dots, it read, CONGRADULATIONS, ANDY, SUZY AND PETE!

"I find it fascinating, but I think you're a workaholic. You haven't taken a vacation in eight years. That's incredible," said Harvey as he picked up a stone to throw into the sea to lend emphasis to his words. But the pebble turned out to be a piece of dog shit so he put it down again, hoping Anita didn't see. She did, and she giggled. He washed his hands in the waves, then splashed Anita and chased her along the beach.

"OK," conceded Anita, "I'll tell you a story about my company - Horwitz and Solomon - I know you'll enjoy. The senior partner who put in millions to start the bank in the early 1900s was a guy called Solomon. Horwitz was just a number cruncher who had plenty of contacts. They put their names together and called the bank Solomon Horwitz Investment Trust. They incorporated, got letterheads printed and were just about to open their doors for business when a colleague pointed out the error of their ways.

"Sooner rather than later people would start to use the acronym S.H.I.T. They nearly had apoplexy. They changed the names round and there they've stayed ever since. Anyway there's neither a Solomon nor a Horwitz now so I don't suppose it matters one way or another." Harvey was laughing before Anita had finished the story.

"There you go, I told you you'd like it. What else is there I can tell you?" Anita pinched Harvey's ass.

"Let's get a pitcher of our favorite beer and talk some more." Harvey tugged Anita in the direction of Scallywags Bar.

"You bet. I'll tell you something else. Horwitz and Solomon finance some astounding projects all over the world. They have clients in over one hundred and forty countries."

"Let me just order the beer then tell me some more." Having arrived at the bar quickly,

Harvey got a pitcher of draught Bud and two frosted glasses. *This is becoming a habit* he thought as he paid the guy. *A habit I can live with!*

Anita continued: "They finance projects like dams, international airports, skyscrapers and bridges. They financed the biggest machine in the world, a four-mile long nuclear particle accelerator." Anita paused long enough to take a draft of frothy beer.

"Why is it you're loath to take even a week's vacation?" asked Bill; "I'd love to take you to Paris for a week, you know, do the Eiffel Tower, Maxims, Left Bank of the Seine and all that. I've never done it myself and it's something I long to do." Harvey topped up both glasses and emptied the pitcher. They both felt a buzz from the beer. *Toasted brains on a hot day. You can't beat it!*

Harvey emptied his glass. "After a few beers on a hot day it's as though you're looking at the world through rose colored spectacles. Shall we get another?"

Anita bought the next pitcher of Bud. Harvey was giggling too much.

"I love watching you walking in a bikini. You know, you really are beautiful. You know what else? I really have a buzz on. Tell me what you were saying about not taking time out from work." Harvey sipped his beer, then took in a whiff of pungent sea air.

"When I started, I took a week off, about six months after I joined them. In the first few months there, I put in place all sorts of systems and controls and took advantage of foreign exchange mechanisms making the bank millions. That's my area of expertise and that's what they employed me for. Then I had a week off. It turned out to be a disaster. The computer went down and we lost all sorts of files, records, data, and clients. It was intensely messy and I had to work twenty-hour days getting it all back together again.

"Now what I do is take a day off during the week. You could say I work a four-day week for a six-day week salary and that's the way I like it. It works for me. That's how we're here today and that is why many times I've been able to spend weekdays and long weekends with you. What doesn't suit me is having all my work gobbled up by the computer the minute my back is turned." Anita rubbed suntan lotion on her tummy and asked Harvey to do her back. She was sensually soft. He couldn't keep his hands off of her. He felt himself getting an erection and had to drag himself into the sea to cool his ardor - as well as his 'ard on!

Each regression brought new revelations about Bishmans' gory past. Harvey now brought two tape recorders. One to tape Bishman and the other to put his private thoughts onto, many of which were quite disturbing:

Bishman had just arrived in Manhattan having got a ride from a guy in Maryland, and had a good feeling he was in for a lot of action.

It was the 28th October, 1982, and if you're a New Yorker you probably remember exactly what you were doing at 7:45 that evening. You'll probably never forget.

As for Bishman, he was walking down Eighth Avenue on 44th Street, juggling with Jesus amongst thousands of blacks, Hispanics, Chinese, Africans, Vietnamese, Puerto Ricans, Haitians, Philipinoes, Mexicans, Cubans and Koreans, all jockeying for position and hustling for a buck. *Just like the third world!* There were also lots of beautiful young hookers, dressed to the nines, their pimps only a stone's throw away.

Suddenly the Big Apple was plunged into darkness. New York had a complete power failure and a major problem on its hands. A lot of New Yorkers thought the Russians were coming. Within a minute Bishman watched a youth snatch a woman's pocket book and disappear into the darkness.

Bishman decided to play it cool. He stood and he watched. A few ideas popped into his head. Police sirens seemed to be coming from every direction. Pandemonium and panic - and the lights had only been out for three minutes. Bishman waited. Within another five minutes the power was restored. Bishman wasn't convinced the restoration of power was going to be permanent. He had a hunch, he kept plotting and planning and his hunch turned out to be reality.

The power failed yet again and subsequently remained off for the next two days.

That night was when the poor got rich, if only temporarily. Within minutes of the lights going out the second time, four stores had their windows smashed and the serious looting had started. Looters were filling up supermarket trolleys with televisions, radios, stereos, whole lambs, hind quarters of beef, jewelry and tins of food. Others loaded up with cakes, records, clocks and fruit. It was an incredible sight, a real live free-for-all, people struggling down the street bumping into one another with televisions and leather-bound sofas, dining tables and washing machines, all under the cover of darkness.

At one clothing store, even the mannequins disappeared into the night along with the cash register, display cabinets and every single item of clothing. Looters were taking orders and going out and fulfilling them, *wholesale!* They'd get you what you wanted, *big discount guaranteed!* The word went out, *time to go to work, let's get busy,* and they did. *Free shopping!*

The first thing Bishman did was to get a gun and he did that by killing a cop. In the blackness, the only light came from car headlights, and what really stood out were the bright blue flashing lights from the police cars.

When the big rattlesnake drive goes down in Texas, they deliberately beat the bushes and grass to make the rattlesnakes 'rattle' and give themselves away. To find a gun, all Bishman had to do was find a blue flashing light.

Bishman approached cautiously. He wanted to ensure the cop's partner was busy and he most certainly was. He was tied up with about fifteen blacks who were putting an empty fifty-gallon drum through a store window.

Bishman crept up behind the cop, by the patrol car and slammed a four-foot section of scaffold pole into his skull. He never knew what hit him. Bishman said to himself: *You thought you could control the city with the lights out, but instead I've stuck your lights out - permanently. He was a fuck-pig anyway. If you've got three cops up to their necks in shit, what have you got? Not enough shit, right.*

Bishman had a problem getting the gun out the holster, but after a bit of fumbling he managed it. It was a Glock-17, that usually held seventeen rounds. Sometimes the police have access to clips that hold thirty-two rounds. *This one did.*

Bishman looked around and surmised there was a certain advantage to being black on a night like this. It was dark enough on its own but the blacks really did disappear into the shadows. *Spooky!* He smiled.

All around were the sounds of huge plate-glass windows getting smashed and big cheers going up. There were lots of gunshots, automatic fire as well.

A lot of businesses were cleaned out that night. By morning, hundreds of stores were stripped clean. A lot of people had had their lights stuck out permanently, too. Bishman killed at least eighteen people that night - maybe more - but the others were just wild shots and he couldn't establish his kills.

Bishman was not the only serial killer on a spree. During the first night he saw over one hundred and fifty bodies. Some maniac had been firing an automatic and you could hear that dull *rat tat tat* all night long, right up until sunrise. On Eighth Avenue and 42nd Street there was a pile of bodies, maybe as many as forty or fifty, in body bags. A special police unit, dressed like a SWAT team, were loading them onto a truck. Bishman noticed that each member of the team carried *three* Colt .45 automatics. One on each hip and one in a shoulder holster. While they were loading the bodies their buddies stood back-to-back keeping guard and carried Uzis and AK-16s as well as the three Colt .45 autos.

During the course of the evening, thousands of gang members made their way over to Manhattan from Queens, Brooklyn, the Bronx and New Jersey. The police had slide-action shotguns on Brooklyn Bridge to deter gang members from coming over. The patrol was taken out with an AK-47 with a starlight scope within ten minutes. They weren't replaced.

Bishman's 'kills' were anyone who came into his line of fire, providing he had at least two escape routes. He was dropping people like flies. The deadly 9mm Glock-17 had almost pin-point accuracy. He fell in love with the gun. Extremely powerful, the Austrians made the gun using seventeen percent non-metallic polymer, making it really light - it weighed in at twenty-three ounces. This was one heck of a gun. You could drop this baby from a helicopter at three hundred feet or leave it buried under ground for a year and it would *still* work. No wonder New York City was the first police force in the country to buy a thousand of them.

Bishman came across some twenty or thirty blacks raping a white girl. Her boyfriend was putting up one hell of a struggle. Bishman fired one shot at him and put him out of his misery. After that he let the blacks get on with it. The time wasn't right to be caught with his trousers down.

In Brooklyn looters were driving cars right out of showrooms without even opening the plate-glass doors. In Queens a liquor store was completely emptied in under four minutes. The youths had organized themselves like a chain gang and cases of booze were shooting down the line like greased lightning, straight into the back of a pick-up-truck they'd commandeered ten minutes earlier. The driver was still lying in the passenger's seat with a bullet in his head, blood gushing from a gaping wound you could put your fist through.

Bishman continued his bloody tour of the city and came across a gang of youths who were lining up to gang bang a girl in a Seventh Avenue parking lot. Bishman joined the line, he was about ninth. Every time someone finished humping, a big cheer went up. The staying power of some of these black guys was incredible but others in the line grew so impatient they jerked themselves off right there and then. That got rid of three of them. It was nearly Bishman's turn. God knows how many guys had gone through the girl before Bishman, but it certainly wasn't a case of sloppy seconds.

Bishman's turn came. The guy in front dismounted, everyone cheered. Bishman was just getting ready, he was about five feet away, keeping well out of the guy's way, when the girl exploded. *Jeeeezus, Fucking Shit*. She didn't explode literally, but she had a volcanic eruption between her legs and a vast column of steaming hot jism shot past Bishman, just missing him. There must have been over a gallon of the stuff, all building up inside of her, and something had to give. It did, with the strangest slurping and gushing noise Bishman had ever heard. Bishman had never witnessed anything like it in his life before and he doubt he'd ever witness anything like it again. He gave her one. He didn't last long and she never said "Thank you."

One of Bishman's 9mm bullets was kept for something special. He'd been waiting for years for the right opportunity to come along. Now it was here. He walked over to Fifth Avenue in the dark, and stood on the top step of St. Patrick's Cathedral. He waited 'till there was sufficient light from passing cars and pumped a single 9mm round into the head of Atlas on the other side of the road. The bullet went straight through the bronze sculpture and smashed the window behind. The window was replaced the next day; the neat 9mm hole in Atlas's forehead still remains today. Every time Bishman was in Manhattan he'd check that it was still there.

One of Bishman's victims was a guy driving a Plymouth. Bishman shot him through the heart when he pulled up to investigate a burning car blocking his way. Bishman thought *the bozos as dead as a dodo* as he put the body in the trunk and drove around Manhattan, the Bronx, Brooklyn and Queens before setting fire to the car at the end of two action-packed days.

From what he saw, Bishman calculated there were over a thousand stores with their windows shattered, three times that many cars burned out and well over a hundred and fifty killed. The more he thinks about it the nearer he puts the figure to five hundred, perhaps even a thousand - there was that much going down.

The smell of cordite hung in the air for days, as did the acrid smell of burning car tires and car upholstery. Police helicopters flew overhead constantly and at least one of them was taken out by automatic fire. Bishman witnessed it crash into the East River. There were SWAT teams and riot police everywhere.

Bishman lapped it up and in those 48 hours took many more risks than he would have done ordinarily, *but when you're on a roll, you're on a roll.*

Sometime later, Bishman heard that the police drained the Reservoir, the vast man-made lake in Central Park, three days after the blackout, and found one hundred and thirty nine bodies all suffering from either knife or gunshot wounds. The lake has remained dry from that day forth.

One thing Bishman does know for sure is that all the burnt-out cars are still being stored in a huge lot in Newark, New Jersey. He found that out six months later when a truckie asked Bishman if he wanted to see the *'Sea of Steel'*. Bishman said "Sure," and the truckie took a detour.

A buddy of his had told him about it. It turned out the *'Sea of Steel'* was a *'Sea of Rust'* but sure enough, about three thousand cars all with New York plates, all wrecked, burnt out and rusty, were being stored. Bishman was pleased to see none of the trunks or hoods were popped. He could only assume the body of the Plymouth owner was still in the trunk.

Nine months after the blackout there was an explosive baby boom in New York, but that's probably another story, right?

Harvey dropped Bishman off in downtown L.A. just by the Greyhound station. He made his next appointment with him and drove off.

Unbeknown to Bishman, Harvey went to Chinatown on a binge and got extremely drunk and violently sick.

Stan Barron, forensic psychologist extraordinaire, was about to take great delight in detailing out the psychological profile of the monster the two of them were so desperate to track.

Barron pushed aside the police files, sickening photographic evidence, pathologists' reports, forensic details and documents that were strewn all over his large oak desk, he picked up about twelve sheets that were stapled together, glanced through them as if to speed read them, then began, as if he'd memorised the document:

"The guy we are looking for often leaves 'mixed' crime scene characteristics; he often uses restraints, ie he ties his victims up, therefore he's organized; but many times he leaves the bodies in full view, allowing them to be found, therefore he's disorganized."

Mainwarring made as if to interrupt or ask some question, but Barron said, "Don't break my train of thought. Let me give you the whole thing, then you come in." He sipped his coffee then added, "Many times he 'de-personalises' a victim, ie mutilates their bodies. That again means he's disorganised, but he takes the murder weapon with him, therefore he's organised. I'm not trying to baffle you with science, Howard - I'm trying to make a point that this guy you are looking for, we are looking for, 'on balance' is organised."

"He's probably an American, but could be a Brit who knows America well and travels back and forth. We haven't come to this conclusion lightly. One of the major aspects of these killings is the periods of non-activity, and we're convinced this is when the Creep's out of the country. The other thing of course, that we have discussed many times is the simalsty betwen the killing here in England and many that have gone down in the States. The agents at Quantico are doing a lot of work on their multi-million-dollar computer, to see if they can get a match with any of their serial killers that stop and start their activities in the States, in the corresponding periods.

"Statistics profile him as white, average appearance and to be of the school 'drop-out' type, possibly unemployed, maybe even self-employed. More likely than not, badly abused as a child."

Barron glanced through his papers once more, hesitated to take a gulp of coffee, then continued, "I think we are looking at a prolific thief and a world class liar, but over the next few weeks we'll be doing even more fine tuning on the profile, when I hope to be able to deliver to you everything except his name and telephone number - but it'll be a damn good starting point.

"He's mature, in his mid-forties, maybe early fifties. He's bi-sexual and he's going to kill again and again until he's apprehended. This guy has been, and still could be, into booze and drugs in a big way, probably has a large pornography collection and his sadistic behaviour points to severe mental problems.

"Take my word for it, Howard, this guy is constantly on the move, knows how to create rapports and is one clever son-of-a-gun and one mean son-of-a-bitch.

"Anyone who consistently mutilates their victims, slashes their breasts, cuts their nipples off or decapitates them is usually doing so through some sexual expression. This guy sometimes collects 'souvenirs' and that's another...

There was a knock on the door and an officer entered.

Stan Barrron was cut short; a n emergency had cropped up and Mainwarring had to go into another meeting, immediately. Some very important results had just come in from the Home Office Forensic Laboratory at Chepstow.

They agreed to meet for lunch together at El Vino's wine bar, on Fleet Street, whereby Stan could deliver the rest of his profile over a few glasses of red wine.

Fucking creep, thought Mainwarring, *this guy's a fucking CREEP*, as he closed the door behind him.

Harvey had the full attention of his I.O.H. franchisees.

"We've all had the experience of smelling a perfume, and the whole experience and feeling and vision of being with a particular person comes flooding back to you.

"You walk past a bakery, smell the fresh bread and get mentally whisked back to your childhood - you see the complete scenario in great detail. Or you may hear a song on the radio, and say, 'That's our song.' That would be an auditory anchor.

"Of course the alcoholic is tied to drinking and reactivating certain feelings and emotions at a given time in his or her life. Then, in the future, every time he drinks, he triggers off those bad feelings and emotions and he tries to drown them with booze.

"I had a client, who, twenty years ago, went to a party with a date. His date was fat and ugly. When he was there he met a gorgeous girl, but because he was with 'Millstone' he never asked the gorgeous one for a date. He did however drink himself into oblivion and continued to do so for the next twenty years. Unbeknown to him, he was firing the anchor of these bad feelings and emotions.

"The easiest way to effect the cure is to hypnotize the client when he's absolutely sober and start a drinking session with him. Use water in a vodka bottle or cold tea in a whiskey bottle and go through the whole scenario with him of getting drunk. Then when he's tapping into all those negative feelings snap him out of the altered state and allow him to access the negative thoughts and feelings of the past events. This will be the first time in his life that he has been able to access those particular feelings, emotions and pictures when he's in the sober state.

"Of course the other thing I do is to collapse his anchors. I access all the negative emotions and write them down on a sheet of paper, I audibly read out to my client what is on the list. Then I harshly slap the paper into the client's right hand. Then I access all the good feelings my client has when he's sober, about what he'd like to do with his future, that sort of thing and I gently read these out aloud and gently place them in my client's left hand. Then all of a sudden I take his two hands together with all these sheets of paper and bring them clapping together.

"I effectively collapse his anchors!

"This will be the first time the client has ever been able to access both the negative and the positive together when he's sober. He'll usually walk around for a while in a complete daze while he's processing all this new information. After a day or two he'll be fine. He'll be able to take a drink, and stop at one. He'll be able to control his drinking habits and be a social drinker like the rest of us. Hic." Everyone laughed.

SEVEN

Often Harvey spent many hours piecing together several of Bishman's regressions, that when edited and scripted, completed a story. This had to be done if he was to get inside Bishman's head - which he fully intended to do:

Bishman's mind was working overtime. He knew his junkie customers wanted more dope. Heroin to be precise. They still owed money on the last delivery and it was a better than evens chance that they wouldn't be able to pay for that. He also knew it was futile arguing with *fuckin' junkies*. He sensed trouble. *Someone is going to get shafted here and it ain't gonna be me*, thought Bishman as he finished off his soda. He was sitting in a coffee bar on Lexington and Fourth Avenue.

"I'll pay cash for my gear, right here and now, buddy, there ya go, two hundred bucks." Bishman handed over four fifties and in return got some heroin and grass. The heroin was in little phials, the grass was wrapped in miniature Ziploc bags. He was going to use the grass himself and sell the heroin to his customers in Brooklyn.

"Gimme another five bucks mon, and take this for yourself." The Jamaican drug dealer passed him a tiny slither of blotting paper the size of a sequin with a funny little picture of Mickey Mouse on it.

"Fuck you pal, you gotta' be shittin' me. Five bucks for that, you must be fuckin' crazy." Bishman pushed back the tiny tab.

"That's acid, mon. With that you'll fucking fly, mon. Believe me." The candy man pushed it back.

Bishman popped the wee paper acid disc in his mouth and slid over an awfully crumpled, dirty, five dollar bill.

"You'd better be fuckin' right, pal. If I don't fly you'll be the first motherfucker to hear about it. Yeah. Boogaloo." Bishman bugged his eyes.

"Hey cool it, mon. You'll fly to the fuckin' moon." The Jamacian grinned, showing a mouth full of gleaming white teeth.

Bishman stuffed the gear into his corduroys and strolled off. He was either going to double his money with this shit or he was going to have fun. He really didn't give a fuck either way. He knew getting money out of junkies was harder than trying to shove butter up a porcupine's ass with a red hot poker.

He was going to Brownsville, which is a particularly tough part of Brooklyn. Brownsville is where the Torture Gang originated, as well as the infamous Murder Incorporated and the

Undertakers Gang. This was one rough area and Bishman's customers were vicious bastards. It was going to be a tough visit - he felt a little weak, so he decided to eat first. He thought he'd drop into McDonald's for a coffee and a burger, and there he started to formulate a plan.

Bishman was thinking what to do, when his Big Mac suddenly started moving across the table. As he stretched out to catch it, it opened up like a mouth that had long, sharp, gnashing teeth inside, that started snapping at him. *Shit!* The burger had turned into a Gremlin. Bishman went to grab it again but his burger grew legs and it started to claw at him. *What the fuck goes on here...*" Bishman looked into the green and red eyes of the Gremlin as it spat smoke and flames at him. It was crazy, vicious. He decided to leave, before he got gobbled up.

"Jesus H. Christ." His shoes were full of water, his feet were soaking wet. Every step he took squelched. He sat on the step of McDonald's to empty his shoes but there was nothing in them. *Shit!*

Bishman slowly walked past a school and about fifty schoolchildren came out running, shouting and screaming like savages. They all had horns on their heads and they were breathing fire. *Great balls of fire,* thought Bishman as he ran like hell.

Slowly but surely he was making his way to Brooklyn, but he could see it was going to take longer than planned. A squirrel from the park ran in front of him and turned into a six-foot-tall dinosaur with huge, sharp claws and started to chase him. *Boooo* screamed Bishman and the squirrel ran up a tree.

He caught a bus and as it went across the river, the bridge actually disappeared and the bus flew like a plane, landing safely on the other side, much to Bishman's amazement and utter horror. All the people on the bus had molten faces - when they opened their mouths their heads disappeared. *Crazy bastards!*

Four bus transfers and a lot of fuck-ups later, Bishman found the house he wanted. It was a derelict building on Rockaway Avenue and Livonia Avenue. The first floor was empty and damp. The junkies lived on the second floor, about thirty of them, and the floor above was kept by a guy who owned hundreds of racing pigeons.

Bishman left a package on the first floor, walked up the stairs and entered, unannounced. There was pandemonium going on. The junkies hadn't even noticed him come in, they were busy slapping the face of one of their buddies who'd O.D'd. To Bishman this was a living hell. Normally these junkies were bad enough, but with the LSD inside him, they were monsters. He could see all their bones and muscles, as though he had X-ray eyes. Their hypodermic syringes started doing the boogie-woogie with each other on the table. One scantily-clad woman had long bright-red finger nails and every time she moved her hands, thousands of tiny red missiles would emanate from her finger-tips. She moved her hands a little too quickly one time and the whole room filled with red polka-dots. *Fuck! Shit!*

The junkie who'd O.D'd had come round and the first thing he asked for was more smack. Bishman had the heroin, the junkies only had a little money - as he'd thought, it didn't even cover what they owed before. He took what they had, gave them the phials and walked downstairs.

Bishman put his plan into operation. He picked up the package that he'd left on the first floor. In Brighton he'd bought a gallon container and filled it with gasoline. Brighton is not on the way to Brownsville but Bishman had ended up there - the fifty-minute trip had taken him five hours. He'd been on a trip of his own, fighting off butterflies the size of 747s, squirrels like dinosaurs and schoolchildren who were going to eat him *alive*.

He liberally sprinkled the gasoline all over the stair-well and floor. No-one came out, the junkies were all too busy shooting up. He threw a match and it went off with a '*whooooompfff*' that startled him. Bishman gently closed the front door behind him.

The return journey took about seven hours, but of course you realize these things are difficult to gauge. It could have taken ten hours, he wasn't sure.

In Manhattan he played a game of pool. Or tried to. The wood grain of the cues and the side of the pool table was breathing - puffing and panting. He hit the first ball and by the time it was half-way down the green baize it was the size of a cannonball; by the time it reached the end of the pool table it had filled up the whole room, and Bishman passed out.

The next day the newspapers had the story about the fire that had killed the thirty-two junkies, but that was overshadowed by the fact that the fire had spread next door and killed a pregnant mother and her five young children.

Bishman went from a state of hypnosis to a state of deep sleep and stayed like that for several hours, while Harvey made himself busy editing, tidying notes and putting his own thoughts on the subject in order - which proved to be quite difficult a task.

"Tell me some more about your tearaway days when you were a teenager in London. I find it fascinating - especially as the world thinks you're the great Dr. Bill, who's helped so many people through cancer, alcoholism and drug problems. They don't know the other side of you. I love it. It makes me feel...alive." Anita kicked some sand with her toes as the seagulls wheeled around in the air and the Californian sun baked down.

Harvey pushed his optical sunglasses further up the bridge of his nose and said, "*Be-Bop-a-Lula* was the record we used to put on the juke box at the Ace Café on the North Circular Road in London. In those days of course there were no speed restrictions and at the Ace Café the road was only two lanes wide. The idea was to put the record on, race outside, start your motorcycle, race up to the roundabout and get back before the record finished playing. To do it, you had to average over a hundred miles an hour, and to average a hundred miles an hour it meant you had to do speeds of about a hundred and thirty. Only the fastest Triumphs, Nortons and BSAs could do it."

Harvey sipped his beer. "All the lads did it. You couldn't be a member of the legendary *69 CLUB* if you didn't. A few of the lads got hurt or died on that one. Then we decided to spice it up, somewhat. The new game was called *Chicken Run*. Two motorcycles would leave the Ace Café and a third machine had to drive between the first two, who would be coming back at about a hundred and twenty miles an hour - that's a closing speed of two hundred and forty miles an hour. It was scary. The crazy thing was, we used to do it late at night, so all you could see was two headlights coming at you at remarkable speed.

"Quite a few of us managed it until one night something went wrong and a Volvo with its two headlights on was mistaken for the two motorcycles. My best mate, Ian Stonehart, on a supercharged Vincent Black Knight, tore into the car at such an unbelievable speed it literally split the car in two. Ian and the four occupants died instantly and that ended the game of chicken. After that we all took up serious road-racing at organized race circuits."

They continued to walk along Venice beach, kissing, cuddling and eating Heavenly Hash ice cream in sugar cones, and talking about their pasts. They got along great. There was a chemistry and an electricity between them that was growing all the time.

Sessions snatched wherever. Sessions that unburdened the one, and held the other in a thrall of fascination. Who needed paying?

"Where did ya say you were from?" The beautiful young hooker, sitting on the bench in Lynn railway station turned her head towards Bishman, but kept on chewing her gum.

"I come from out West originally but I travel a lot." Bishman stood up as if to stretch, but he yawned instead.

"Have ya been to Lynn before? Fuckin' dump, this place, I can't wait to get outta here." She pushed her golden hair back and tossed her head. Good looking girl, knew how to use make-up too.

"You live here, then. Brought up here, were ya?" Bishman sat down and lit up two cigarettes, he passed her one.

"Yeah all my life." She drew down on the cigarette and blew the smoke out, neat, through round lips, like women do.

"I've never been to Lynn before. I've been to Boston lots of times though. I'll probably never come here again. I got a ride with a guy and I've been travelling in the wrong direction. It happens all the time, I was on the wrong side of the freeway. Story of my fucking life." He looked around. At three in the morning the place was desolate.

"You know what? Lynn's a fuckin' dump. It's the only place in America where McDonald's went bust. They had to close the place down. It got robbed every week for about a year. Yeah - Lynn, Lynn, City of Sin they call it." She laughed and smiled at Bishman.

"I've never heard that one before. My sister used to work in McDonald's. She O.D'd way back on smack or some other shit." Bishman rolled a joint.

"I still keep in touch with a friend of hers whenever I can," he went on, "She works for the CIA in Virginia. You should hear some of the things she comes out with. Incredible!" He lit the joint, took a long toke and handed it to the eager recipient.

"Yeah, like what sort of things? I've never known anyone in the CIA."

Bishman coughed on the joint. Then cupped his hands around the smoke and inhaled it like that, rather than puffing the joint directly. "She doesn't work out in the field. She works in the headquarters, in the computer room." He'd had enough of the joint and lit a cigarette. The girl put her hand out for one and smiled nicely. He handed her a cigarette and she lit it with a slim silver lighter.

"Brenda, my friend at the CIA told me all about the moon rock samples. They've landed on the moon dozens of times you know. But most times it was on secret missions. They've brought back all sorts of rocks and samples. They've already proved the moon was part of the Earth and the craters are from a nuclear war, three thousand years ago. Blew the fucking place sky high and the moon split off from the earth. The Chinese and Arabs. Not the Americans and Russians. They've proved it and hushed it all up. The CIA controls NASA. They blew the shuttle up because NASA wasn't handing over all the samples. They do now. They've learnt their lesson." He tossed the half-finished cigarette onto the track.

"Like the fucking AIDS scam, another big CIA hush-up. They know the Russians developed and released the virus here in the States. The CIA and KGB are in cahoots. They've already got the vaccine for AIDS but it's a big hush-up job." He put his hand on her lap and she held it, gazing into his eyes, taking it all in. *Awesome*.

"They keep letting it rip because it's wiping out all the blacks. People don't realize it but it's already wiped out over sixty million blacks in Africa. They reckon by the time AIDS has gone full circle there won't be any blacks left."

She squeezed his hand and moved closer, as if to cuddle up. She put her face closer - he felt her *Juicy Fruits* breath and smelt her cheap, sickly perfume. "What do you mean, full circle?" she asked.

"Well, they're all fucking each other, and the babies come out with the AIDS. The prostitutes never use any birth control, they don't believe there is such a thing as AIDS. Soon there won't be anyone who isn't infected in the whole of Africa. The other thing is the CIA wants all the gays wiped out in America, it always has done, so they let it carry on in this country too. Brenda reckons it'll be another six or seven years before they release the cure to the public."

"You know what? You're the most interesting guy I ever met. You're kinda neat. I like that in a guy. You wanna fuck me, for free I mean."

"Yeah, you bet, where?"

"Round the back here, that's where I always go." She took him by the hand.

He went round the back of the station and fucked her. Then he went down on her, and as he did caught the odor of oily sardines and thought, *I can smell it from here*.

She gave him a blow job. "Try sucking instead of blowing," said Bishman, "I don't want to end up with a permanent hump in my back!" Then he fucked her again. When he'd finished, he strangled her. He was hungry and went off to look for a McDonald's. He never found one.

On the drive back from Santa Barbara Harvey gave Bishman detailed feedback on the events to date, but when Harvey actually looked at Bishman he noted he was sound asleep and in the foetal position.

"Dr. Bill, I'd really like to see some more hypnotic phenomena. Can you oblige?" The question had been asked by Patricia, an extremely attractive woman of about thirty-five.

"Why sure, I suppose you'd like me to get you to do all sorts of naughty things." Harvey laughed and came over to her with a warm smile.

"No, I want to see some more of the funny stuff. You know, like you did a few weeks back."

After a short induction and inserting a quick suggestive program into selected subjects, Harvey stood back and looked at his students, then casually walked to the back of the room. He unexpectedly turned back and touched each of the volunteers' shoulders one after another. As he did, all hell broke loose.

Tom and Carol started shouting at each other, a major argument about something trivial like where they would eat lunch. David gave his rendition of *Blue Suede Shoes* and although he didn't know all the words, what he sang of it was pretty realistic. He sang it over and over again, even strumming an imaginary guitar.

Patricia was getting wolf whistles as she slowly and sexily lifted her skirt up, giving the guys a pretty sexy eyeful of wonderful long thigh. She had legs that went all the way up to her ass. Harold was punching an imaginary George Foreman and shouting that he was the greatest. It was pandemonium and the class loved every minute of it.

All except Tom. Everybody had forgotten about him - until he stood up and they could see he was trying intensely hard to prise his eyes apart to see what the hell was going on, but to no avail.

Harvey found himself listening patiently to the hours and hours of regressions that were often ramblings and bits and pieces of shattered lives that all had to be pieced together, and because of the severity of many of Bishman's tales he felt he couldn't tell Anita *too* much, even though he would have liked to unburden his own heavy heart.

At a kiddie's park in Topeka, Kansas, one bright July morning at about 11:am., a group of about a dozen youngsters were playing. Some were on creaky metal swing sets; two were running up and down a slide the wrong way. A number were chasing each other through a tunnel made from lumber. Two young lads were having a friendly argument.

A few dogs ran around, sniffing each other's asses and trying to hump one another. Two obese women stood talking, a man sat on an oak bench smoking a pipe and reading a newspaper. The sky was a pleasant shade of deep blue; birds sang in the trees and occasionally came and had a dust bath in the playground. Every now and then a lively squirrel would chase the birds off.

A woman was ordering her husband around. "Little Eddie wants to go to the bathroom, take him over to those bushes."

The man did as he was told and lifted little Eddie into the clump of bushes. When the little lad had finished defecating he came out and said to his father, "I hope some dog treads in it." His dad missed the humor.

A police car pulled in and the cop, who was wearing Ray-Bans, started looking around for someone in particular. A woman walked towards the car.

"Ma'am, is the fella still around? Tell us about it." The cop lent out of the car, sucking hard on his cigarette.

"Well, like I said over the 'phone, I've been here over three hours, watching my kids play in the park. That's them over on the swings.

"As I was watching them I thought I saw a man in the bushes over there, but thought to myself it couldn't possibly be, because no-one's come into the park since I arrived. It must have been a tree or something. A branch maybe.

"Anyway, my curiosity got the better of me, and I eventually walked right over there, to that clump of trees, and sure enough, it was a guy, like a statue, still as a tree, just staring at the kids in the park. Even when he saw me he never moved. He must have been there three hours at least. He had light-blue death eyes. He wasn't jerking off or exposing himself or anything. He just stared at me, it was really cre..." The cop interrupted her.

"Well ma'am, you did the right thing to call us. We'll drive through the neighborhood to see if we can find anyone. What we need is a description, tell us what he looked like." The cop tossed the cigarette out of the car.

"He had death eyes, he must have been about thirty-five years old, he wore corduroy slacks, a white sweatshirt and sneakers, and he had death eyes. I felt a shiver go down my spine. What could he be wanting here - none of these kids are over ten? He has a neatly trimmed moustache. Yes, that's right. A small moustache and death eyes."

"Ma'am, that description fits just about everyone on the block, you must be able to give us some distinguishing marks or something. Not only that, he hasn't done anything yet. Even if he was standing in the bushes and staring at the kids playing on the slides, that isn't exactly a crime." The cop took a few notes in a little black pad. He lit another cigarette and looked over the top of his Ray-Bans.

The woman stepped back. "I'm telling you this man had death eyes, he's dangerous, I just know it. I just feel it. The thing was, when I looked up the next time, he'd vanished. Then I thought I'd better call the cops. You know how it is, right?" The woman turned to look at her kids who were clambering over some climbing apparatus by a rusty merry-go-round.

"Thanks for calling us, ma'am. You keep a good lookout for your kids, ya' hear. If we find anything we'll let ya know." The cop was already driving out of the park. He felt good in his Ray-Bans.

102

Harvey was feeling good and when Bishman eventually came round he took him to dinner at a Greek restaurant in Westwood Village, where they talked volubly for over three hours.

Harvey was enjoying his talk as much as the franchisees. He edged his gold-rimmed spectacles up a fraction, pushed back his prematurely gray hair, took a sip of water, and the forty-five year old genius began:

"In the last ten weeks you've gone through a whole variety of learning experiences. Today I just want to consolidate a few of the concepts that I and the other hypnotherapists have told you about.

"Today, I'll be touching on rapport, trances, alcohol abuse and reframing. If there's enough time at the end of the session we can bat around a few questions and answers. I'll ask the questions, you give me the answers."

The room filled with spontaneous laughter. They'd grown used to Dr. Bill's humor. Although Bill Harvey was not actually a doctor, over twenty-five years as a practising hypnotherapist, the title had been endowed and stuck. He'd even given up telling clients and students that he wasn't a doctor. He had, however, probably cured more people of cancer, alcoholism and phobias than anyone else in the world.

"What have you learned from that last story?" asked Harvey, markedly slowly and deliberately.

A well-dressed man of about forty put up his hand. "I think the most important thing I got out of it, was that when you carry on in that monotone voice I can hardly keep my eyes open. But other than that, yes, I understand fully what you say about reframing." He put his hand down.

"EXACTLY!!!" Shouted Harvey, clapping his hands at the same time, and shaking the audience out of their relaxed state, "EXACTLY!!! Half of you have gone into an altered state by listening to that hypnotic drone - and it was my *tone of voice* that did it, *not* the actual words I used.

"You can sit here on the rocks as long as you like, feeling the emotions, listening to the voices and looking at the pictures. See if your mind wants to tell you something. Have a look. You can do that now or in your own time. No biggie."

Harvey pressed the 'on' button of his Panasonic cassette recorder as Bishman started his dialogue:

Central Park during the day is one of the most pleasant spots in the world where one finds respite from an incredibly fast-moving city. You go there to get away from the hubbub and anxiety that city life causes.

Lovers stroll hand in hand, tourists gawk, executives and secretaries jog and old people feed pigeons and ducks. People from all walks of life, from all over the world, are drawn there. They eat ice cream, munch trail mix and pistachio nuts, and drink sodas and beers from cans in brown paper-bags.

You can even go for a delightful ride through the park on an old-fashioned horse and carriage. Mind you, if you have romance in mind, make sure you tell the coach driver before you start that you don't want his long-drawn-out verbals about Manhattan, Central Park, the IRA, the IRS, the Dow Jones, the release of Mafeking and the release of hostage Jesse Turner from Lebanon, whose home town is Boise, Idaho. *Well it would be, wouldn't it!* Some of those Irishmen who drive the carriages have more mouth than a cow's got...., but that's another story.

Residents of Manhattan go there just to get out of their apartments and breathe the fresh air, which sometimes isn't so fresh.

A school teacher from the Bronx brought her class of kids, about fifty of them, and as they walked into the park, by the statue at Columbus Circle, the smell of urine was unmistakable. All the kids were holding their noses and making poo pooing noises. The teacher said, "I can smell Jasmine!" and all the kids giggled.

But at night, Central Park becomes a whole different world. You wouldn't even know there was a city out there, other than being able to hear police sirens in the distance.

The whole giddy-up is different. It is proven that death lingers and lurks behind every tree, shrub and wall and under every bridge.

The crime and violence in Central Park increases dramatically when it is a full moon. The official version of the increase is thirty-two percent. The true figure is that it increases over eighty percent and what goes down in Central Park is horrific.

Walking through the park at night is a frightening experience for anyone. There are delinquents out there with guns, knives and garrotes and others with twenty-power starlight scopes. The electronically amplified light from the full moon, stars and Manhattan street lighting give a picture a grey-green hue, kind of eerie. Sometimes when looking through a starlight scope you see someone looking at *you* through a starlight scope...*Fuck!*

Bishman walked through the park. The moon was full, a solitary duck swam on the pond. In the background there was a drunk shouting "Buck, give us a buck, need a buck. Buck!" *Who the fuck's going to give a drunk a buck in Central Park, full moon, two in the morning? God only knows.* All of a sudden he was silent, someone must have bottled him.

Bishman walked around the edge of the lake and started toward the bridge. A man standing on the bridge was silhouetted up against the skyline. Bishman gripped his marine knife, not too hard. He kept walking toward the bridge, the solitary figure stood still. They looked at each other and Bishman kept walking slowly, determined, alert. Once he had started to cross the bridge he was committed. The guy was a six feet two, three hundred and ninety pound, black guy, broad shouldered, built like a brick shithouse. His street name was 'Barbarian.'

Bishman kept walking, the plastic bags over his sneakers making a rustling noise. They looked at each other and simultaneously nodded an acknowledgement. Barbarian pulled his stomach in, as a signal to say *walk past*. Bishman looked him in the eye and said "Booo...", walked straight past and didn't look back. Central Park after dark has its own code of unwritten laws. This was one of them, whatever it was.

Suddenly a huge owl swooped down low and snatched up what appeared to be a field-mouse. Its wings made a frightening flapping sound. Bishman stood still to regain his composure, his heart was pounding. When he looked up he saw his target in the bushes, standing still, also waiting for a victim, waiting to try out psychotic behaviors.

The guy saw Bishman too, and *knew* he could take him. He could plainly see the knife Bishman held in his right hand, but this guy was strong and fit, he worked out every day, lifted weights, took care of himself, the last of the hard men. Mr. Body-Perfect. He puffed himself up like a bullfrog to make himself look even bigger and confronted Bishman, who was raising his marine knife. The hard man grabbed Bishman's wrist with both his hands. The knife and wrist were locked solid, there was nowhere to go, nothing to do.

"Jesus H. Christ!" The man let loose the most hideous, frightening scream you ever heard. He released his grip to clutch at his stomach. Warm, sticky blood trickled through his fingers. He hadn't seen the serrated bread-knife in Bishman's left hand, the one that had been pointing backwards. He let out a prolonged, blood-curdling scream of terror. Bishman had ripped into his gut with the bread-knife and twisted it. He was wailing like a mental patient. As the hard man released Bishman's right hand, the marine knife in that hand came flailing down too. A ghastly smell permeated the air as his bladder and bowels simultaneously released, as they often do in violent death.

Bishman left him for dead with thirty-seven knife wounds. He would arrive in the Bronx Hospital as a D.O.A. The newspapers wrote up the murder, calling it a cowardly, frenzied attack. No mention was made of why the victim was in the middle of Central Park at four o'clock in the morning. At the age of twenty-nine, the guy had owned and controlled a computer company operating out of Queens, with a turnover in excess of fifty million dollars. But he still enjoyed being in Central Park around the time of the full moon.

His name has been withheld to protect his family, who are still in the process of squabbling over his estate.

Bishman retraced his footsteps that led him to the edge of the park, he didn't want to go any further. *Not with all those fuckin' whackos, weirdos and psychos out there, no way, boogaloo,* he thought.

Just before the exit, he slipped the plastic bags off his sneakers and took off the old tracksuit top and mismatching bottoms that had streaks of blood splattered over them and stuck them deep inside a trash can. Bishman knew the trash would be emptied before seven o'clock that morning.

On the way out of the park, at the exit by West 72nd Street, Bishman noticed a terrible itching on his left wrist, right by his scar. Of all things he'd been bitten by a mosquito and it itched like hell. Bishman dug his thumbnail deep into the insect bite and then dug it in again, at right angles, to form the sign of a cross. *'Well it always worked before,'* thought Bishman as he dug his thumbnail in again to reinforce the sign.

Bishman tried hard to remember who told him that little trick but he couldn't, so he started humming *Mack the Knife.* He was half way through his tune when he remembered, *Yeah, it must have been that cretin, Michael Shwartz. Same guy who told me dragon flies would zip up my eyes and I'd attract rattle snakes to me if I meditated in the forest...Yeah! Michael Shwartz, my ass! Fuckin' cretin!*

Bishman spat a groobly on the ground. He couldn't tell whether it bounced or not...it probably did.

109

Harvey would give Bishman feedback at opportune moments. This was one of them:

"Good stuff, Bob. I know we've talked a lot, with you both in the trance state and in the conscious state. The important thing to realize about the feedback that I give you is, that it's *no biggie*. Don't try to find answers in it, just let your subconscious mind assimilate it. Like I say, just relax. You don't even have to listen to me, because I'm not talking to you. I'm talking to your subconscious mind.

"The thing about drinking is this: All the counsellors have been asking you *why* you drink. I don't think *that's* important. I would like you to ask yourself the question: *What would I do if I didn't drink?*...Simple as that, no biggie."

Many times Bishman would ramble for many hours, all recorded by Harvey, only to come up with one coherent experience right at the end of a regression. This is *one* of those many sessions:

Chicago is known as Windy City, and for good reason too. The biting North wind comes sweeping right in over Lake Michigan and the towering skyscrapers, causing howling vortexes that are unknown anywhere else in America. In winter, the place gets bitterly cold. This particular day, there were plenty of *dead umbrellas* and plenty of *dead rainbows* too.

110

The dead umbrellas are obvious: the cheap flimsy things, that are all too often made in China these days, just can't hack the pressure of Windy City. At the end of each windy day the streets are littered with them. The dead rainbows are from Bishman's childhood. His sister, Ghislaine, when she was alive, used to point them out to him. Whenever it rained, the patches of gasoline in the street would turn all the colors of the rainbow. Hence the expression, dead rainbows.

The day Bishman found himself in town was a particularly windy one, and it was the bitterly cold wind and driving rain that had forced him into the first bar he came across, after the truckie dropped him off.

Pussy Galore is probably the roughest bar on Chicago's notorious East Side, in a seriously rough neighborhood known by Bishman as the Combat Zone. It could even be the roughest bar in the whole of the States.

The minute he walked into Pussy Galore he realized he'd made a big mistake. To quote Julia Roberts in *Pretty Woman*, "Big mistake, huge!" Everyone glowered at him. He was obviously a stranger in a strange place. All the usual weirdos, whackos, alkies and druggies were there. Bishman, King of Serial Killers, could pick up the vibes, even the barman's face said *drink up and go, post haste!*

There was sawdust on the floor and the walls were decorated with hundreds of photographs of Al Capone and the prohibition era. There were cased Thompson submachine guns, the old "Tommy" guns, decorating the place - fixed firmly to the walls. A huge mural of the St. Valentine's Day massacre adorned the main wall. Pictures of George "Machine Gun" Kelly and "Pretty Boy" Floyd, toting Tommy guns, seemed to be everywhere. Pictures of Dillinger with his tiny gun, posing as though it were a brand-new toy, hung over the bar.

There was even a large cartoon of "Baby Face" Nelson getting gunned down by G-Men holding Tommy guns. He got hit with seventeen bullets. In the cartoon he was being asked if it hurt, replying: "Only when I laugh."

Bishman sipped his bourbon, slowly. He had a memory pop into his head. *Once he'd wandered into a restaurant early one Sunday morning, in Shreveport, Louisiana. Of the two hundred diners he was the only white man, all the rest were black. He didn't walk out, he carried on as though everything was cool, which it was. He ate two breakfasts, paid the tab and left. No problem.*

However, he did have a problem here and it was getting progressively and aggressively worse. By the time he had ordered his fourth Jim Bean he had goons sitting either side of him. The meanest son-of-a-bitch, a guy by the name of Sonny Claymore, reputed to have killed over seventeen hoodlums for various mobsters in Chicago, stared coldly into Bishman's eyes. Bishman stared back, pale blue eyes bugging out, jutting his chin forward and said "Booo..." in a scary sort of way.

Claymore ordered himself a whiskey and judging by the way he did, you'd surmise he knew the barman pretty well.

"Just how hard are you?" grunted the steely-eyed Claymore, looking Bishman straight between the eyes, not backing down for a second, at the same time thrusting a NATO Bowie knife with a ten-inch blade deep into the bar counter.

Blunt as a boar's ass, thought Bishman as he pulled a Spanish switch blade from a sheath in his sock. He pressed the release button and an eight-inch blade flew out of the end and locked firmly into place.

On the Cobra Mk 8, which Bishman happened to have, you could put that sucker up to someone's throat, press the release switch and the blade would sink its full depth into the victim. *Nothing* could stop it. That's what you *paid* over $300 for, *certainly worth stealing,* which is exactly what Bishman had done earlier that day. A knife for the serious blademan only. A powerful, lethal bit of kit, stiletto pointed, hollow ground and razor sharp, both edges.

Bishman held the knife. Claymore and his buddy couldn't help being impressed with the speed the blade came out. It was electrifying. Claymore put his hand around the big Bowie knife that was well lodged into the bar. Bishman took his Cobra in his right hand, held it up slowly and deliberately, and proceeded to pull its razor-sharp blade across his own left wrist. He ordered a Jim Bean, a double. When the barman brought it over, he sent it back.

113

"No, make it a triple," said Bishman pushing the heavy glass back over the bar.

He continued drinking. He had three more triples and about nine cigarettes. While he did, the blood continued to ooze from his wrist, dripped onto the bar and trickled onto the sawdust-covered floor. Bishman didn't bat an eyelid. Claymore and his buddies were long gone, so were most of the other hard cases. He left the bar sketching a farewell wave to the barman. He found himself humming the Alka Seltzer commercial and singing the words, *plop plop, fizz fizz, oh what a relief it is!*

As he went outside he had to hop over a big splattering of vomit. He knew intuitively it belonged to Claymore and his buddies.

EIGHT

Harvey noticed that Bishman was always punctual and as requested, never turned up to an appointment under the influence of booze or drugs. This in itself was quite a feat, and Harvey made a number of notes concerning this and the fact that Bishman was always exceptional in the areas of personal hygiene, always clean and his clothing was relatively clean and fresh too. It was not the normal behaviour of someone in Bishman's situation. Harvey concluded that Bishman must stash clothing somewhere or constantly steal new clothes - maybe from victims. Harvey was not one to have the wool pulled over his eyes and made a note to study the anomalies in Bishman's story:

Bishman walked up Fifth Avenue and sat on the top step of the Marble Collegiate Church. A few years previously he'd heard Norman Vincent Peale talking about goals and getting things done, right here in this particular church. Bishman had goals and he wanted to accomplish great things. He wanted to be a billionaire and be famous. He tried the doors and they were locked. *Fuck, shit!*

He continued walking up Fifth Avenue, battling his way through secretaries briskly exiting their offices for lunch, executives hurtling into stores and tourists practically throwing themselves at cabs.

Bishman walked up the steps of St. Patrick's Cathedral and pulled on one of the astonishingly heavy doors, *Shit, these motherfuckers are heavy*, he thought.

He sat in a rear pew. Two hours of cogitation brought a revelation to his mind, to wit: *Why do women have tits? So men will talk to them!*

Bishman's train of thought was broken when he saw out of the corner of his eye a cop the size of King Kong. He didn't have his gun drawn, but he looked as though he could, and would, without too much provocation. Bishman's asshole puckered. The cop escorted the priest around while he emptied all the collection boxes that were on the walls all around the Cathedral.

Lucky I stole the two votive candles before King Kong came in, thought Bishman as he closed the heavy door behind him.

Harvey noted this item as unfinished. He anticipated that *sooner or later* Bishman would come back to it.

116

Anita lay on the bed naked. Harvey had changed from green swimming trunks back into stunning bright yellow boxer shorts. Anita was expecting to make love with Harvey for the first time. She wanted a lot more foreplay, but she really didn't know what to expect next. They'd just come from a long session in the Jacuzzi.

"Roll over on your front and pull your hair from your back. I need to get to the back of your neck."

"How's that?" Anita rolled over and pulled her long blonde hair to her front.

"Yes that's good, I don't want to get baby oil all over your hair."

He warmed baby oil in his palm and gently massaged her neck and shoulders. Powerful hands, working slowly, gently, lovingly.

"Keep you hair pulled back, I'm not finished yet." He warmed up more oil. She felt relaxed and loving. Harvey moved slowly down her spine, separating the discs, traversing the length of her back. He gently brushed over the cheeks of her ass, then massaged each thigh thoroughly.

Harvey warmed more baby oil and caressed her calves and then her feet. He moved back up her legs and started on her thighs again, going right up between her legs - right up to her pussy but not quite. Anita's groin area throbbed and she opened her legs slightly, but not obviously. He then worked back up to her neck and worked his magic on her neck and shoulders again. More oil was called for.

117

He went down her back, slowly and this time very gently massaged her ass. Each cheek separately, then both at the same time, then gently flicked an oiled finger across her asshole. She quivered and groaned in appreciation. He worked her thighs again, right up to her pussy. She sensed that he actually touched her pussy lips but it was so gentle she wasn't sure. He worked her calf muscles again. She was in heaven.

"If you turn over, I'll do your front. Would you like that?"

Like it? She was purring. "Like it? I'd love it."

Harvey warmed more oil. He started on her neck and then her front, carefully and deliberately keeping away from her full, beautiful breasts, that had lost their shape, because she was lying down.

He spent time gently working the oil around her belly button and her flat tummy and down to the pubes. He deliberately brushed the bush of golden pubes, the Bermuda Triangle he called it, full of mysteries of the deep, and pulled back quickly.

Anita lay there, loving it. He had been over an hour, and he was still at it. She hadn't been pampered like this for a long time. A long time? *No, never!*

This Dr. Bill knows all the erogenous zones, she thought. Anita was lost in thought and lost in lust. *And he's still not made love to me.* Little did she know his jism was backing up his spine to his brain, making him go all pasty white.

118

"If you sit up now, I'll massage your front again. He snuck behind her and she waited while he was warming up more baby oil. He breathed softly on her neck and then in her ears. *Sheer magic!* She could *feel* him through his yellow boxer shorts. He slipped his hands around her and he rubbed her belly and then slowly moved up to her breasts: this was what she had been waiting for. This was what he had been waiting for, too. He gently massaged and felt and groped, and she sighed to let him know her appreciation. She loved it and he kept going, lifting each breast, caressing it, playing with huge brown nipples that were getting larger and firmer. He felt each breast for shape, size, texture and he got to know those tits intimately. *These breasts could satisfy a man*, he thought.

"I want to make love with you," he whispered in her ear, "But if I do, I know we'll regret it, it's too soon. Let's get to know each other. If we decide to make love later, we'll both enjoy it more - I promise."

She didn't doubt him for a moment. She slipped on her black lace negligée, and felt so relaxed she floated out of the room; she fancied herself to be in heaven, she fancied herself to be in love.

Bill Harvey's seminars at the Springfield headquarters were proving a resounding success. He loved flying there, his Lear jet was earning its

119

keep. He was glad to keep his home and personal base in California. That was one of the best moves he'd ever made. He kept reminding himself not to get too involved, that Max was the prime mover now.

The multi-millionaire wizard of hypnotherapy pushed back his prematurely gray hair, loosened his tie and began: "Lack of sleep affects homeless people the same as it does the alcoholic. Because they sleep on park benches or on the street they very rarely get sufficient sleep. Eventually, their waking and dreaming states get out of phase.

"The drunk suffering from delirium tremens may very well be seeing Zulu warriors and boogy men right there in the middle of Main Street with his eyes wide open. He'll actually be seeing the traffic and the hallucination both at the same time, which of course is extremely dangerous. He won't be able to tell the real from the dream.

"As for getting to understand states of consciousness, you don't *know* things until you *know* them, and you get to *know* them by *doing* them. I suggest every one of you lives on the streets for five or six days, in winter, when it's too cold to sleep in the parks. You'll know a little more about waking and sleeping states, and why so many people talk out loud and scream in what would *appear* to be the most inappropriate situations."

NINE

For sessions with Bishman, Harvey used a wide variety of places because he hated being tied to his office, or for that matter, to any single location. He often used hotel or motel rooms, the beach, the rear seat of his Rolls Royce, and more often than not the warm and inviting wilderness of the majestic Californian countryside. He made a conscious decision never to invite Bishman back to Pinewood.

On every occasion that Bishman went into an altered state Harvey would take particular note of his facial expressions, tears, smiles, body odours, breathing rates and any other hypnotic phenomena that would always be apparent. He also noted Bishman's almost casual acceptance of violence:

It seemed that every time Bishman decided to take a walk in Central Park, it was a full moon. This particular evening was no exception.

Bishman was humming, as was his way. His tune for the night was *Soldiers Who Want To Be Heroes Number Practically Zero, But There Are Millions, Who Wanna Be Civilians.*

There was no-one about. No-one he could see at least, although intuitively he knew he was being watched. *So what!*

A solitary cricket made a loud 'cric' then stopped. Bishman stopped by the cricket hoping it would chirp again, but it didn't. If it had, he'd have crushed it underfoot.

Bishman continued his walk along the path which was lit by a street lamp every fifty yards or so, enough to keep boogy men away, perhaps. Bishman got half way through humming his tune for the hundredth time when he heard somebody running up behind him...*Shit!*

Someone's trying to put a make on me and I haven't even got a gun on me. Balls! thought Bishman as he started looking around for weapons. Trashcan lids, wire, branches, rocks, bottles, *anything...Fuck!*

He knew timing was crucial. If he turned around too soon he may very well get blown away, extremely quickly. *There's all sorts of jerks in this park. Lord only knows what they all do.* He kept cool. Just when he thought the timing was perfect he spun around to confront his would-be-assailant. About six feet away and closing fast was a guy in his early twenties. He looked worried, even scared. He was right out of breath, panting like hell. He ran right past Bishman as though he didn't even notice him and kept right on running. He ran even harder. This guy was in a big hurry.

Bishman's ears pricked up. *Hell!* He could hear somebody else running just as hard as the first. *No, harder*. A second man ran right past Bishman, he was also out of breath, a big gun swinging with the arc of his hand - *Colt .45 revolver by the looks of it*.

Bishman watched as the second man gained on the first; only yards separated them as they reached the next lamp-post; hundreds of moths were flying around it. The second guy stretched out his arm, aimed and fired. The first guy was spectacularly lifted clean off the ground, about four feet, with the impact of the bullet, hanging there momentarily before crashing to the ground. The gunman was now walking towards his victim and Bishman, keeping in the shadows, moved closer. The gunman coolly and calmly stood over his victim and pumped in another five bullets. Each bullet made the body writhe, such was the impact. The report from the gun was loud enough to awaken the dead, but it didn't waken the guy on the ground.

Bishman froze. He had a succession of thoughts whizz through his mind. *Even if he has one shot left he'll be shooting at me in the dark, he's the one who's in the light. I'm gonna get that son-of-a-bitch if it's the last thing I do*.

Bishman walked toward the gunman who was still standing over the body. He didn't move, it looked like he was frozen. It was kind of eerie, the dead man just lying there with the gunman hovering above him. The kind of vision that would stay with Bishman for ever, especially as he was unarmed. Bishman closed. Another cricket chirped. Bishman had definitely stopped humming. The gunman stood stock-still, triumphant, like the Grim Reaper. *Thirty yards*. Bishman kept right on moving. *I'm going to kick that guy's balls so far up his ass he'll have to put his hand in his mouth to scratch them*, thought Bishman. *Twenty yards*.

Suddenly, without any warning, the guy on the ground leapt up and burst out laughing. The gunman burst out laughing too and the two of them legged it off through the park like a couple of jack rabbits.

Bishman froze like a statue. He could hear peals of laughter way off in the distance, hoots of snickering, prankish cackling, two youths roaring in hysterics. It seemed to get louder and more raucous the further away they got. Cackling, hooting, snorting and cracking up, these two youths were having a blast with their big guffaws.

Bishman had a bad taste in his mouth. He didn't like it. He didn't like it at all.

When Harvey took Bishman into hypnosis he never knew whereabouts in the country Bishman would start or finish. Bishman however, was usually exceedingly articulate and took great delight in labouring precise details:

Texas is the serial killer's killing field. Bodies disappear overnight. Unlike New York City, where murder victims usually turn up in trunks of cars or in the Hudson River, thousands of victims disappear in Texas never to be seen again.

A recently published report in *Texas Medicine,* the magazine of the Texas Medical Association, revealed that during 1990 three thousand, four hundred and forty-three people were killed by guns in the state of Texas.

In reality, the figure is probably two or three times higher, because Texas is the center point of the figure-of-eight loop that serial killers use as their circuit. Texas is also a state where there are no handgun restrictions, or extremely few. When you buy a gun there is no state law that requires a background check. *Texas: Serial killers paradise!*

Bishman had walked for miles. He knew he'd find some action but he wasn't sure what. He just knew he'd recognize it when he found it. This is exactly what Bishman was thinking to himself, as he happily hummed a tune he didn't know the name of, when he spotted an eerie glow in the sky that told him there was a large fire - maybe three miles off. Certainly no more than four. He could sense excitement and danger. This was what he had been looking for, he just knew it.

The flames attracted him like a moth to a lamp and as Bishman quickened his pace it reminded him of a joke. A labourer from Boise, Idaho, was helping his wife deliver their first baby. They lived out in the boondocks - no electricity, running water or gas. You've got the idea: Boise, right. As the wife was having the baby, the labourer held up a kerosene lantern to make sure everything was going well. It was a perfect delivery. The wife even ate the placenta.

All of a sudden the wife started to moan again and the labourer held up the lamp again - and a second baby popped out. Soon after that the wife started to groan again and once more the labourer held up the lantern and a third baby appeared. The old labourer said, "I think it's the light that's attracting them." Just then Bishman remembered the name of the tune he was humming. It was *All Things Bright and Beautiful.*

"What are you doing on ma property?" bellowed an angry voice. Bishman jumped. He'd arrived sooner than he had anticipated. He snapped right out of his internal joke-telling and humming session.

"I just came to see if I could be of any help." Bishman spoke in a voice designed to calm down the angry farmer.

"Well, now that you've seen the fire is under control, you can fuck your butt right off ma property," said the farmer wielding a double-barrelled, twelve gauge shotgun.

Bishman could now clearly see the farmer and the shotgun - they were illuminated by the light of a gigantic fire that was in the shape of a huge horseshoe. It was about thirty feet high with flames shooting twice that height.

"My name's Bishman. I didn't know the fire was controlled. I thought you could use some help. What's that you're burning? I've never seen a fire like it." Bishman was trying to start a conversation and it wasn't easy.

"I'll tell you what it is, it's five thousand head of fuckin' cattle worth over a million bucks and ordered to be destroyed by the FDA because of hoof and mouth disease. The foreman and crew all fucked themselves off outta here when they heard I was wiped out. The bastards."

Bishman wiped the sweat from his brow. "So I *can* help you. You not only need a hand but I might be able to give you some ideas about starting over. I doubt the FDA will allow cattle on your ranch for at least two years so you gotta be thinking of doing something else." Bishman lit a cigarette.

"Something different my ass. All I know is beef." The farmer pointed his shotgun to the monumental horseshoe of fire.

"Don't give me that bullshit, I know lots of fellas making lots of money doing a host of different things. Beef's only one of the games they play. I'll give you a few ideas. Garlic's one, mushrooms is another, organic farming is three and hydroponics is four, onions is five. If you can't play beef you gotta play one of the others. You don't have a choice." Bishman inhaled deeply.

"My ass, you got that right, fella. All I've been thinking about is quitting. You've just given me some damn good ideas to get me up and running again. The insurance will give me a grub stake to get started. Sure, not as much as I'd have gotten if these fuckers had gone to auction in the fullness of time. But nevertheless enough to get me started on a new venture. What did you say your name was again?" The farmer put out his hand, Bishman shook it and said, "Bishman. Bob Bishman."

"Jack Jervis. My friends call me J.J., want a drop of this? It's fine Tennessee whiskey. I think you'll like it." He passed the silver hip flask to Bishman.

"Don't mind if I do." Bishman took a long swig, then another. It was good and it hit the spot.

They talked and drank and the flames shot about thirty feet in the air. J.J. explained to Bishman that the five thousand head of cattle had been bulldozed into position and covered with a thousand gallons of gasoline supplied by the FDA. Once it was ignited there was enough heat in the cattle to sustain the fire. The heat was so intense Bishman could smell his sneakers roasting and feel them melting. It was awful. J.J. said even the bones would reduce to ash, Bishman believed him, the sweat was pouring from him. He mopped his brow again.

They finished the silver flask and J.J. went to the Suzuki jeep that was parked about a hundred yards off to get another bottle to top it up. They sat and drank some more. It was a good way to pass the time. The fire raged.

Bishman took a long swig and lit a cigarette. "Last time I was in Texas was about six months ago. I went to see an airshow. I can't say exactly where it was, but it sure was good. Some crazy bastard flew over the airfield ten feet off the ground in a Grumman F-14 Tomcat, *upside down*. He must have hit the wrong button because the rockets on his ejector seat fired and blew him clean out of the cockpit. The plane crashed about twenty miles away."

"Kill him?" asked J.J., knowing the answer already.

"Kill him! It punched a fuckin' hole in the ground twenty feet deep. Nothing left of the guy except for jelly." Bishman suppressed a burp, then changed his mind and let it out.

J.J. went off for a piss, then strolled over to the Suzuki jeep to get another bottle. He had lots of ideas mulling over in his mind: *The future doesn't look so bleak after all. Odd how sometimes a stranger can come into your life at the right moment and change it completely. This guy seems to know his stuff. Perhaps I can tap him for some more ideas.*

On his return he was greeted with two barrels of the Winchester twelve-gauge shotgun being fired from a range of about six feet. J.J.'s vital organs all but disappeared and his body was practically severed in two. The smell of cordite was lost in the smell of roast beef. That tickled Bishman, who went to the Suzuki, picked up a shovel, a groundsheet and another bottle - the one J.J. had brought back with him had been vaporized in the shotgun blast.

Bishman scraped up the remains onto the ground sheet and threw them onto the fire along with the shovel and the shotgun. He was amused at how light the body was. He must have blown away more of J.J. than he realized.

He drove the jeep to San Antonio and parked it in a back street that was full of cars. It would probably be there a month before it was discovered. As an afterthought he wiped the steering wheel, gear lever and door handle with some Windex and tissues he found in the glove compartment.

He got out of the Jeep, dropped the keys down a drain and walked away. *Garlic my ass*, he thought, and started humming *Rawhide*.

As an after thought he went back to the Suzuki to collect the last bottle of whiskey.

By pre-arrangement Harvey met Bishman in downtown L.A., then drove five hours to a quiet spot in San Fransisco. Harvey often used different locations that were off the beaten track. He seemed to have a nose for discovering desolate places.

Harvey made a note that the dialogue was beginning to sound like the continuation of a previous story. He was right, and yet another piece of the jigsaw fell into place:

Bishman had had enough of Central Park. He had another plan in mind. He walked briskly up Second Avenue, carrying his carefully wrapped ten-pound package as though he hadn't a care in the world, as far as East 120th Street, turned right and walked down to First Avenue. Just before First Avenue he saw what he was looking for. In fact he heard it first. *Montego Bay* was blaring away from the crumbling brownstone. It was four in the morning, there would probably be about a hundred and twenty people, mostly blacks, Hispanics and Puerto Ricans, in the club, The Grape Escape. But outside, there was no-one around. Bishman knew there wouldn't be...*Intuition!*

He carefully opened the door and scattered the contents of a trashcan that he'd brought off the street and emptied half the gallon of gasoline he'd bought earlier. The gasoline went all over the trash, up the walls and over the painted door. About three feet away from the gasoline, he deftly made a fuse from one of the votive candles he'd stolen from St. Patrick's Cathedral. He carefully arranged the paper against the candle, figuring that he would have about four minutes to do what he had to do next. He carefully lit the candle and blew out the match, closing the door quietly and deliberately behind him. The door opened outwards onto the street so he wedged the empty trashcan up against the door handle.

Bishman calmly walked around to the back of the brownstone and did the same to the back door, using up the remaining half gallon of gasoline and the second St. Patrick's candle. He lit the candle carefully and nestled it in amongst some old newspapers he found by the back door. He pulled the papers over to where there was plenty of gasoline. Bishman had used this technique before and had nearly cremated himself when he lit the match - the flame had actually tracked across the gasoline fumes and ignited the whole shooting

131

match. That was in Michigan. He'd learned a valuable lesson. Keep naked flames well away from gasoline, even the vapors can ignite from an open flame from as much as ten feet away, especially on a hot day, à la Michigan.

The front door should be firing up just about now, thought Bishman as he closed the back door behind him, wedging it firmly with an old wooden board.

As Bishman suspected, the place turned out to be a fire trap. The fire exits were padlocked to stop gate crashers getting in for free and the windows were boarded up to keep the place dark. He didn't wait around. He'd read about it in the newspapers the next evening.

There were no survivors. The police and fire crews worked till nine in the morning taking out one hundred and forty-seven victims in body bags, many of them never formally identified.

Bishman took Harvey through five hours of jokes and ramblings, of which this was the *only* memory of any consequence:

Bishman had his thumb out; he was humming *Hitching a Ride*. He was in good spirits. His blond wig was just the thing he needed to attract the guy who was to be his next victim. He'd had a close shave and he smelt good too. His make-up was just right.

Many vehicles drove past as the sun started to go down. It looked like the Earth had the Sun for supper that night, the way it gobbled it up. Crickets chirped, the evening was humid.

A dark red panel van pulled up; the signwriting on it was painted over roughly and Bishman could see a driver but no passengers. He approached it cautiously, looking out for any dudes in the back. It wouldn't be the first time a hitchhiker got in a vehicle to find there were five or six motherfuckers ready to rape and pillage.

He poked his head in as he talked. Everything was cool. He got in and the driver moved off.

They looked at each other. The driver was wearing a blonde wig too. *They both knew!* The driver turned up the rock music full blast. Heavy metal, Deep Purple. Bad news. He started to haul ass!

"You fuckin' asshole, child abuser, homo, sadist, killer," screamed the driver at the top of his voice right in Bishman's face, spit, froth and foam coming out of his smelly mouth.

"You fuckin' cocksucker, motherfucker, son-of-a-bitch," screamed Bishman venomously, pushing his face right up close to the driver's. Adrenalin levels began to rise.

The driver gassed up, really hauling ass. The road was clear for the next thousand miles...at least. Just three hundred and sixty degrees of tumbleweed and cornfields plus the occasional billboard.

"You scum-of-the-earth, fuck pig, queer, moron, motherfucker, murderer, asshole,

133

jerk-off," the driver screamed with unbelievable anger and vehemence. The hairs on both their heads, necks and backs were standing on end. Four hate-filled eyes, spit and foul breath.

"Gobshite, fucker, shithead, bastard, animal, child molester, ripper, asshole, shit-faggot," screamed Bishman, spitting froth, foaming at the mouth. Their hearts were now pounding with fury, hate and anger. The tension rose a few more percentage points.

"Swine, slasher, bitch, asshole, ripper, motherfucking shit-head, bastard, jerk," yelled the driver, snarling and hissing, his nose nearly touching Bishman's nose. Bishman could feel his hot foul breath washing over him, feel the spit spraying his face. He could hear the words way above the heavy metal. They screamed and shouted like this non-stop for twelve minutes. Twelve hair-raising, heart-pounding minutes of terror, high intensity shouting-match, the driver hauling ass all the way. They very nearly popped their rivets. If pure evil exists, this was it.

Suddenly, without warning, the driver hit the brakes and Bishman nearly went through the windshield. It was sheer luck that he didn't. No judgement involved. He thought to himself *I'm outta here, pal,* as he opened the door. Before he could slam it shut, the driver was gassing it hard, the door flapping in the breeze.

Bishman stuck his finger up at the van disappearing in the distance.

"Sit on that and spin you fuckin' cocksucker!" he shouted. Then he thought, *See ya later, pal...much later.*

Bishman sat down by the side of the road, trembling. His hands were trembling so much it took three paper matches to light a cigarette. He was still sitting there an hour later and his hands were still trembling.

TEN

Harvey now had over three hundred audio cassettes and twenty-seven notebooks of jottings and scripts, representing over two hundred sickening hours of regressions. He called them the Bishman Files. He took Bishman into hypnosis:

Things don't just happen by accident, although on many occasions they may appear to. A panhandler doesn't necessarily ask everyone for money. He targets certain individuals in certain places at certain times, when he thinks he stands a good chance of getting money.

The serial killer doesn't kill everyone in his path. He deliberately goes walkabout, looking for stragglers and potential victims who are on their own, naive people who have left themselves wide open to be approached. Bishman had walked up Fifth Avenue and was just approaching the big super toyshop, F.A.O. Schwarz. Across the road a guy was drumming for all he was worth. His street name was Harold - he was the *Junk Yard Band* and probably the best drummer in Manhattan.

The young man who was sitting on the toy-store's steps was transfixed by the drummer. He was searching, and Bishman knew he was onto a winner.

"Cigarette?" offered Bishman.

"Yeah, thanks."

"See the sign up there on the top of that building? That's 666 Fifth Avenue." Bishman lit up, always smoking, ever the conversationalist.

"What does that mean then?" asked the guy.

"666. It's the Sign of the Beast. I thought you'd know that." Bishman paused to allow them both to listen to Harold, across the street, who was now building up a good head of steam for his grand finale - a raucous crescendo where everyone, hopefully, drops a dollar bill into the hat.

Harold the *Junk Yard Band* eventually quietened down and Bishman started talking.

"When we were kids we used to get out a Ouija board and ask it all sorts of questions. Nothing happened, but we stuck at it. We'd almost given up, when one day it slowly started spelling out letters. We put them together and it spelled out LUCIFER. We dropped the board and ran like hell." Bishman laughed.

"You're shittin' me?" The impressionable young man was glazed over.

"What d'you do? I mean other than sit on the steps of F.A.O. Schwarz and smoke other people's cigarettes?" He took the hint and passed a cigarette to Bishman.

"Not a lot. Panhandle for small change. What about you?"

"Same as you, but I also help people make a lot of money. Those who want to, that is."

"Yeah, like how? I've never had any money, but I sure could use some." The young man lit his cigarette.

Bishman wiped his forehead. "You see most jobs need skills that you haven't got, or pay 'commission only' for selling some stupid fucking knickknack that no-one wants in the first place. How people really make a lot of money is just by talking to people, or more to the point, just by listening to people. Do you reckon you could do that? I never met anyone who can't." Bishman stood up.

"Of course I could talk to people and listen to them, but how would I get paid?" The young man could see the dollar signs.

"Have you got a buck on you? Get me a coffee and a donut and I'll tell you the whole scheme. You can make a hundred, two hundred bucks a day. Maybe more."

"Where do I get the coffee from?" The young man stood up and looked around.

"From any one of the thousand vendors. Look there's one over there." Bishman pointed about fifty feet away. They were everywhere. *Where has this cretin been all his life?*

"Cream and five extra sugars. I'll be here."

The youth must have been nineteen or twenty. No job, no goals, no hope, no nothing. If you don't stand for something you'll fall for anything and this young man was just about to make the biggest fall in his short career.

"There ya' go, I got you a jelly donut."

"Good one. That'll hit the spot. People don't realize how important coffee and donuts are. I'll explain it to you. You know everything is made up of atoms. That's all we are, millions of atoms. An atom is made up of protons, neutrons and electrons, and they're all held together in some sort of cohesive glue.

"The scientists have always been baffled by this ocean in which everything floats around because it can't be measured as matter, it's more like units of energy. Scientists call this cohesive glue, 'gluon' - but they've got it all wrong. What hangs everything together is coffee and donuts.

"Take the coffee and donut vendors off the streets of Manhattan and the very fabric of society would disintegrate. People would walk around in a daze." Bishman smiled and licked his fingers free of the sugar that came off the jelly donut he'd been eating while he told the story.

Bishman finished his coffee, which had become cold. "D'you realize there are thousands of old people and invalids out there who have no-one to talk to. They live in nursing homes and hospitals, many times their own homes. A lot of them have plenty of money and their own families have deserted them. You don't want too many clients. You just want a few - with money. You go around to their place and just sit and listen to their boring reminiscences for a few hours at a time. If they ever dry up, which is decidedly rarely, all you have to say is: *What happened next?* That'll keep them going for another few hours - they'll start rambling away again. At the end of four or five hours you pick up your fifty or hundred bucks, it's up to you. Then you make the appointment for the same time next week.

"You see, the secret is just having a few clients who pay you hard cash, week after week. Are you interested in becoming a conversationalist?" Bishman waited for an answer. It didn't take long.

"Yeah, it sounds too good to be true, but it makes a lot of sense."

Bishman burped, bringing up some acid and donut. He swallowed, then wished he hadn't. "Think about it. No-one knows how to handle the plight of the old people. I've laid it out on a silver platter for you."

"How can I start? What do I have to do? I want to become a conversationalist!" The young man could see a *thousand* bucks a week, *easily*.

"Look, I'm out of time now. I've got to see someone else and get them set up as a conversationalist. Meet me over at the corner of the park at around ten tonight. I'll be done by then and we'll talk. I'll give you all the names, addresses and phone numbers you'll need. I'll see ya later," said Bishman pointing to the corner of the Central Park.

"Yeah on the corner about ten. What's your name?"

"Call me Richard," said Bishman.

140

"I'm Wally. I'll see ya at ten."

"Yeah, see ya then." Bishman went off humming *Who Wants to be a Millionaire?*

The theme was hearts. The bath was heart-shaped, the jacuzzi was heart-shaped, the sauna room was heart shaped. It was fantastic. It was like one of the honeymoon suites in a motel in the Poconos. This was the room Anita had fallen in love with when she first met Harvey at his party. She was inspired by the elegance and enchantment of the room.

They soaked in the jacuzzi, drinking pink champagne and talking. The night was still young. They'd had an incredibly relaxing day together.

"What's the latest on Bob?"

"How come we always end up talking about Bob?"

"I don't know, but you've always got more to say about Bob than you have about Max - and Max is pulling in millions while Bob's not even paying you."

"Bob's like a drug in a funny sort of way...I can't get enough of him, I've thought about it myself. You know my interest is people and psychology.

"Bob told me the nurses in the psychiatric ward found him the most interesting case they've ever worked with. I can understand why. Everything he tells me is interesting. Mind-

141

blowing actually. He still keeps saying, 'No biggie' and 'Boogaloo' practically every other sentence, and bugging his eyes out. It's quite frightening, but I'm used to it now." Harvey topped up Anita's champagne glass, then his own, then plopped in more strawberries from a crystal dish.

"Go on." Anita fished out a huge strawberry with her fingers and popped it into Harvey's waiting mouth.

"Are you sure you really want to hear more?" Harvey attacked his strawberries too, and fed one to Anita. A small one; it was a joke.

"Yes, really, I'm as fascinated as you are. He sounds really cree...I don't know, weird."

"The other night I took him out to dinner, nothing fancy, a small Greek restaurant in Westwood Village. The place was pretty busy. A few weeks earlier he'd asked me about making money and what the secret was. I had told him what I believe, that you have to have a burning desire to make something happen. Not just a plain wish but a real *burning* desire. We had this conversation in my office, just the two of us. To emphasize the point I smashed my fist on the table and screamed *'Got to have it! Must have it! I'll die if I don't get it!'*

"He seemed to take it in and I thought no more of it. Until we were having our Greek meal. He suddenly looked up at me and said, 'I really do understand what you meant about burning desire.' At that moment I knew we were doomed and there was nothing I could do to stop him. His fist came crashing down on the table as he screamed....'*I've got to have it! I must have it! I'll die if I don't get it'*... full pelt at the top of his voice, and of course Klefticon and Souvlaki and a pitcher of draft Bud went flying everywhere. I just carried on eating. Every head in the place turned and looked at us. But I pretended nothing had happened - probably the best way to play it. It was really quite bizarre." He topped up the champagne again and smiled.

"Jeeeez, it's enough to give you the willies. D'you think he's dangerous?" Anita splashed Harvey for fun.

"I reckon he could be if he was pushed. I want to see where the whole thing leads. It's my most fascinating case yet." Harvey splashed Anita back and that started a grand splashing contest.

"You ready to get out? I want to show you the rest of the bedroom."

"Yes sure, shall we take the champagne with us?"

"You bet. Is there any more in that bottle...no it's empty, I'll get another. I'll be back in two seconds, probably less. You can shower if you like, then make your way to the bed. I'll be right with you."

Anita showered and got into the heart-shaped bed: luxurious pink silk sheets, heart-shaped duck down pillows. *Surely he'll make love to me tonight,* she thought as she rubbed herself on the smooth silk sheets. She couldn't wait. She wanted to *see* him as well.

Harvey returned: "Let me just get the cork out and I'll be right with you." For fun, he deliberately popped the cork loudly and let the cork hit the ceiling. He poured two glasses that literally overflowed everywhere. There were still strawberries in both glasses.

He slipped his bright red boxer shorts to the floor and Anita gasped. He stood there for a moment while she took it all in. It wasn't the length of it so much - eight inches perhaps - it was the thickness of it. She felt herself go all weak. If she hadn't been laying in bed she would have fainted. It was like a baby's forearm. Her pupils dilated and her eyebrows went up in the air of their own accord, while her eyelashes fluttered uncontrollably.

Her throat was dry. She was intensely excited. As he climbed into bed, she took hold of it and she couldn't close her fingers around it. It looked magnificent as he slipped in between the sheets. He took her in his arms and gave her the longest, slipperiest French kiss they'd ever had. Anita was fully turned on, her heart was pounding.

He gently eased her on top of him and pulled back the duvet. "Slide up here - no, more, higher." Harvey's strong arms pulled her up his chest. She straddled across him, willingly.

"You want me to come higher?" Anita wasn't sure what the game plan was, but she was up for it.

"Sure, come all the way up - that's it, even more." He could smell her odor although they had just gotten out the shower, and he nuzzled his face carefully into her crotch.

He licked his tongue in and out, very gently teasing the flaps of her pussy. He did it for what seemed ages. He fondled her breasts and felt the shape of them. Full breasts, nipples getting firmer and firmer. Anita made herself more comfortable and pushed her pussy into his face as if to say *more...harder...now*.

Harvey was not to be rushed. He kept teasing and gently running his tongue over the lips. Then he started to go a little harder and then eased the lips apart and licked them from one end to the other. His tongue flashed in and out of her, into all the crinkly bits as well, slowly but surely.

Every now and then his tongue would touch her clitoris and she would let out an appreciative sigh or moan. He just kept teasing, their breathing getting heavier all the time.

He eventually allowed his tongue to find the hood and play with it ever so gently. He licked, sucked and swallowed on it, and kissed it and increased the pressure until it was unbearable. She put her hand behind herself to feel him and she couldn't believe it. She played with him exceptionally gently, slowly working her hand up and down, and every now and then played with his balls. The more she felt him, the more she got turned on. She was soaking wet.

He continued working on her breasts and licking her clit. She exploded into a wild orgasm, a wave of ecstasy showered over her body. He kissed her pussy over and over again, incredibly gently as if to say *thank you*, bringing her down very gently. She thought it was over but it had only just begun. All Harvey needed was a recharge.

"Let's just top these up," he said as he filled the glasses, took a long sip, then another.

"You know what, Bob always says *Antibodies* when he raises his glass. Quite funny, really. I've never heard anybody else say that."

Anita toasted Harvey and said: "Antibodies - ha ha ha."

"Don't you start, that's all we need, two psychos."

"Why did you say psycho? Jeeez, you worry me. Is he safe? Are you all right with him?"

"Of course I am." Harvey started playing with Anita's tits. They were baby soft.

"I love your breasts, they're the most beautiful tits in the world." He caressed, kissed and played with them as he marvelled at their tan, texture, shape and fullness.

"I want you to turn around." His strong arms helped move her, she wasn't quite sure what to do.

"That's it, I want you down there, where I can eat you properly."

Anita stuck her ass in the air and she took Harvey in her hand. He was laying on his back, with her pussy nuzzling in his face. *Purrrrfect!*

Harvey gently started the procedure again...licking, teasing, probing. Crinkly bits as well. Anita slowly took Harvey in her mouth, licking and sucking, gently, slowly but surely taking it all in. It was huge, the texture felt perfect, no ugly veins bulging out. She licked it from the top of the helmet right down to the base, teasingly slowly, then from the top again. It was her turn to tease, and she did it wonderfully. She took him in her mouth over and over again. Her jaws actually ached, but it was so good she wasn't about to complain.

He kept teasing and probing her and gently started to finger her. First one finger, gently probing, then a little more licking of the lips and the clitoris, all over, slowly, just the right pressure. Anita came time and again. Sometimes she let Harvey know by breathing hard and others by squealing with delight and other times she came and didn't let on at all.

She tried hard to get her hand around his cock, but no matter what she did or how hard she gripped she couldn't. *How is this thing going to feel up inside me* she was thinking and as she did she came again, her whole body shuddering with ecstasy, juices flooding out like sluice gates being opened.

Every now and then Harvey would just gently kiss her pussy and the cheeks of her ass. She and Harvey were perfectly in tune, as though they had been lovers for years.

They stopped for a moment. "I've never come so many times in my life, I can't believe it," she said.

They both took a sip of champagne as if to recover for a brief moment, then got back on the job. They assumed the same delicious 69 position, Anita carefully and sexily nuzzling her dripping wet pussy in Harvey's face. The aroma was scented heaven. Sheer, delicious, delightful, love juice. *A drink from the furry cup.*

Harvey used four fingers and massaged them in and out of her soaking wet orifice. Every time he plunged his fingers into her he made sure he nudged her clit, so as to stimulate it. Anita went up and down, flicking her tongue over the top of his helmet, and gently caressing his balls. He could feel himself coming and to warn her, let out some "oohs" and "aaahs" and a few other symptoms and groaning sounds. She took the hint and went right down on him faster. He gently pulled back the hood to expose her clit, fingered her and flicked his tongue around her exposed clitoris in a circular motion, getting the pressure just right.

They both came together and when they did Anita knew her pussy was connected to her brain. He belted spurt after spurt of hot cum deep into her throat and she swallowed every sweet, precious drop. She could feel every inch of that cock in her mouth and she'd never felt anything so sensational in her life before.

Anita eventually turned around and came up for air, they kissed and nibbled each other's ears, and Harvey quickly fell asleep.

On his return from Springfield, Harvey's first concern was to have a session with Bishman. When they met at Harvey's office, after a short relaxation induction Bishman went into an altered state and, without any prompting from Harvey, continued the dialogue about Wally, the guy he had met outside the toy shop on 5th Avenue.

Harvey always felt he was making progress if Bishman actually finished the tales because in that way the jigsaw would become complete:

At 10:pm, the duly-appointed hour, Wally arrived at the corner of Central Park. Bishman was already there. He'd forgotten what he'd told Wally his name was. He thought he'd wait and see if Wally called him by name. Wally had come for details about being a conversationalist; really it was an appointment with death, but how was he to know?

Immediately Bishman took the lead and started walking and began talking about going to nursing homes and hospitals and listening to old folk. Bishman made a real effort to explain to Wally that he must give value for money and even if these old people bored him he must listen to them. "Who knows," he said, "You may even get asked questions and if you haven't been listening you've had it."

He sold the story over and over again, *All you have to do is talk and listen and you could earn a hundred or two hundred bucks a day. Easy, right?* Of course Wally kept wanting to know addresses and phone numbers, where to go and how to start. Bishman kept him hanging on. They seemed to walk for hours. From the busy streets they wound their way through back alleys, all the time further and further away from anyone who could notice two guys just walking along, talking intently. They stopped behind a disused warehouse. Wally hadn't noticed that, now, there was no-one around. The place was deathly quiet.

149

Bishman talked Wally into going down on him. It seemed a reasonable deal and, as it happened, Wally gave good head. No-one's going to give you the details of how to earn two hundred bucks *every day* without getting *something* in return, right? He got Wally to drop his trousers and bend over, splaying himself over a trash can. Wally thought he was going to get butt-fucked. Instead he got gun-fucked.

Bishman rammed the .45 Colt automatic up Wally's ass and then, as Wally shrieked *Richaaaaaaaghhh!!!!*, Bishman pulled the trigger three times in rapid succession. The body acted as an efficient silencer. Bishman was amazed at how muffled the sound was. He was also amazed at the gaping holes that appeared as exit wounds in Wally's back. Usually the .45 would inflict huge wounds but these were absolutely enormous, jagged, and the bullets had torn out huge amounts of bone and tissue.

Earlier, Bishman had been bored; with the rest of the afternoon to kill, he had played with the gun. He had emptied the clip and noticed the bullets were the flat-nosed lead variety. He carefully cut a deep cross into the lead with a razor blade and effectively turned them into dumdum bullets. The pain inflicted must have been excruciating. He left the gun up Wally's ass and walked off, thinking, *Conversationalist my ass, talk your way out of that...pal!*

Bishman had got the gun that same afternoon, from another aspiring conversationalist who thought a Colt .45 was a small price to pay for such a good business opportunity. However,

Bishman never kept his second appointment with him. By that time he was in Michigan, in the Purple Pussy Cat, sipping a Coors and talking to some guy who thought he too might like to earn a hundred bucks an hour by being a conversationalist.

Sometimes Bishman would seem to be set for a long session but then would only just come up with a tiny piece of the jigsaw puzzle. When this happened Harvey felt short-changed:

Bishman took out the .41 Smith and Wesson Model 57 revolver from the brown paper bag. He looked at it as he played with it. It was heavy and comfortable.

He'd stolen it three hours previously from an empty house, at around ten that evening. There had been lots of guns there - all loose and all loaded. This one wouldn't be missed for days. He wondered how any sensible adult would believe that a house was burglar-proof and that guns would not be stolen. *Guns get stolen every day of the week*. He fondled the gun and walked over to the stolen Toyota. It had been left in someone's drive with the keys in the ignition. That was in Trenton, New Jersey.

He started the car and joined the freeway, heading South toward Willingboro on Route 295. When he was sure there was no-one behind him he indiscriminately fired at the oncoming cars, taking careful aim at the driver's side windshield. He knew he got lucky when he could see yellow and red lights in his rear view mirror going in all directions, pointing ways they shouldn't have been, like across the road, into the sky, that sort of thing. *Carnage! Mayhem! Murder! Boogaloo!*

He parked up within ten miles, in Cherry Hill on a side street with a lot of other cars, and hid the empty gun in the top of an old elm tree that had rot in it. Presumably, it's still there.

The account that you probably read in the newspapers was that a twenty-eight year old nurse by the name of Millicent Toulanger had had her spinal cord severed by a .41 calibre bullet and will be a paraplegic for the rest of her life, a life that would be spent in a wheel-chair.

Harvey made some notes about Bishman...they weren't *all* good.

ELEVEN

The immaculate yellow Rolls Royce pulled into the drive and Harvey parked. As usual, he went around to the passenger's door and offered a hand to Anita. Always the perfect gentleman.

The Rolls Royce cooling fan came on; the motor twanged as it cooled. Fireflies lit up in the warm Beverly Hills air as, arm in arm, they walked to the house. Anita was wondering if this was the night he'd make love to her. She'd finished her period two days before. *Perfect timing*.

"I fancy a swim - are you up for that or would you rather do something else?" Harvey asked as he slid a plastic card into the electronic security mechanism in Pinewood's front door.

"Depends on what the something else is. Let's swim now and do the something else later," she giggled and gently pinched his ass.

The outdoor swimming-pool was full-size Olympic and the water was cool and fresh. They played and joked and swam. After an hour the novelty wore off and they went back into the

153

house, leaving the smell of the freshly-chlorinated pool behind.

"Champagne, Bucks Fizz, Bloody Mary or what?" asked Harvey.

"It's OK. I'll fix the drinks, you tell me what you want," said Anita, already popping a cork from pink champagne, anticipating Harvey's answer.

"I'll have my usual, strawberries and pink champagne. You know I'm drinking far too much lately. I'll end up like Bob."

He took the drink and said, "Bob seems to know the Los Angeles area pretty well. Mind you, he must have been around the States about twenty times from my reckoning, maybe even more." He sipped his drink and hooked out a sweet juicy strawberry with his tongue.

"What on earth does he do? How does he make money? Surely he doesn't survive on panhandling alone?" Anita sat next to Harvey on the soft white leather-covered sofa.

"He sure does. Mind you, he can talk. Charm the knickers off a nun, our Bob."

"Really, you wouldn't think so. I thought all these alkies and druggies and weirdos and whackos were out of it."

"Don't you believe it." He topped up the champagne, took a drink, and topped it up again.

"Let's go to bed, I'm as horny as hell." Harvey stood up.

"Me too, but I didn't want to say anything." She tugged him for a kiss.

Although they'd never actually made love, they felt as though they had, and Harvey's plan of waiting had worked wonders. They had become good close friends and had a lot of things in common.

They went hand in hand into the Charlie Chaplin room and Harvey picked Anita up in his arms and carried her across the threshold. She loved it.

Memorabilia were everywhere. This was a fun room: a cane, an old pair of boots, old suits. Sepia stills from the movies *City Limits* and *The Immigrant* and *Kids' Auto Races at Venice,* the movie in which Chaplin established the famous Tramp character, decorated the room. The bed was an old four poster that could easily have come from a Chaplin movie.

They spent a long time in the shower gently lathering each other and spending lots of time on slow, deep, wet French kisses. Harvey got out first, as was his manner, always assuming the woman would want to spend more time in private, cleansing various parts of her body. That was his theory, anyway. *Getting all the yogurt and cream cheese out of the flaps and crinkly bits, hopefully.*

He waited under the silk sheets thinking pleasant thoughts and when Anita finally came, she looked radiant. She wore a beautiful black negligée, and had put on a black lace bra and black lace frilly panties.

"How come you've still got your bra and panties on?" asked Harvey, as he sipped his Champers.

"I know how much you like to take them off," she giggled and munched a strawberry.

He took her in his arms and passionately kissed her. Then he slipped her bra and panties off. *She's right, I love taking her bra and panties off.* He gently caressed her breasts, breasts that had retained their shape because of the way she was lying, on her side facing him. She took him in her hand and slowly worked him up. She slid down the bed and went down on him. Her jaw was still aching from last time, but no complaints. She fed the huge quivering cock into her mouth rather slowly, stopping every now and then to delicately take one of his balls in her mouth. They would only just fit, one at a time, and she did it tenderly. She licked his scrotum for what seemed an age, then she slowly went down on him again. It was hot under those silk sheets and she was in heaven.

Harvey reciprocated and Anita just laid back and enjoyed Harvey's tongue darting around the most sensitive parts of her body. *Sheer heaven.*

He then lay on top of her and carefully slipped his helmet inside her. She thought she was going to get the whole thing, but it was not to be. He took his huge cock in his hand and gently massaged her clit and her pouting pussy lips, tantalisingly slowly. He slid down the bed and went down on her again; it was sheer ecstasy for both of them. After a while he brought himself up again and just slipped the helmet inside her once more. Then he massaged her with it. He slid in an inch more, then restrained himself. Anita was breathing noticeably heavily and trying to pull him in. *No way, José.* Harvey pulled out despite himself.

He went down on her yet again and licked and kissed and fingered her engorged bud, which was standing to attention like a little man in a rowing boat, and Harvey's tongue probing the delicate folds of flesh of her vagina.

Once more he lay on top of her, this time giving her a long wet French kiss. He ran his tongue over her pearly white teeth, their tongues dancing together in silent melody.

He slipped in about three inches of his stiff cock and she groaned, whimpered and screamed as he left it there for a few minutes, teasing, tantalizing, tickling, playing, driving her wild. She loved it, he loved it, it was driving him mad, but *still* he contained himself.

Harvey was driving Anita wild, teasing and playing with her mind as he went down on her once more and licked up juices that were pouring out of her. He fingered and licked, then gently put four fingers up inside her and brought her off again. "First you tell me you won the *Golden Hands Award for Massage*, now you tell me you're the *President of the Amateur Muff Divers' Club*. You come up with the funniest expressions I've ever heard," said Anita, and promptly started 'Ohooooing' and 'Ahhhhhing' again.

He carefully straddled across her; this time, he slid his throbbing cock right up inside of her. He lay there, he didn't move, but he took his full weight off her with his arms. The lovers just hung onto one another for a full five minutes, motionless. They gazed into each other's eyes, and he studied the beauty of her eyes and her

157

complexion. *Sheer exquisite beauty*. Their bodies were welding together with sweat and passion.

Harvey wanted to regain his composure, and he did. He now started thrusting in and out very slowly, caressing her breasts, kissing her ears as he went.

He slowly fucked her for forty-five minutes, then started to increase the momentum and build up speed. He thrust into her right up to the hilt. She felt fulfilled. Anita could feel an orgasm in her clitoris, it was ecstatic, she could feel another in her G-spot, it was as though she were peeing herself, and she felt every fold, crinkly bit, muscle and nerve ending in her vagina explode in a starburst of wonderous sensations. Her eyes rolled around in her head, waves of ecstasy coursed through her body and mind. Harvey kept pounding and humping, shooting huge spurts of jism straight up inside her pussy.

It felt like a pint of fluid, maybe more. Anita could feel each hot spurt. Her head was seeing stars, she was floating on clouds, the endorphins had released. *Morphine within*.

Every time their bodies pulled apart there was a vulgar burping sound, the sweat was rolling from them and they were slowly collapsing in a heap. They kissed slowly and softly, and brought each other down. He left it in to soak for about twenty minutes while they whispered sweet nothings in each other's ears. The smell of sex was intense; *Serendipity* perfume, the sweat, the jism, the pussy juices, two bodies welded together. It was sheer unadulterated heaven, snuggling together in each other's arms.

Bishman always had plenty to say about settings and was keenly observant. On many occasions he amazed Harvey with his vivid eyewitness accounts and the descriptive language that he used to illustrate an event:

New York is brusque, glorious, bawdy, chic, spectacular, lovable, majestic, inspiring *and* also a haven for serial killers. It offers everything: plenty of potential victims, escape routes, lots of hubbub and every opportunity to get lost. It's one of the highlights of the figure-of-eight circuit. Probably ten people a day are murdered in New York and no one seems to know, or for that matter care. Many of these are committed by the professional serial killer.

Penn Station 10:pm, the naked city reveals some of its seamier side. Many of the city's homeless are filling the place up. They file in from all the entrances in ones and twos. The place already has plenty of Indians and Pakistanis looking for seats by the telephones, where they make free calls all over the world by billing other people's accounts.

The homeless sit among the weirdos, whackos, freakaboos, cretins, winos, drug addicts, the occasional plain-clothed Amtrack cop, panhandlers, urban nomads, troglodytes, nocturnes, sneak-thieves, unemployed,

159

unemployable, hucksters, shysters, prostitutes, scum-of-the-earth, alcoholics, sleazeballs (males), sleazebags (females), mentally deranged, the occasional serial killer (although you wouldn't know it), human flotsam and jetsam, and about ten percent (certainly no higher) regular train passengers.

At about 1:30 am, there are about three hundred people sitting in the seats. Four police officers look on. *Nearly shakedown time.*

One guy, about forty, has a small rubber lifebelt around his neck, another sitting next to him is frantically sucking a pacifier. Two foreign students, pretty young girls, probably from Sweden, look on in absolute amazement and horror.

Bishman went to the bathroom to wash his feet. He had washed the dirt from one foot when a scuzzy wuzzy informed the janitor.

"Hey fella, no washing feet in here. It's for face and hands only," said the janitor gruffly. Bishman put his sock back on and left the other foot dirty. He'd have to wait until he got to Central Park before he washed that one. He didn't look at the retard who fingered him. He didn't want a confrontation. *The guy will never know how close he came to getting a pencil jabbed in his throat.*

There's always plenty of people who talk out aloud and this night was no exception. One black guy was shouting out to all and sundry, "Shut up, or I'll kidnap your brain. If it's any good, I'll use it...Your wife sent a message, she say don't go home just yet. The milkman's still there...They should have drowned you at birth! Shut up, or I'll kidnap..."

Six large trolleys of fresh donuts were pushed through the station by two guys for the three Dunkin' Donut stores in Penn Station, all ready for early morning commuters. They were guarded from the hungry homeless by a private security guard, who carried a pump-action Remington 870 shotgun with a twenty-one inch barrel and a seven-round magazine.

Bishman closed one eye and left the other one open. He looked over at the four police officers as they pulled on fingerless, weighted leather gloves and took out their night-sticks. It reminded him of the Gestapo. He started thinking about Adolf Hitler, saying *'All I want is peace,'* as he pointed to a map of Poland and said *'That piece!'* He started thinking about Nazis, Poland, Gestapo, Jews and Germany, and other weird and wacky things:

The idea is that too many homeless are sleeping on the park benches. First you close down Bryant Park, under the guise of doing extensive repairs and renovations. Then you close down Madison Square, and seal it off. Then you close off Tompkins Square Park, and eventually all the parks are sealed off. You burn down the Staten Island Ferry Terminal, a favorite with the homeless. Bishman could almost smell the smoke and see and hear the crackle of the flames in the roof timbers. Then you board up the few remaining vacant buildings and vacant lots that are left. You bulldoze down all the shanty-towns.

Then all you have to do is tighten up the panhandling laws.

One day the homeless decide to get organized and unite. All one hundred thousand of them prepare to leave Central Park and march down Fifth Avenue to get some food and maybe a little money, too.

Of course the police don't like this idea, so when they see the homeless crowd getting agitated and organized they call in reinforcements. The State police line up at the entrance and all of a sudden you have a frightening confrontation on your hands. Next day, the *New York Times* runs its headlines: **STATE POLICE SHOOT SIXTEEN HOMELESS IN CENTRAL PARK.**

You pick up the *Daily News* for the complete scoop and the headlines there tell you more or less the same thing: **STATE POLICE MASSACRE NINETY-ONE IN CENTRAL PARK. REINFORCEMENTS CALLED IN**.

And finally, because when something big breaks you always buy all the papers that count, you grab the *New York Post* for the latest on the situation. **CENTRAL PARK MASSACRE: HUNDREDS KILLED, MILLIONS HOMELESS, BLOOD AND SHIT ALL OVER THE PLACE, TANKS CALLED IN!**

Penn Station 3:am. Four police officers move in for the kill. It's time to move all the passengers sitting in one seating section so the cleaners can get in. Half the people are asleep.

Two officers bang their night sticks to get attention.

"All of you who have tickets for trains move to the other seating area. This section is now closed. Anyone who doesn't have tickets, now is the time to move on."

Bishman had inadvertently nodded off while visualizing the Central Park massacre. *Sometimes* when the mind is done in by booze and drugs, the subconscious mind works a whole lot better.

"Wake up!" growled the officer, kicking Bishman's foot. "If you have a ticket move over to the other side. If you don't have a ticket for the train it's time to move on." The leather-gloved police officer banged his night stick on the wall and for a moment Bishman thought he saw a German Gestapo officer complete with helmet, jackboots and leather gloves. He thought, when they say *'Never again,'* you can't be sure they *really* mean it.

Just at that precise moment one of the police officers raised his arm in the air and pointed to the departures timetable. It looked as though he was saluting, *Heil Hitler*. Bishman was convinced.

How would they ship a hundred thousand homeless out of New York? Maybe in Greyhound buses, their windows blackened. Maybe they'll use some freight trains and ship them out from Penn Station direct, Warsaw to Treblinka fashion. The Gypsies were the first to go in Poland, about one and half million of them, and only then did they start on the Jews. In Poland

163

they did it by offering food, showers and work - *just what the homeless in New York need!*

"It's that time again, gentlemen. Time to move on." Two more officers started banging their night-sticks on the wall and eyes started popping open and people started to pick up their worldly possessions in plastic bags and move to the other seating area.

Bishman moved to the other seating area and sat put. He blended in with his corduroy trousers, white sweatshirt and sneakers. He could have been a commuter, or he could have been a street person. He blended in real good. To all intents and purposes he was invisible. *He was a chameleon.* In actual fact he was more like a trap-door spider waiting for the right moment to come along before he sprung on his prey. The way the evening was going, it wasn't going to be too long:

Harvey noted and numbered the session. As in many cases he had an intuition that something exciting would come out of this episode. He wondered how many days or weeks it would be before Bishman mentally clicked back into the story, if indeed at all. He waited with bated breath, *knowing* and *hoping* that some action would come.

At Bishman's request, Harvey dropped him off in Pacific Palisades by a derelict building that was covered in brightly colored graffiti, including: FUN SUCKS, I HATE FUN...DRY HUMP FOR PEACE...NEVER PLAY LEAPFROG WITH A UNICORN...MARY POPPINS IS A JUNKIE...SUCKS SYNTAX and NO GRAFFITI HERE. Harvey swung his Rolls Royce around and when he looked in his rear-view mirror, Bishman had gone.

"This is one of the main secrets of making a really good curry. I promised I'd show you, didn't I? - Can you pass me the champagne?" Harvey poured some corn oil into a large cooking pan.

"You're not going to put champagne in there as well, are you?" Anita giggled.

"No, I just want to top up my drink." Harvey carried on chopping up two large onions, stopping momentarily to sharpen a knife which was *far* too large for the job but looked ever so macho. The onions never made Harvey's eyes water. But when he'd finished chopping them, he had to go to the bathroom, and caught his helmet in the zip. Now *that* made his eyes water!

Harvey took a long draught of pink champagne and hooked a tasty strawberry out with his tongue. "You see, you musn't be frightened of the onions or garlic - two large onions and two large garlic, not just a clove of garlic. You'll never get anywhere like that."

Harvey finished chopping the onions and garlic and threw them into the hot oil, stirring them until they were half brown.

"Now here's the real secret for really good curry. Plenty of curry powder, three heaped tablespoons for flavor. You see the heat is not in the curry powder, that's just the spices, the flavor.

To get the heat you put some of this in." Harvey gingerly sprinkled in a teaspoonful of cayenne pepper into the pot.

"I know you may not like it too hot. On my own I usually put in two tea-spoonfuls or more. Burns like hell, brings you out in a sweat. According to Lance Weil, it actually alters your state of consciousness." Harvey laughed as he stirred up the mix in the bottom of the pan. The curry powder quickly absorbed all the oil and the mix was now good and dry.

"Now you add the potatoes which should be nearly cooked. Even if they're not, they'll finish off in here." Harvey added a panfull of small new potatoes complete with the water they were cooking in, as well as a tin of peas, a tin of red beans and the flesh he'd cut from four chicken breasts.

"Now this is the important thing."

"What's that?" enquired Anita, thinking she must be missing some great gourmet secret.

"This!" Harvey topped up the two champagne glasses and plopped in more strawberries.

They laughed and cleared up the mess they'd made. In truth, Harvey made the mess, Anita cleared it up.

"I found out Bob makes money in other ways than panhandling."

"What?" Anita wondered what on earth Harvey was talking about now, her mind still on chicken curry.

"You know, the other day, we were discussing how Bob sustains himself through panhandling. That's what I'm talking about. He's sold his blood and semen too, you know, for money. He's also done a little drug dealing. A long time ago he even made love to a girl who had no tits for money."

"No tits?" said Anita, squeezing her breasts flat with her hands.

"That's right, this girl had had a mastectomy and no-one would touch her, so her girlfriend paid Bob for giving her one. I think it's incredible. The things this guy comes out with under hypnosis are outrageous." Harvey laughed and stirred the curry.

"I think what's even more incredible is that someone goes to a sperm bank thinking they're getting an Einstein, a Mozart or a Shakespeare and really they getting a Bob Bishman or a Son of Sam." Anita grinned. Well, grimaced actually.

"I reckon he's a lot more clever than he lets on. He told me when he was at school he had to talk about Aristotle and Plato. He told them Aristotle was known as the Greek Tycoon, a shipping magnate, and Plato was a character from Disney, a dog with big floppy ears. You've got to be pretty smart to come out with an answer like that. I also found out that he spent time in England to get out of the Vietnam war. A lot of his buddies, although they were alkies and druggies, still got passed with an A1 fitness record and got sent to Vietnam, regardless.

"Bob didn't take that chance. He went to England and spent seven years there. He never really talks about it, he just mentioned it under

167

hypnosis. He intimates he spent time at Findhorn, which is a retreat in Scotland, but he's never actually mentioned the name. If he has spent time there, it would explain why he's got such a lot of esoteric knowledge. He also knows one hell of a lot about firearms and explosives and because he has a lot of time on his hands he spends a lot of time in libraries, wherever he is in the country. I think his favorite book is *The Anarchist's Cookbook*, he's really quite a character," said Harvey as he stirred the curry and continued with a mouth full of strawberries.

"Regressions are truly strange and they affect different people in different ways. Most of what's coming out under hypnosis is stuff that he's perpetrated here in the States over the past seven years." Anita knew better than to ask, *"What stuff?"* She'd learned that when Harvey wanted to talk about certain things or divulge certain information he would. But he didn't like being quizzed, particularly about Bishman.

Harvey opened up a little more. "It looks as though his life runs in seven-year cycles. From seven to fourteen he was badly abused; from fourteen to twenty-one he was into booze, drugs and sex in a big way; from twenty-one to twenty-eight he tried awfully hard to put himself back together again in England - detox, seminars, mental institutions, group therapy, frontal lobotomy, electric shock treatment, various medications, just about everything you can think of. The last seven years he spent traversing the States. He's been in Los Angeles over a year now, seems to have settled down a lot. I'm glad you find his case as interesting as I do."

Harvey lifted up his champagne glass as if to say "Antibodies", which is exactly what he said.

They both collapsed in each other arms laughing and had a quickie on the strength of it.

"I smell that curry!" Harvey lifted the lid and added more water but not before he gently popped a small piece of chicken curry into Anita's mouth for her to taste. She "mmmmed."

"I've got to put up rice and lentils. Lucky I'm organized, isn't it?" He turned on the self-igniting gas under the rice and lentils.

Anita laid the table in the dining-room with solid silver cutlery and set the table off with long red candles in solid silver candlestick holders and a beautiful flower arrangement she'd made from some delicate little yellow flowers she didn't know the name of. Harvey tipped out the rice and let the lentils cook a little longer while he fried a dozen popodoms until they were crispy brown. When they were ready he dished up the lentils. He popped the cork from another bottle of champagne and took it through to the dining-room along with a bottle of mango chutney.

When they finished the most scrumptious chicken curry of all time, they cleared the dining-table and Harvey laid Anita on it. Then they had each other for dessert!

169

Harvey was always delighted when Bishman would pick up from a previous regression. This is exactly how he put the pieces of the jigsaw puzzle together. When this happened he felt he was making progress. Other than that he was getting bored with some of the sickening filth and rantings and ravings that Bishman was producing.

Harvey deduced that Bishman had picked up the thread from when he was in Penn Station visualizing the Central Park massacre:

Maggie, a five-buck-a-time hooker, homed in on a guy who had been hanging out in Penn Station; he was drinking beer from a can wrapped in a brown paper bag. He was a big guy, somewhere in his late forties, a Vietnam vet, getting quite drunk. She went up to him and asked him for a cigarette. He supplied it, with pleasure.

"Got a light?" She held the cigarette up to her mouth.

"Yeah, sure." He got out a disposable Bic lighter and lit her cigarette, while he lit one himself at the same time.

"Where are you off to? Not going to Long Island are ya?" She stuck out her ample breasts.

He noticed them. He couldn't help but notice them! "No, I'm going to North Carolina, I go home to see my folks about once every three months." He blew smoke rings that weren't quite perfect. *Not bad for someone atoxicated by incohol,* he thought.

"What time does the train leave? It doesn't go for a while yet, does it?"

"Nah, ya got that right, about another two hours. I always get here early though. Get my ticket, have a beer, smoke. You know what it's like." He stared hard at her breasts.

"Want to do something? With me you don't even have to hold back, you know. Sometimes a guy likes that."

"How much?"

"Blow job - for you honey, how about five bucks?" She pursed her lips, he got turned on.

"Sounds good to me, let's do it. Where?"

"My place is just around the corner, you sure you got money?"

"Sure I got money." She was already walking out of the station, toward the Eighth Avenue exit. He followed quickly. Blow job for five bucks! Wouldn't you?

"Just down here, on the left. Buy me a beer first. What's your name? Mine's Maggie." She lead him into a liquor store and picked up two Budweisers. He paid two dollars forty cents, cash.

"It's not far now, just down here." She pulled back the ring on the Budweiser and took a deep swallow. He did the same with his.

She led him into a narrow section of scaffolding that led into a building site off 34th Street.

"You sure this is OK? Is this where you live? Is it safe?" He tossed the empty can onto the street.

"Yeah sure, you're going to like this."
She took his hand and guided him into a room at
the back, it seemed quite safe and dark. The only
light came through from a fluorescent sign from a
building across the street. She lent up against him
and caressed his cock through his trousers. He
already had a hard-on. She dropped to her knees
and started kissing his crutch at the same time
fumbling his belt undone.

"Gimme my five bucks." She continued
stroking him and rubbing him and unzipping and
pulling his trousers to the floor. He was getting
extremely excited. He stuffed five bucks in her
hand. She got his trousers to the floor and planted
a big kiss on the end of his cock. He was ready for
this. He was so ready for it, he didn't realize
Maggie was rifling his pockets and had emptied
them of cash, train ticket, cigarettes, everything.

She stuffed the money into her pocket,
got up, and walked off.

"Hey where ya going?" He tried to pull
his trousers up.

"I'll be back in five minutes, I have to
do something. Five minutes, just wait?" With that
he waited.

"You sure you'll be back?"

"Sure, I'm sure." *You asshole!* she
mumbled under her breath.

The drunk fumbled with his pants, and
she was gone. He fiddled with his pants some
more and in a state of bleary-eyed confusion left
them down around his ankles, he decided to wait.
Surely she'll be back.

Bishman who'd watched her pick the guy up at Penn Station, followed her down the road. He walked alongside her and smiled. He got the cigarettes out and offered her one, they got talking. After a while she started coming on.

"Do ya want to do something?" She pursed her lips.

"What did ya have in mind, a fuck, a blow job or what?" He drew heavily on his cigarette.

Four blacks in a bright red Bronco drove past. It was full of tweeters and woofers, it *deaf*initely had two zillion watt speakers in it, and the occupants probably had blood trickling from their ear-drums. The music they were playing was crap, or was it rap, probably a bit of both!

"Blow job for five bucks and you don't even have to hold back."

"Sounds good to me. Let's get a beer first." He led her further down the road and then into a liquor store on the corner of 29th Street. He bought two Coors. He gave her one.

"Where you from?" He took a long sip of the ice-cold beer.

"Puerto Rico." She pulled the ring on her can and it broke off.

"You have this one, I'll get that one open." They swapped cans.

"Na, where ya from now?" asked Bishman, struggling to open the can, eventually managing it, wishing he hadn't swapped in the first place.

"Oh, from Brooklyn."

He led her into a boarded-up building on 29th Street. The back door was broken in. It was vacant.

"I know this place," he said, "I've been staying here, it's cool."

They drank and smoked.

"Give me five bucks, or give me ten and you can do what you like - no holding back, right."

"No holding back, right." Bishman handed over his last ten bucks, all he had left was some small change. The place was *deathly* quiet.

The place had a distinct smell of damp plaster, but every now and then the zesty aroma of freshly-baked bread drifted into the place from a nearby bakery.

She was just about to drop to her knees and was looking straight into his eyes - which is why she never knew what was coming. Bishman let his right fist drift backwards as far as it would go, then piled it into her stomach, using a rabbit punch, which involves letting the forefinger knuckle protrude in front of the other knuckles and exerts tremendous pressure on impact. When the fist is twisted, which is exactly what Bishman did, it has the effect of rupturing vital organs and causing internal bleeding. As she collapsed forward he brought his knee up frighteningly quickly and smashed it under her chin, loosening a lot of teeth. Her head flew backwards. He put both hands around her neck, and in under thirty seconds she was dead.

He stuffed his hands into her pockets and took the money, train ticket and cigarettes.

174

Waste not, want not. Blood was trickling from her mouth, from where she'd bitten the tip of her tongue off and from internal bleeding. The rabbit punch had had a devastating effect.

He lifted up her sweatshirt and felt her breasts. He undid her belt and pulled down her jeans, slid her pants off and examined her pussy. *Looks like a cat with its head cut off,* thought Bishman. He looked at her ass and felt her tits again, *seen better tits and ass on a snake,* he thought. The light was not all that good, so he might have been wrong.

He finished the two beers and took the cans with him. The whole operation, from the moment he hit her, had taken under ninety seconds.

He walked to the door and a huge brown rat ran in front of him. For a moment he was startled. Bishman jumped as well! He carefully opened the door and peeped outside - there were two black guys talking on the sidewalk. *Shit!* He decided to wait. For an hour and half, he just stood there. Not smoking, not doing anything. Just silent and uncomfortably still.

He remembered the stories about the vets in Vietnam: if they were in the jungle with gooks all around, it was fatal to think about the gooks or even try to look at them through the thick undergrowth. The gooks were able to pick up the vibes and would start shooting in their direction. Time after time troops got shot, until they realized what was happening. Bishman didn't want to *attract* anyone to him. *It worked.* The next time he carefully opened the door, they'd gone. He slipped out, wedging the door shut behind him. It would be a long while before they found *her* body.

Bishman walked down 29th Street, then up Ninth Avenue. He gave the two empty Coors tins to a bum who was going through a trashcan filling his plastic bags up with cans at five cents a pop. The smell of rotting garbage and filthy sidewalks permeated the humid early morning air.

Street people go through the trashcans for beer and soda tins they can exchange for cash at the supermarket. They also look in every bag for food, including those with dog shit in them. *So much for the scoop the poop law in New York*, thought Bishman.

It was five thirty on a beautiful morning. Bishman lit a cigarette and as he walked he counted out his money. *Got my ten bucks back, less the two dollars sixty cents for the Coors, that's $112 profit. Killing, it's a living*. He started to hum *Money Makes the World Go Round* from *Cabaret*.

Three weeks later a cat dove through the extractor fan in the bakery where the smell of fresh bread had been coming from. It came out shredded onto the sidewalk on 29th Street. That little item got three column inches in the *New York Post*. Maggie's murder only got one.

Everything was going well for I.O.H., money was rolling into the coffers. Max Hatfield had everything under control. He was everything

Harvey could have wished for in a business manager, the man was a dynamo, and then some!

Bishman was also getting on well at his sessions. Harvey thought they were making fine progress. Bishman held back nothing. Harvey gave feedback in accordance with how the sessions went; a good bond had developed between master and client.

Harvey's relationship with Anita was smooth, like velvet. They wined and dined in all of 'Tinsel Town's' finest eateries, their favorites being Pennyfeathers on La Cienega Boulevard and another restaurant owned by the same people, Café Sushi. They had fancy picnics and trips all over the place. Harvey was catching up on some favorite haunts.

Anita discovered that Harvey was not a great socialiser. One on ones he liked much better; strange - for a man who spent so much of his time talking to and at people, in a crowd, he was usually remarkably reserved. When it was just the two of them, he was just the opposite.

Perhaps the great "Dr. Bill" persona was just that: someone Harvey could confidently present to the world, leaving his real self intact, inviolate. As the weeks wore on and Anita got further and further under Harvey's skin, she sensed there was a lot more to him than met the eye - a depth of character that would take a much longer relationship to reach. For the moment, she was content with the pleasures readily available.

They had just finished making delicious wet love in the Star Room where there had been thousands of stars and a full moon, all lit up like a miniature planetarium, and controlled by computer. Harvey was topping up the champagne glasses. They toasted. He put his arm through hers and she reciprocated and the two clinked glasses.

"Darling, I want to ask you something," said Harvey as he stroked her breasts through her beautiful blonde hair, that he had pulled to her front. He blew sexily in her ear.

She stroked his cock - it was already becoming hard again. "Of course, you want to borrow ten bucks, right?" She teased and continued caressing him.

"No, that wasn't quite what I had in mind. But if I tell you and you don't like it, I promise not to pursue it any further. I promise, honest." He caressed her breasts, this time underneath her long blonde hair. He liked the difference in texture of how they felt through her hair and without it. He found it incredibly sensual. So did she.

"Go on, tell me." She nibbled his ear, then took a long sip from her glass while he continued. "I think we've known each other long enough to talk openly. I'd like to tell you a fantasy of mine that I've had for a long time, and if you like it, we'll act it out. If you don't like it, I'll never mention it again." He took a sip of champagne.

Anita laughed. Not a sneering laugh, that would have put Harvey right off, but a sexy laugh. A very sexy laugh indeed. "Of course I'll like it, I like it already, I'll do anything for you, Bill, you know that." She gave him a big kiss and squeezed his dick. "Tell me what it is, your fantasy. I've got a few of my own I wouldn't mind acting out. Mind you, you've fulfilled most of them already." She kept on caressing his cock.

Harvey ran his hand slowly up and down her thigh. "I've always wanted to go to a high-class hooker. Of course, I never have. But I've fantasized about it over and over again. I'd like - you to be the hooker. We'll both pretend we've never seen each other before. You dress up in all sorts of lingerie and work me over, good and proper. I'll pay you cash, that's all part of my fantasy."

"I love it. When can we do it? I've always fantasized about being a hooker! I've got some interesting ideas of my own." They went into a kiss but burst out laughing instead, before making delicious, hot slippery love - probably on the strength of the hooker fantasy.

TWELVE

As usual, the New York City police are ultra busy. It's usually only the humor that keeps them going. There's a lot of it around, and the night Bishman killed Maggie was typical.

One drunk, absolutely spifflicated, left his club around four in the morning. The vodka he'd been drinking had made his numbs go all cheek.

He got out to his car, a nice clean Honda Prelude complete with custom paint job. It was quite frosty outside and his windshield had iced over on both sides. He fumbled around for what seemed like an eternity in his glovebox and eventually grabbed what he thought was the de-icer aerosol. He liberally sprayed both the inside and outside of the windshield and started to make his way home. Like all drunks, their cars know their own way home. This one was no exception...*Thank Christ!*

Windshield wipers going full tilt on the outside, hot air blowing on the inside, the drunk had never, ever, in his whole life, driven through such thick fog before. But he persevered.

This really was the foggiest night he'd ever seen, he was congratulating himself that he'd only bounced off about a dozen stationary cars in the last five miles and now he was nearly home. Unfortunately the last car he glanced off was a cop car...*Isn't it always the way?*

They pulled him over and when the cop opened his door he literally fell out onto the street, passed out, *non compos mentis*.

The first cop pulled his buddy over from the patrol car and they were there a good half an hour. What they wanted to get to the bottom of was why the driver had sprayed the inside and outside of his windscreen with grey paint. They didn't get a coherent answer.

The other noteworthy incident of the evening was that during the day, the traffic signals on Tenth Avenue and 23rd Street had been completely ripped out by a truck that was hauling a huge load of cardboard. The truckie never even stopped and he dragged the whole traffic light about a hundred yards down the road in a mighty shower of sparks and loud grinding metallic noises before they disentangled themselves from the bottom of his truck.

All that was left at the scene of the accident were the live electrical wires coming out of the ground.

Apparently, shortly after midnight, a woman had been walking her dog - a little Chihuahua by all accounts - and the damn thing pissed on the two live wires. The dog literally exploded in a huge puff of acrid smoke and the woman just stood there holding the dog's leash, howling hysterically. She wasn't too happy about it. She wasn't too coherent, either, when the police arrived to take her statement.

The police officers put the charred and smoking remains of the mutt in the trunk of their patrol car and drove off, making some quip about *mustard or sauerkraut with your hot dog, madam?*

BOOK

TWO

ONE

Harvey surmised Bishman was talking about a previous event that had left Harvey dangling half-way through a story. When this happened, Harvey couldn't help but be excited, his adrenalin level rose:

Bishman felt good about himself. He bought a twenty-cent razor and a five-dollar black sweatshirt with the slogan on it, **WELCOME TO NEW YORK**, in white letters along with the outline of a murder victim, like the police use. This appealed to Bishman's sense of humor.

He walked up to the Port Authority where the Greyhound buses leave from, went into the downstairs bathroom and spruced himself up. He threw the razor and his old sweatshirt into the trash and walked out into the cool air of Eighth Avenue, feeling good about having a little over a hundred bucks to his name. *Maggie's money! Killing, it's a living!* Thought Bishman, as he popped three tabs of acid into his mouth.

He walked as far as 97th Street. It was cool, four-thirty Friday afternoon. He decided the time was right to put his thumb up. There was a lot of traffic. Everyone was vacating the city at the same time. This was usual. Every time a police siren went, Bishman thought *I'm not leaving this place any too soon, yeah, boogaloo*. He was lost in his own thoughts.

Wrapped up in the busyness of his mind he only just noticed the Connecticut plates on the black stretch Cadillac which had pulled up and stopped. He'd only had his thumb out a matter of seconds. He was expecting a ride to take somewhat longer; *but when you're on a roll, you're on a roll*. For a single moment he had a flash of nervousness. *Is this maybe three or four black dudes in a limo, who just want to take me for a ride, perhaps play with my mind?*

A tinted window rolled down and a distinguished looking businessman of about fifty-five enquired: "Where ya heading, fella?"

Bishman thought quickly: "Outta town, probably Connecticut, but outta town definitely."

"Jump in, buddy, I'm going to Groton. You can drop off anywhere along the way or get out at Groton and pick up your route."

The limousine lurched into the traffic, somewhat aggressively. Bishman and the businessman introduced themselves. There was instant rapport. Two interesting guys, both wanting something from each other. Company, conversation, excitement, adventure, something out of the norm maybe.

"I'm Leonard Prendegast - good to have you aboard. Cold in the city, isn't it? I'm glad to be getting out for the weekend, what did you say your name was?"

"Bishman, Bob Bishman. Yeah, thanks for the ride. It's too cold for me in Manhattan, this time of the year. I'm looking forward to hitting the road again."

"What do you do, Bob? Just travel around, checking places out? That must be a great life. I'm tied to a desk for eighty fuckin' hours a week."

Bishman noticed the guy's Rolex President with diamond face, bezel and strap, and some ostentatious but enormously appealing diamond rings. *This guy is made of money,* Bishman just *knew* it.

He could also sense a number of other things. Although the guy was stinking rich there was no barrier. He was talking to Bishman on his level and Bishman knew it, and appreciated it.

The interior of the limousine was plush. There was a small television and a fully-stocked drinks cabinet that Bishman's eyes had fallen on.

"Wanna drink?"

"I'll force one," replied Bishman.

"What do you fancy after a hard day's work at the office?" he chuckled.

"Oh, whiskey for me, straight, lots of ice."

"There you go, buddy, just help yourself. Take plenty of ice too, you deserve it." Prendegast operated a switch at the side of the cabinet and ice cubes plopped out, one cube at a time. They were shaped like a pair of woman's tits, which Bishman thought amusing, although he didn't say anything. He'd never seen anything like that before.

He took the whiskey, thanked Prendegast, held the glass up and looked at it ruefully, then toasted: "Antibodies." He smiled, and took a long sip of the whiskey full of ice tits.

"Call me Leo. Everyone calls me Leo." Leo gave an encouraging smile.

Traffic had been pretty slow and they were only just moving through Harlem.

"Not many folks go up to Harlem these days unless you fancy getting your fucking head blowed off, ain't that the truth? New York, what a city, where the weak get eaten and the strong grow rich!"

The 'phone went. It startled Bishman.

"Excuse me, Bob, I must take this, the West coast still keeps going for another three hours and I need to tie up some loose ends." He picked up the phone and lit a cigarette with a solid gold lighter.

"Yeah, of course it's Leo. And I know who that is. Well at least I think I do, I hope it's you, Arnold. You got my message OK? The deal's do-able. I outlined it on my fax, you and I go in fifty-fifty with the money. We cut the other guy in for fifteen percent of the action and always keep him at that level, no voting on his shares, but we do need him for his creativity.

"This new magazine will fly. You get the guy's drift. With a name like *Tycoon*, all tits and ass, better material than *Playboy*, *Mayfair* and

188

Penthouse put together. There's some real neat pussy shots, just getting wet, but still quite legal and the detail is clearer than anything you've seen before. This guy knows what he's about. This is the latest technology. It's all filmed in Denmark. That's where they make the plates and we can print anywhere in the world. That's right. Yes! Yes! Yes! You got it.

"Listen up, will ya? We'll use Interstate Distributors and our own people will sell the advertising. The most wonderful thing about this magazine is that all the copy is about making money. Now if you think about it, what does every red-blooded fellow think about ninety percent of his waking hours? Only two things right! Money and pussy, and not necessarily in that order, right! And now you can get them both in one monthly magazine, *Tycoon!*

"We're all highly excited about it this end. They've spent a lot of money on the mock-up, it's superb! I've also read it from cover to cover. If they can keep up the standard for a few years, this will be worth a few hundred million to us. I've been longing to take Bob Guccione and Hugh Heffner head-on, and this is our chance.

"I know you'll come in - I've already committed you! Four million a piece, right. Yeah, the guy's name is Jon Golding. OK, Arnold, have a great weekend. Yeah I know, you're in Manhattan next Thursday. And it's your shout for dinner, you old rascal."

Leo lifted his weight to one side, away from Bishman, and let rip a loud fart. "It's still working," smiled Leo.

Leo inserted a tape into the tape deck. It was screwed up and played at a funny speed. It was playing a squeaky rendition of Gene Vincent's *Be-Bop-a-Lula.* He ejected it and inserted another cassette which played perfectly: *The Man Who Sold The World,* sung by Lulu. He turned down the volume so they could talk over the top of it.

Some people just know how to get people to open up and talk and make conversation and life flow smoothly. Bishman was one. Leo Prendegast was another.

"Tell me about yourself Bob. You obviously like travelling, seeing a bit of the country. What else do you like?" Leo was probing, ever so gently.

"I'd like to be a Disciple of Mammon. I've never had two cents to rub together. All I've ever done is panhandle for small change and get myself around the country a few dozen times. Living by my wits. You must have *some* advice." Bishman was serious. He would like to be a billionaire. He'd been on the streets for far too long. He knew he had a mind, but he didn't know how to use it.

"Well if you're asking advice I don't really have any. I could be facetious and say 'You make a billion here and a billion there and it soon adds up.' But I won't. I've worked hard for over thirty years building the empire that my father left me and his father left him. If there's one thing I've learnt it's this. You've got to have options, escape routes, back doors and weasel clauses. And the greatest thing of all is knowing how to turn disaster and failure to your advantage - but more than *that*, read positive thinking books like *Talk and Grow Rich.*

"The other thing, Bob, is you gotta work out of Manhattan. You know many Americans think Manhattan is the capital of America. They've got it all wrong, it's the capital of the fuckin' universe! Mind you, I love that saying of yours, Disciple of Mammon. My ass! Where did you get that one from?"

"It just popped into my head," said Bishman. Which it did.

Soon the open road was getting them nearer to Groton and further away from Manhattan. Bishman had already learned a lot about Leo, who was a compulsive talker.

"You know what, Bob? You're more than welcome to stay the weekend at my place. I've got a large estate, you'll have a lot of fun. I know we've still got quite a few miles to go yet but if I know you're staying over, I can get some dinner organized. I like to give the chef a little time to get prepared. Not only that, I like to eat when I get in the door, not two hours later. It would be my pleasure to have you as a house guest.

"Not only that, I promise to have you sucked and fucked and blowed in more ways than one. How about it?"

"Let's do it," replied Bishman, but not without reservation. He *knew* this was going to happen. He could *feel* it. *What the fuck am I getting into here?* he thought.

Answering Leo about taking risks, Bishman replied, "Yeah, sure I take risks. Living on the streets is a risk every day you go out there, what with all the wierdos and whackos about. There's some right fucked-up people out there you know, Leo, some real funky people too. Yeah, sure I take risks, but not as many as I used to when I was heavy into booze and drugs."

"You seem to have come out of it all relatively unscathed, Bob. You don't seem to have suffered at all. Some people who've been into the drug scene are crazies. Living in Manhattan you see it all the time. In New York we get about a hundred murders a day. It's criminal, if you'll excuse the pun. What we've got is a glut of serial killers and a dearth of good detectives."

Leo told a filthy joke, Bishman countered: "A guy went to huge party and desperately had to use the bathroom only to find that it was already overflowing with menstrual turds, toilet paper, faeces, used rubbers and piss. He had to take a shit because he was about to explode. The toilet bowl was already level but he carefully balanced on the rim and took a dump. Just as he finished he slipped and his ass dunked in all the shit. The thought of it made him violently sick. Well, you know how a syphon works?" Leo topped up drinks, spilling half of them with laughter. They were having fun and they knew it.

The car swung over to the right and pulled in over some railway tracks. An Amtrack train sounded its horns - long blasts - and rang its bells. Bishman looked out and could see the ferry: *The Chautaugwau*.

Harvey was biding his time, his decision being made. He switched off the tape recorder and completed his notes on paranoia, and the fact that Bishman had developed a nervous tick in his left eye and his nostrils flared continually through the regression.

Bishman stayed in an altered state for another six hours and twenty minutes without saying a word, but snoring remarkably loudly.

It was the end of one of those hot, hazy, smog-filled Los Angeles days. The wind was just coming up and the slight breeze made the evening more bearable. The yellow Rolls Royce pulled into the parking lot at the back of Buccaneer Street in Venice. The driver got out, carrying with him a wide crocodile-skin briefcase.

He knocked on the door and in due course the door opened. He stood staring at a beautiful young woman.

"Are you Lyn? I'm Trevor Stanton," said the grey-haired forty-five year old.

"Yes of course, come right in, I've been expecting you." She turned her cheek as if to be kissed, which he did. He could smell her perfume and was immediately attracted to her. He'd never experienced such arousal. She'd fingered herself beforehand and rubbed her vaginal juices behind her ears, like the hookers used to do in the old days. *There must be some truth in the animal magnetism of natural body aromas,* thought Lyn.

"Come right through...make yourself comfortable. Can I get you a drink? Whiskey maybe, gin, vodka, rum and coke?" She went over to the drinks cabinet and waited for his reply.

"I usually drink pink champagne and, as it happens, I've got a couple of bottles right here." He opened his briefcase. "They're both cold, they haven't been out of the refrigerator long, but perhaps you'd like to chill this one down for later. Oh, while I'm at it, here's the money. I'd rather get that side of things cleared up now. Fifteen hundred dollars as agreed, right? Cash, count it if you like." He threw the money onto a polished ebony coffee table; it landed on some art books. Fifteen hundred dollars, with the bank wrappers still around the three bundles. A lot of money. For that, he'd expect a lot too.

"Want something in that? Strawberries, maybe?" She smiled.

"Yes, that would be great." Stanton looked around the graciously appointed apartment where everything spoke softly of wealth and class. *Exceptionally tasteful,* he thought, *for a hooker.*

"What is it you do exactly?" she asked, as she passed him his drink, deliberately coming closer than she really needed so he'd pick up the pussy odour again. "Work in the film industry, or what?"

"No, in fact I'm a consultant from London. All sorts of management consultancy, helping companies get out of debt, that kind of thing, saving them from the predators. Creditors, right - we call them predators, ha ha ha." Stanton popped a couple of strawberries into his mouth. They were cold and delicious, even crunchy.

"Sounds good. Why don't you bring your drink through to the bedroom and we'll have a little fun." She led the way and waited.

"Why not indeed. That's what I'm here for, right?" Stanton took his drink and followed Lyn into the bedroom which was tastefully decorated in pink - incredibly feminine too.

Lyn cast off her evening gown and revealed a long, slender figure. She was wearing black stockings, black panties, black suspenders and a black bra.

"If you just sit there and relax, I'll put on a little show for you. Would you mind if I played a little music?" She turned on the stereo. Eurythmics, *Sweet Dreams Are Made of This*, played at just the right volume.

"No, you carry on." Trevor Stanton took a drink, then topped the glasses up with champagne. He made himself comfortable: he could already feel himself becoming hard.

The music was obviously chosen because it suited her dance routine. Lyn rolled her hips and body in the most suggestive movements imaginable. She went right up to him, simulating intercourse by rocking back and forth, still in her lingerie, practically letting her panties touch his face.

Lyn then started to undress conspicuously slowly, one stocking at a time, rolling it down, carefully taking it off and placing it delicately over Stanton's arm. She did the same with the other stocking. She wiggled her hips and moved graciously back and forth like a professional belly dancer, all the time *Sweet Dreams Are Made of This* played rhythmically, hauntingly, in the background.

She slipped off her bra and stepped backward, then built up a circular movement so that her full breasts where swinging around and around. Stanton was transfixed. This was what he was paying for.

She dropped the bra on his lap and, accidentally on purpose, brushed his hard-on that was now bulging in his trousers.

Then carefully, slowly, she undid her suspenders and, just as slowly, slipped off her black lace panties. She walked toward Stanton, briefly brushed her golden bush in his face then pulled back.

She went to the side of the room and brought around a big pile of lingerie. All sorts of goodies. She took them behind a screen, just three yards from where Stanton sat, a screen that came just up to her shoulders - the gauze-like material, aided by carefully-placed back lighting, letting through a willowy silhouette topped by two delightfully full breasts that grew even larger as she bent over to slip on her panties. Stanton had the double delight of seeing the shadowy figure slip off the last remnants of one ensemble and just as sensuously slip on the next...before presenting herself. The bulge grew even harder.

"This is the famous Frederick's of Hollywood collection," said Lyn as she emerged in *Secret Appeal*, a sexy cami-top pant set of exquisite black and gold lace. She turned around, slipped out of the outfit and laid it across Stanton's knee.

Then she put on *Unforgettable,* an exquisite black gown, with its satin bows and lace ruffles. The skirt had a slit up the side. She slowly, sexily, paraded up and down, her long blonde hair setting the whole thing off to perfection. She slipped off the skirt and handed it to Stanton.

Next was *Beautiful Bows*, a lace catsuit complete with convenience crotch. She made sure Stanton knew the meaning of convenience crotch; she got him to bring her off by fingering her through the slit. She was still dripping wet when she put on *Triple Dare*, a horny three-piece camiset, fishnet stockings and G-string in jade green.

Stanton was bursting out of his seams. Lyn kept going. "This is the *Velvet Lace Ensemble*," cooed Lyn from above the screen. It turned out to be royal blue and had a sexy tulip-cup bra, garter belt and stockings. Lyn kept wiggling around so Stanton could see both the front and the back. She turned slowly and somewhat carefully slipped the whole thing off onto Stanton's lap.

Lyn came over and dropped a silky pair of French bloomers on his lap, but this time her hand stayed on his trousers, pressing. She slowly took his fly and unzipped him, leaving his trouser belt still done up. She took his grand cock out from his boxer shorts and caressed it ever so gently. "Gee whizz, fella, you are a big boy. I'm glad you're circumcised too, I'm not all that keen on guys who aren't. You know, when you pull back their foreskin and there's all that smegma there. I usually tell them to go and wash up. Or if it's a john who's paying me a lot, I may get a warm flannel and do it for him. Smegma, ugh!

"Reminds me of an article I read in the *Los Angeles Times* last weekend, about a shipwrecked sailor they discovered on a desert island after five years. All he had to eat was acorns and cheese."

Stanton knew he'd fallen for it, but he couldn't stop himself. "Where did he get the cheese from?" he asked.

"Under his foreskin." The hooker laughed, so did Stanton.

While his palms followed the curve of her breasts, searching for her nipples, she sucked and gently licked the helmet, taking the thing in her mouth, deep down. He felt those tits of hers as though there was no tomorrow, while she plowed that monumental cock into her mouth up and down, never stopping. She went at it relentlessly with hungry intensity, and when he started to come she didn't ease up. She squeezed his balls harder and harder. *Hurt me gently,* thought Stanton, as she took the whole thing in her mouth. She sucked him dry then carefully tried to put his semi-limp cock back in his trousers and zip up the fly. She couldn't because he was still too firm, so she left it.

Lyn went through the whole routine again with some more lingerie until Stanton had a big erection. She suggested they lay on the four poster bed. He carefully lent over to kiss her: "Hey, no kissing, fella." Lyn pulled back and he tried again. "No kissing, fella, fuckin' only." She slipped off his shirt and trousers.

Lyn straddled across Trevor Stanton - he had a wicked hard-on. She carefully opened up the lips of her pulsating, dripping wet pussy, and gently eased his giant prick into her soaking orifice. She then started to ride him wonderfully slowly making sure that she went right to the top, nearly coming out each time, then slowly, all the way down to the hilt. Her thighs and legs worked overtime. She rode and rode. He just lay there, taking it all in. Occasionally he reached up his arms and gently played with her full, perfectly textured breasts and large brown nipples. She went up and down like a steam train, really working it, really doing her job, doing all the work.

He watched her pussy ooze out white creamy slip-in-easy-juices and he could feel the muscles of her vagina gripping around his cock. He was sure she was doing it on purpose. The gentle, musky aroma of her juices kept wafting toward his nose. He just lay there - it was a dream come true. When Stanton started coming Lyn started humping, bucking and heaving even more frantically and he could feel the explosions. She could feel the hot jism hitting her insides and she just kept right on going, never faltering for a single moment until Stanton was well and truly spent. He'd never experienced such a powerful orgasm. Eventually she slid off from his still immense cock, although it was now slowly going down.

"We're through, fella." Lyn got up and went to the bathroom and brought back a warm flannel and mopped him up.

He tried to kiss her - he tried all sorts of manoeuvres - but he was told "No kissing, fella!"

Stanton picked up his briefcase and went to the front door. Just as he was about to leave, Lyn turned her cheek and allowed him to give her a kiss. She then slipped a small, prettily wrapped package into his hand.

"See you again, I hope," said Stanton as he walked towards his car, clutching his gift.

"I hope so too," said Lyn as she smiled sexily and closed the door on the warm Californian evening. She went to the refrigerator and took out the remaining bottle of pink champagne and thought, *profit!*

Trevor Harvey headed up Santa Monica Boulevard, towards Beverly Hills. On the way he ripped open his gift. It was a cassette. He inserted it into the deck: *Sweet Dreams Are Made of This*. He suddenly did an illegal U-turn and headed back towards Venice. He drove to a spot along the Pacific Coast Highway by Topanga Canyon, parked the Rolls and strolled down to the beach. He walked for a while then took off his shoes and socks to let the sand squelch between his toes. Bill Stanton was in heaven.

Suddenly he heard a voice from behind, quite a way off. "Bill Harvey, Dr. Bill, can I join you? It's me." Bill Harvey recognized the voice. He snapped out of his trance, *Bill Stanton, Trevor Harvey, Bill Harvey, that's me*, he thought.

"Hi, Dr. Bill, I hope you don't mind me joining you - I saw your Rolls parked up the top and I thought if you were on your own, I'd join you. Been out for the evening, have you?"

"Sure have, Bob. What about you?" Harvey jumped over a small dead shark.

"Yeah, nothing much. I've been strolling around. I know this area pretty good." Bishman lit his customary cigarette and they started chatting about this, that and the other. Nothing heavy duty. Small talk.

Harvey and Bishman walked and talked until the sun, appearing just below the horizon, turned the deep blue above it into rose. The moon, robbed of its power, started to fade. It was morning, with that chill in the air that always seems to precede the sun's first tentative rays.

"Hey buddy, you up for some breakfast? My shout." Harvey got up and dusted the sand from his trousers and put his shoes back on.

"I hope my Rolls Royce is still there, ha ha ha."

"It'll be there, the joyriders only like BMs, Corvettes and Porsches," said Bishman, as he rubbed his arms and lit another cigarette.

They walked across the sand and went up to the highway. His car was still in the parking lot. A lone yellow Rolls Royce, untouched by human hand.

They drove for a few minutes and pulled into Patrick's Roadside Café, with the green shamrock symbol outside. The smell of delicious 'Wanda' burgers and roast coffee filled the air. They had eggs-over-easy with sausage, home fries, a full stack of pancakes with maple syrup and a bottomless cup of coffee. When Bishman had finished, he polished the plate with two slices of pumpernickel toast, and ordered the same again.

Harvey sipped strong black coffee. He was thinking two things. One: *by golly, that Lyn can hump*, and, two: *when you have a frontal lobotomy, the brain cannot tell when the stomach is full.*

That day Harvey sent Anita a cuddly four-foot-tall teddy-bear clutching fifty red roses and a little note in one paw that read, 'In appreciation, with love and kisses from Trevor Stanton.'

TWO

It was unusual for Harvey, but he actually coaxed Bishman into picking up the tale about Leo Prendegast, the seven previous sessions having been nothing but verbal diarrhoea, and Harvey was becoming increasingly impatient. Bishman obliged. *Thank Christ for that!*

Lenny the chauffeur drove hard for twenty miles to catch the 9:30 ferry. He just made it.

"Some people get out and stretch their legs and pick up a drink at the bar," said Leo. "My custom has always been, over the years, never to leave the limo. We can just sit here and chat for an hour, I hope that's OK. I think it creates mystery. They all know who I am, but they never see me, only what they've read about in the papers. More whiskey, something else?"

For forty minutes they told an endless string of filthy jokes, each one trying to outdo the previous performance.

The stretch Cadillac bumped off the ferry and Lenny drove quickly for about twenty minutes to the far side of the island, which was practically deserted.

They passed mansions, palaces and castles on the way. The *really exotic* residences can't be seen from the road because the driveways are too long. The ones that can be seen from the road are known as hovels. It's a local joke.

The Cadillac swung into a pair of large wrought-iron gates that were just opening and two guards with black AK-47s and dressed in black tracksuits and black balaclavas, just like Ninjas, moved in behind the Cadillac as the heavy gates immediately swung shut. Bishman craned his neck. He didn't want to miss a trick.

The gates had had the words SKYBO CASTLE worked into their pattern of iron.

The stretch Caddy shot down the dead straight quarter-mile gravel drive, wheels spinning all the way, the chauffeur obviously enjoying himself. Either side of the drive was a vast expanse of well-kept lawn that had been groomed and landscaped with the occasional shrub or small tree.

Bishman could see the magnificent castle coming into view, its huge towers and turrets silhouetted against the skyline as clouds scudded eerily across the face of the full moon. It was truly awesome, like someone had gone to England and taken apart one of the largest, most majestic castles and brought it back stone by stone and rebuilt it on Fairfax Island. And of course that's *exactly* what Andrew Prendegast had done in the early 1900s.

The air was decidedly chilly and Bishman hadn't realized just how foggy it had been. But it was a pleasant evening. In the background you could hear various fog horns on the Sound and the occasional bell sounding on a buoy. As they talked their breath hit the air. It was good to get out of the limousine, no matter how luxurious it was. *What surprises are to come?* thought Bishman.

Leo walked with a casual air of ownership and led Bishman into the castle to be greeted by Madelaine, a stunning cheerleader type woman of about thirty-five, wearing a bright yellow miniskirt and tight-fitting black top that showed off her voluptuous figure. Madelaine showed Bishman his suite, where he promptly showered in a massive bathroom that was full of green ferns, shrubbery and appointed with solid gold faucets.

He slipped on a dressing-gown as directed. It was heavy black silk, more like a kimono. It had a multi-colored dragon embroidered on the back. He felt like Bruce Lee as he went downstairs.

Leo arrived at the same time - also comfortably dressed in a dressing-gown - and switched on the full-size organ that had been converted at great expense to play as an electronic player organ. The piece he chose was *Prelude and Fugue on the Name of B-A-C-H* by Franz Liszt. It was frightening, and awesomely loud. Leo let it blast for a full five minutes of sheer hell. The whole castle reverberated.

Madelaine came through and showed them into the dining-room.

The dining-room was brilliantly lit by two dazzling chandeliers. The dining table of polished mahogany was fully twenty feet long, set with a solid silver candelabra, with three red candles blazing merrily away. Two places had been set. Each setting had three crystal glasses and solid silver cutlery. A waiter, dressed in a pink suit, pink bowtie and pink shoes, surprisingly casually and somewhat effeminately, came in and served them both with hot Kilpatrick oysters on a bed of crushed salt. Madelaine attended to drinks - she was now wearing a powder blue mini-skirt and tight-fitting pink top that showed off her ample tits.

They ploughed through a succession of courses: thick juicy steaks, succulent lobsters, sorbets, oysters and various other platters, and a scrumptious cheese board, washed down with vintage port. Leo expounded in detail the great pleasure of fine food and wine, then lifted his weight to one side and let rip. "It's still working, ha ha ha."

Harvey was pleased that Bishman's mind had finally clicked into gear, but was disappointed that he hadn't finished the story. He never let on, but he was growing increasingly impatient: *time was not on Bishman's side*.

Harvey and Anita enjoyed an uncommonly special relationship. They both enjoyed long, protracted sessions of steamy sex and they both enjoyed *quickies*, which could be anything from thirty seconds - less on occasions - to a full five minutes.

This particular Sunday afternoon, they found themselves at Pinewood and Anita suggested to Bill that it was her turn to give him a massage. Who was he to say "No"? He was in the bedroom quicker that you could say, "I'm coming."

In the luxury of the mirrored bedroom, he took her tongue deep in his mouth and worked away at it until Anita pulled away. By this time Harvey was fully erect, no mistake about that. Anita had something special in mind. She told Harvey what she was about to do was called *The Tunnel of Love*, and quite frankly he thought about coming just at the thought of it - whatever it was.

Anita used four police-issue handcuffs to tie up Harvey, spreadeagled on the four-poster bed. He loved it. She warmed an ample supply of baby oil in her delicate hands and gently proceeded to massage his balls.

She warmed more oil in her palm and slowly started to work on his giant member. She was highly systematic, with a definite technique - one she was exceedingly good at.

First, she pulled his cock into the bolt upright position, so it stuck out of his body at right angles. Then she started, extremely slowly and quite deliberately with one hand at the base of his mountainous cock, slowly working him upward, and as she got to the helmet she made sure her fingers slipped over it, the rim, the tip. Every sensual part of the end of his dick was gently and tantalisingly caressed. Before she took her hand away from the helmet, the second hand was at the base of his great cock gripping it quite firmly but gently with lots of lubrication, and beginning to work its way slowly up the shaft to the helmet.

What made it even more special was that everywhere Harvey looked he could see their reflections in the hundreds of mirrors that were on the walls and ceiling. That was an incredible turn-on! *Like having a hundred dicks,* thought Harvey.

Harvey was writhing in excitement and she'd only been going about five minutes. She kept going and going. Even when she put more oil on her hands, which she did frequently, she wouldn't miss a beat at the same slow, tantalising speed, with her perfect slippery grip, always right from the base in amongst his pubes, and slowly covering every single centimeter of the helmet with sensual, caressing movements.

Harvey thought he'd died and gone to heaven. The feelings in his cock were exquisite. They never stopped because Anita made sure there was some stimulation all the time, and the stimulation varied. At the base there wasn't much, but markedly it would increase the nearer she got to the helmet. No matter how much he 'Ooooohed, and 'Aaaaahed' she wouldn't increase her tempo. *Bitch...If anything she's going slower!* Of course, when she got to the helmet she deftly caressed every part of it, sometimes opening up the very end of it and gently massaging inside of the tip where he peed out of.

After about forty wonderfully slow and luxurious minutes, Harvey thought he was going to explode. Still Anita *did not* and *would not* increase the tempo. She kept going, then suddenly Harvey blew his bolt, like a sperm whale, the first spasm shot over six feet in the air, narrowly missing her face but she kept going ever so slowly, definitely not speeding up or going into a frenzy like you'd normally be tempted to. The magic was the slowness and now he was blowing his bolt again, another six-foot spurt of steamy hot spunk, booof!...boof!...boof!...bof...bo...b. He wondered when he was going to stop, as he watched the whole thing for himself in the magical array of mirrors. Eventually he did, but Anita kept going right until the very end, until Harvey actually *pleaded* with her to stop.

Finally, she uncuffed him, got a warm flannel, mopped him up and he fell asleep in her arms.

Another time, another place, on the city limits of San Bernardino. Bishman had no hesitation in picking up the thread of the Skybo Castle story:

After dinner, Leo and Bishman retired to a comfortable smoking-room where a huge log fire had been stoked up with chunky pine logs that were spitting and crackling and emanating a lovely pine smoke smell that tended to clear the nasal passages. The room was not overly hot, but perfectly comfortable with its huge armchairs upholstered in rich oxblood-colored leather. Leo tried to entice Bishman to take a cigar and cognac, but Bishman had the taste for wine.

"Bob, I know it's getting late and you're probably whacked but I'd like to show you around the place a little.

"I want to show you the gun collection because there's a range here and we can let off a few rounds. It's kind of traditional, every Friday night I let my aggressions out in the armory. I blow all the cobwebs out of my mind. It's my therapy. The armory's in the basement."

They walked down a flight of stairs. The firing range was enormous. Just like a police firing range where six people can shoot at targets. The gun collection stood in cases and racks around the walls. Hundreds of guns everywhere, none locked up.

"Help yourself, have a good look around. Don't mind me. Make yourself at home." Leo motioned to Bishman to pick up some weapons.

Bishman picked up a .45 Colt automatic. His favorite weapon. It was heavy. It had a good feel about it. He put it down. He got the feel of a .38 Smith and Wesson - *a Saturday Night Special!* thought Bishman.

"Boogaloo."

"What?" said Leo.

"Nothing."

"Have some fun, fella. Get those aggressions out!" Leo was fiddling with about a dozen firearms all at the same time.

Bishman picked up the .45 Colt auto and let off three rounds. He was off target. The next three shots all hit the target within a half-inch of each other.

"Where the fuck d'you learn to shoot like that?"

"Picked it up along the way. Besides, that's my favorite piece of kit."

Leo let off a few rounds with a Colt .45 revolver, stopped, then continued with rapid fire from an Uzi submachine gun. He let loose with twelve different guns, one after another. The noise was deafening. Any bullet travelling over 1,100 feet per second, which is over the speed of sound, will of course be like a tiny jet plane and break the sound barrier, causing an ungodly din quite independent of the noise the actual gun makes. "Use those shooters-baffles if you like." Leo pointed to a corner full of equipment.

Bishman noticed a pile of equipment and materiel including; grenades, launchers, rockets, bulletproof jackets, holsters, explosives, fuses, live ammunition and blanks, automatic rifles, submachine guns. A job lot by the looks of things, that hadn't even been sorted. A distinct smell of marzipan permeated the air, over and above the smell of cordite and cigarette smoke. Bishman made a mental note: *explosives, dynamite.*

He put on a pair of ear-muffs and gripped a .44 Magnum with a ten-inch barrel. This was the same gun "Dirty Harry" used. Dubbed *the most powerful handgun in the world*, this gun still crushes the competition, delivering 971 foot-pounds of energy at the muzzle. *Awesome!*

211

This will go through one side of a Chevy engine and out the other. The Chevy would stop, make no mistake about that. This gun will stop a three-hundred-and-fifty-pound man who's coming at you full of drugs or liquor. Take his limbs clean off, blow away vital organs, crack or no crack that may be overriding the nervous system and bestowing superhuman strength, this gun would stop the meanest son-of-a-bitch. Bishman knew what he was talking about although he never said it out loud. The gun felt good, as though it belonged. *It soon might!*

The smell of cordite now permeated the atmosphere, despite the powerful air-conditioning.

"I don't think I've ever seen anyone enjoy themselves so much with my toys. It's good to see the killer instinct, Bob - have you ever killed anyone?" The question was asked with a lot of enthusiasm and in a half joking, half serious manner.

"Let's say that I've been around a long time and when you've been around, things happen."

"Let's get out more of those automatics. They're noisy but a lot of fun."

"Let's do it," retorted Bishman rubbing his hands together.

Leo handed Bishman a Skorpion Model 61 submachine gun, which has the cyclic capability of firing at the rate of 840 rounds per minute; it was the type used by the Red Brigade to slay Aldo Moro, and Bishman could see why. He let off twenty rounds and severed three of the human-shaped targets in half. Targets that were a hundred and fifty yards away, well within the Skorpion's range of two hundred and twenty yards. The firing range at Leo's was four hundred and forty yards: a full quarter of a mile. You could electronically set targets anywhere you wanted them, and retrieve them fast.

"I can see you enjoyed yourself, I'm glad. Now let's go have ourselves some *real* fun." Leo was already heading towards the door.

"Let's do it." Bishman didn't know what he was going to do, but he was up for it - whatever it was.

They walked through halls and rooms, and at the end of the castle reached a chrome-and-velvet-lined elevator which expressly took them to the cave room, some three or four floors up.

"This is the Castle's main attraction and another of my Friday night traditions. Of course when we have house guests from the city I hardly ever bring them here, unless they have been friend's for many years. Arnold Rustemeyer loves this place; the cave room and wind tunnel were his brain-child. You'll be able to fulfil *any* sexual fantasy you've *ever* had. I just hope you're up for some frolicking in the wind, so to speak."

They walked in and the effect was staggering. They were in a magnificent, spacious cave that had many smaller caves leading off it. It was truly awe-inspiring, with colorful cave drawings and decorative hieroglyphics on the walls, just right for stimulating the emotions of primitive, raw sex.

There was a dazzling waterfall at the far end and *The Flight of the Bumble-Bee* was playing gently. There were smaller waterfalls and fountains around the other walls of the huge cave. Colored lights - cleverly and discreetly placed - created hues of red, green and purple around the rocks, waterfalls and the colorful rock plants and delicate flowers that were growing. As the music changed so did the lighting. *A perfect setting for sex games.*

A profusion of phallic-shaped stalagmites and stalactites added to the eerie cave-like effect and Bishman thought; *you can always remember which is which because girls tights always come down.*

Bishman explored each of the caves. They varied in size and each had its own feel and its own décor. The larger caves had waterfalls and reflecting pools. All were full of furs flung over king-size beds. The lighting in all the caves was controlled by dimmer switches on the wall, the lighting creating wonderfully warm effects. Each cave room had showers, hot pulsating water at the touch of a button, no faucets in sight - the water looked as though it was coming out of the rock and created a waterfall that you showered under. *Someone's spent millions on this place,* Bishman was thinking when he heard Leo laughing and talking:

"Bob, come and meet some young friends of mine, my sex slaves. Carol, Mandy, Debbie, Patty, Wendy and Bobby. The young lads are John, Max, Eddie, Richie and Peter. This is Bob, and I want you to make him feel at home. They all know the *rules* here - there aren't any, ha ha ha!"

These were real youngsters, the oldest was about sixteen, the youngest about twelve. None of them had any clothes, other than the same type of kimonos that Bishman and Leo were wearing. All had colorful Japanese designs on the back: dragons, eagles, tigers, humming-birds, all beautifully embroidered.

There was a lot of giggling. They were all standing about in the main cave, around what appeared to be a huge wishing well. "This is the magic wind well. It's been designed for reduced noise and maximum pressure," Leo said as he switched it on by pressing a row of colored buttons in a side panel. The well was thirty feet deep and twenty feet wide. At the bottom was a mesh of heavy wire in three-inch squares. A gush of warm air started to rise as the fan in the bottom built up speed. The noise was wonderful and the rush of warm air invigorating.

"This is what we do for fun at Skybo Castle," shouted the eccentric billionaire over the noise of rushing air. Each of the sex slaves was holding a bottle of baby oil. They derobed. "Anything goes here, Bob, you just enjoy yourself." With that Leo dropped his robe, farted loudly, shouting "It's still working!" and dove over into the wind well. Everyone roared with laughter. Bishman looked over the edge, but Leo hadn't gone far - he was literally floating on a powerful column of warm air that was gushing upward. "When we get a power failure the fan loses speed and we all crash to the bottom. Thank God it doesn't happen too often!"

"What?" Bishman never heard the reply.

Mandy and Wendy dove over next, and so did Richie and Peter.

"Never mind, come in join the debauchery, the wind is fine!" Leo was already groping his young sex slaves.

Bishman dropped his kimono to the floor and dove over the side. He was surprised he wasn't suffering from brewer's droop, he'd drunk so much, but the sight of all those nubile bodies had already given him a handsome hard-on. For a moment his heart fluttered - he thought he was going to hit the bottom, but there was no way: the powerful, warm jet of air supported him and he felt just like a sky diver. He popped up like a cork, the pressure of the air making his eyes water.

Everyone was shouting and screaming and laughing, baby oil was flying in every direction. Mid-air collisions. Bouncing off the red and blue velvet padded sides. Hands grabbing asses, tits, pussy and cocks - it was a marvellous orgy. A wind well of interlocked human flesh.

Leo was the first one up and out and over the side, satiated. Bishman followed him; the youngsters were still fucking and sucking each other.

While they had been cavorting, refreshments had been brought in and laid out buffet-style on a long trestle covered with a white table-cloth. Chicken drumsticks, vol-au-vents, oysters, king-size prawns, lobsters that were cracked open, a hot garlic butter dip being kept warm over a small candle, and popcorn. Bishman ate, drank, smoked and chatted to Leo.

Both of them laughed as the sex slaves carried on cavorting, totally oblivious to Bishman and Leo watching them over the side.

"I like looking at youngsters fucking each other, turns me on. You know what, Bob, we've got two-way mirrors throughout the castle in all the bathrooms and bedrooms. When we throw a party you'd be amazed at what some of these women get up to in the bathrooms. Frigging themselves off, combing their pussy hairs, picking scabs, shitting, hiding sores with powders and fucking around in general. Fucking and tonguing each other and dragging the occasional guy in there and fucking his brains out. Outrageous!" Leo roared. Bishman laughed louder.

"I like making films of it all, I can't get enough of it. You like films, Bob?" Leo dunked a huge lobster tail in the hot garlic butter dip.

"Yeah, sure I like films. What kinda films you talking about?"

"You know, films. *Films!*" Bishman still didn't *really* know what Leo meant, although he did have his suspicions.

"When you've had enough victuals, we'll have a couple of sex slaves each and go our separate ways. I want more of that Debbie, she's got the softest tits I've ever felt, and those freckles, Oh! those freckles. After that you can have whoever you want." The hedonistic Leo picked up another large lobster tail and belched loudly.

"I'll have Wendy and Peter," said Bishman with a lecherous grin.

"OK, done, I'll take little Eddie, he gives the best head, and he has such a tight little ass. In

217

the morning come down to breakfast at about nine-thirty, ten - no later - because we've got a long day ahead of us. I want to give you the complete five-dollar tour of Skybo Castle. I hope you've enjoyed yourself so far." Leo burped.

"Too fucking right I have, I'm shagged out already, I don't know what you think I can do with Peter and Wendy."

"You'll think of something. See you in the morning - hang loose, babes." Leo took Eddie and Debbie and wasn't seen again until morning.

Bishman took Wendy, a delicious fifteen-year-old blonde with big tits and Peter, a twelve-year-old boy who had the cutest face and a tight ass to match, to the cave that he'd chosen. A waterfall, reflecting pool, green lights, a king-size vibrating bed covered in furs and a mirrored ceiling were the cave's main attractions. The three of them dove in the waterfall shower and started soaping each other up and splashing around.

After the three of them were satiated, Bishman wanted to talk. He started before the others had chance to fall asleep - it had been a long, horny session.

"How come you guys got to know Leo. Where did you meet him?" Bishman asked in a coaxing, gentle way. He was great with youngsters, he created instant rapports. He found it easy. He knew where he was going to lead with his line of questioning but he decided to do it in a roundabout way rather than come out with direct questions.

"I was panhandling in Brooklyn. His chauffeur, Lenny, gave me some money for coffee

218

and cigarettes. He got talking. He asked if I'd like to get away from Brooklyn and live in the country and do cleaning work for cigarette money and a little dope. At first I refused but I just fell into it after a while. He brought me here about six months ago, I've been here ever since. It's quite a good deal compared to living on the streets." Wendy smiled beautifully, she put her dressing-gown back on.

"Same with me," said Peter. "I used to live on the streets in Queens, until I met with these guys. Lenny gave me money and food then brought me here. I've been here longer than Wendy but I don't know how long. What's your name again?"

"Call me Bob." Bishman smiled at them but really he was smiling to himself as he *sensed* oncoming action.

"How many others are there?" asked Bishman.

"How many what?" Wendy asked with a questioning smile.

"Well, for a start, sex slaves that I haven't met; cooks, cleaners, guards. The place is a fortress." Bishman stubbed his cigarette.

"Well, there are probably about another twenty sex slaves you've not seen, but they all live in the same quarters as us," said Wendy. "As for guards, there must be forty or fifty of them, but the place is so big, you never see them all in the same place at the same time. When we play in the tennis courts and walk in the grounds you see them dotted all over the place.

219

"The staff is a regular ten and we know all of them. They do all the cleaning - we don't do any of that, although we thought we would. We're only used for sex."

"What do you think of that?"

"Tonight was OK, but sometimes Leo brings people here to make films with who are right bastards. They really hurt."

"Yeah, that Walsh guy was a right bastard!" Peter winced.

"Yeah, and another guy he brought here ages ago, Roger - he was *mean*."

"What kind of films does Leo make? He keeps telling me about films."

"Don't know. Whenever he makes a film with a guest and some sex slaves we never see them again to ask them." Wendy was smiling again and her tits weren't quite covered.

"What do you mean, the sex slaves go off to make a film and then you don't see them after that. They go back to Brooklyn or Queens or wherever they came from?"

"I suppose so, I've never been able to ask them," said Wendy.

"I'm tired." Peter yawned. He wasn't quite getting the drift of an important and dangerous conversation.

"Yeah, so am I. Good to know you guys. Let's talk some more tomorrow."

Peter fell asleep. Bishman kissed and cuddled Wendy, a soft and sensuous fifteen-year-old, not the kind of girl you fuck just once. He could feel himself getting hard again. He fucked her one more time and rolled over. He whispered in her ear: "Just in case I don't see you in the morning, during the day have a look around the place and see if you can find me some of the videos that Leo's made. I want to see them for myself." He fell asleep with his finger up her ass.

Harvey let the emotionally and physically drained Bishman sleep for the next nine hours while he played back tapes and made copious notes about extermination of human garbage.

THREE

Three days later Bishman's mind kicked into gear. He needed no prompting from Harvey, who was struggling with his own innermost turmoil:

When Bishman awoke everyone had gone. The time was 9:30 am. He had thirty minutes to wash and shave. Fresh clothing was laid out in the cave room. He had to freshen up quickly. He mulled over the night's activities. His subconscious had processed a lot of information. He knew he was treading on dangerous territory here. He was going to be lucky to get out of here alive. He knew what kind of movies were made here...*snuff movies!* He went down for breakfast.

Madelaine met him as the elevator door opened and she took him to the breakfast room. Leo was already there complete with navy blue blazer, trimmed in leather and highly-polished brass buttons that had the Skybo Castle motif on them.

"I trust the sex slaves kept you up all night, ha ha ha?" Leo was stuffing his face with French toast. This guy had an appetite for food, sex and life. It was good to see. Bishman wondered if Leo had an appetite for dying as he loaded his plate with steaming hot, mouth-watering goodies.

I'm shagged out! I don't know how you keep up the pace, Bishman was thinking. *This guy's at least fifteen years older than I am and he's up and raring to go before I am...Shit!*

They ate, read newspapers, drank strong Megalodora coffee (that Leo called mud) and smoked, and as usual, when the Demon King had finished breakfasting he let rip..."Well at least that bit's still working!"

Leo looked up. "Today I want to show you more of the collection and some of the grounds. Tonight we'll have some more fun. You enjoyed the wind-well, right?"

"You got that right." Bishman stubbed his cigarette and lit another.

Leo led Bishman into the courtyard which was now clearer to see in daylight, although it was still foggy - it really was a tremendous place. The Cadillac had been garaged. Each of the giant rooms surrounding the courtyard was an individual museum or exhibition. The one adjoining the actual castle was the motorcycle showroom: Leo's pride and joy. A collection of over five thousand motorcycles which covered a vast area, rows of motorcycles from every country in the world, going back to the early 1900s.

Bishman was absorbed as they walked through the showroom. They stopped occasionally to gawk and read labels and get a closer look. Every machine was immaculate.

"This is a Brough Superior. Each of these machines is connected to an electric starter, so that by pressing a button it will burst into life. It cost us a lot to do but the result is fantastic. Every one of these five thousand machines will start at the touch of a button. There's a three-minute delay, caused by the fuel pumps being switched on and the starter motors building up speed."

Leo hit the switch for the big Brough and shortly the huge machine burst into life. A blast from the past, roaring away in the nineties. The machine revved up and down fully, of its own accord. The noise was awesome, the whole place reverberated.

"Of course there's a master-switch that fires the whole lot up at one time: we did it once and nearly bust our eardrums.

"We could spend all day in here, Bob, but I want you to have the complete five-buck tour - let's go next door, I think you'll find this interesting."

The showroom next door was a museum with costumes of the world. Neatly laid out in aisles were glass cabinets with models, about twenty inches high, of people dressed in their national costume. Bishman and Leo walked up and down those aisles taking it all in.

"For what it's worth, I get a buzz showing people the bikes, costumes and coins. Everything gives me a buzz, but I still like the sex slaves best of all. Seen enough? Let's move on to the coin collection."

As they walked back out into the courtyard, the sun was breaking through the fog and warming up the air. Bishman mulled over the events of the previous night. He knew *something* was up and he was trying hard to put his finger on it. He was instinctively preparing himself, mentally and physically, for a major *something*, he didn't quite know what. But for the moment he was caught up in the fantasy world of the eccentric billionaire, Leo Prendegast.

Leo led the way into the coin museum. A vast open area with cases laid out with literally tens of thousand of coins from every country in the world.

"These are my favorites. I had them specially minted in solid gold to commemorate my father's death. The trouble we took in getting permission to get gold coins minted was totally out of order, but at least I can say we've got our own currency."

Bishman heard footsteps behind him and turned. "There you go, guys. I brought you out a snack and a beer." It was the buxom, beautiful Madelaine. *When she farts, I bet the hairs round her ass crackle like a bullwhip.* Bishman smiled at the thought.

Leo peeled back the cellophane that was covering the tray of sandwiches. Prawn and avocado, smoked salmon and cucumber, and roast beef with mayo. On the tray there was a six-pack of Budweiser and two frosted glasses. *Magic!*

Leo caught Bishman smiling. "Surely you don't fancy her, after going through all those sex slaves last night?" He laughed heartily.

"No, not really, but variety is the spice of life." Bishman devoured the prawn and avocado and snapped open a beer.

Madelaine came back. "Leo, I've got lots of messages for you. The usual stuff. Nothing important. The only thing you might need to know is there was an electronic bank transfer to your Monaco account for four million dollars from Arnold Rustemeyer. I thought that would make you happy." She walked off.

"You got that right. Bob is wondering if you know how a syphon works!" Leo shouted in Madelaine's direction, then continued with a raucous belly laugh. Madelaine never heard. At least she continued walking as though she'd never heard.

"Eat up, drink up and we'll move on. We get looked after here, see what I mean? The place is like a magnet. I keep coming back for more when I know I shouldn't. I really ought to be out there exploring the rest of the world, while I still have the time and energy. I'm no spring chicken anymore and I haven't seen half the things I want to see or done half the things I want to do. This place has turned into a millstone for me, and you never know when your number's up."

Bishman swallowed his last sandwich. "You never know." *You never fuckin' know, pal. And it may be up sooner than you think.* Bishman mused, bit his lip, then took a swig of ice-cold beer.

"Leo, with all your money you can do what the fuck you like. You don't have to come back here every weekend. But I know what you mean, I suppose that's why I keep on the move. Sometimes, though, I think I'd like a place to go back to every weekend, maybe even settle down." They both laughed and finished off the beer and sandwiches. It was like they'd known each other for a lifetime. In fact, it hadn't quite been twenty-four hours.

They walked into the courtyard, where the sun still hadn't penetrated the fog; although you could feel its warmth, the morning was still chilly. Bishman hucked up a big green and yellow golly which he gossed out. When it hit the ground it bounced. It must have had a bone in it. Bishman thought *get out and walk*.

Bishman was following Leo, expecting him to go into the next building. Instead, Leo looked at his Rolex.

"We've really got to get over to the zoo now, otherwise we'll miss feeding time. You like animals, Bob?"

"Yeah sure, I'm up for anything." Bishman lit a smoke and coughed.

They strolled over to the zoo, a fifteen-minute walk from the courtyard, through acres of artistically-sculpted rose gardens - all in full bloom, but probably coming to an end. You could even have smelt their subtly differing fragrances, if you'd put your nose up close enough. Neither Bishman nor Leo did. Bishman did however sniff his fingers, and he could still smell the delicious Wendy.

The sun still wasn't quite hacking it, the sounds of the foghorns could still be heard on the Sound. Skybo Castle was an eerie sort of a place.

"This zoo is the largest private zoo in America," said Leo.

"What about snakes?"

"Yeah, sure, we got a reptile house - there's more snakes in there than a dog's got fleas. You wanna see snakes? Let's go."

"This section houses Australian snakes," Leo told Bishman. "People don't realize it but we are lucky, most of the snakes in America are non-venomous. In Australia only a couple of the snakes are *not* poisonous. All the others are lethal. That one there, the Taipan, can kill a man in about ten minutes, although the antivenom is available. People who live in the bush actually carry snakebite kits with them all the time. That's one mean snake. That's the favorite of Billy-Bobs, the zoo keeper. He actually handles the son-of-a-bitch. I don't mind looking, but I keep well clear!"

Bishman was taking it all in, lethal snakes; nothing locked; gun collections, all loaded; guards with AK-47s, that looked like Ninjas; publishing magnates; sex slaves; snuff movies; billionaires; tigers; seventeen acres of prison camp. *Shit! Fuck! Boogaloo!*

"Bob let me tell you the program. I gotta tell ya, we're running out of time: I wanted to show you more before dinner but all we've got time for is the Chamber of Horrors - we'll walk over there now."

On the way they walked past Leo's shining Sikorsky helicopter.

228

Once in the Chamber of Horrors Leo eagerly started to point out exhibits: "This guillotine actually works, unlike most of the models here which are strictly for show purposes. They're made of wax, plaster or glass fibre - but all tremendously realistic as you can see." Leo passed Bishman a joint, they lit up, and moved on. The tour was a silent one. The place was dark and remarkably eerie. Each exhibit had its own lighting and looked decidedly realistic. All the normal stuff: a guy being tortured on a rack, a water-wheel with spikes on it that was dragging on a naked man. Another victim was stretched out, with a cage strapped to his belly that had rats in it.

Madelaine broke abruptly into Bishman's reverie. "Hey, you guys! Are you eating today or what? No lunch and now going to miss out on dinner?" You could tell her tone was particularly friendly and she was trying hard to elicit a favorable response.

"We're not only done, but we're hungry. We'll walk back with you." Leo put his hand on Bob's shoulder and Bishman flinched. Leo felt him flinch and took his hand away. "Let's go eat, buddy."

"Let's do it," concurred Bishman. The three of them walked back to the castle. Nothing was said until they reached the entrance, "Bob, take a quick shower, no falling asleep. You've got half an hour. We can get a couple of hours' sleep before tonight's shenanigans after dinner. Does that suit you?" asked Leo, chuckling.

The two cohorts dined gluttonously in spectacular style and Leo finished off by letting rip, as was his way: "At least that bit's still working, ha ha ha."

After a much-needed nap and another long shower, Bishman met Leo downstairs. They arrived in the cave room, both pregnant with excitement. The sex slaves were ready and willing, same crowd as before plus a few new faces - a couple of them even younger than before.

Leo started up the high-powered wind machine and they frolicked away. Baby oil, tits, asses, pussies and pricks, and all the crew flying around like sky divers. A cesspool of human flesh.

"Enjoy yourself tonight, Bob. Fuck as many of these nubiles as you can. We start filming in the morning."

"What?" The powerful gushing of warm wind, screaming and laughter drowned everything.

"Tonight we fuck ourselves silly, tomorrow morning we start filming, whaddaya reckon?"

"You know me, I'm up for anything."

After three hours of shagging, sucking, fondling and clambering out every now and then for a glass of wine or a joint, the party wound down. Everyone was fucked in more ways than one.

"Right, Bob, your shout. You pick first tonight, take three or four of the fuckers, make 'em work you over rotten."

"I'll settle for Wendy and Peter. Also this time I'll take Debbie." Debbie was another young nubile of about seventeen. Big tits and a genuine redhead, the collar and cuffs matched perfectly. She had wonderful freckles all over her boobs.

"Good choice. All you other young lads come with me, the girls go back to your room and no messing around, understand?" The girls went off giggling, and the lads followed Leo to his cave. Bishman was trying hard to picture Leo fucking the asses off six young boys all at the same time. *I suppose he knows what he's doing*, thought Bishman as he marched Debbie and Wendy up to the cave, little Peter trailing behind. They jumped under the waterfall shower - it was almost routine.

Wendy was longing to talk, but Bishman wouldn't let her. They groped each other instead, and after a long wet kiss with Wendy with Peter and Debbie trying to get in on the act, they turned off the waterfall-shower and rubbed Bishman down with huge white fluffy towels that had a gold monogram of Skybo Castle in the corner. "All part of the service," said Debbie.

"I know you want to talk," Bishman whispered in Wendy's ear as she went down on him. "But we've got to carry on exactly the same as we did last night, until I know Leo's asleep. All these places have two-way mirrors. Leo told me himself. We carry on like last night and talk later." Bishman stared at her coldly.

"But it's Mur..."

"I know what it is, that's why we talk later. Let's get fucking, right now!" With that and a big laugh, he rolled right over on top of Wendy and gave her one.

After some heavy-duty sex they dove in the waterfall-shower and freshened up. By the time they finished, Leo's cave was *deathly silent*. Bishman pulled some furs together on the huge circular bed and the four of them sat around pow-wow style smoking a joint. Their state of consciousness was enhanced because of the vibrating bed. Little Peter was as high as a kite already, and the others were kind of mellow.

"Can I talk now?" asked Wendy. "I'll be ever so quiet, it's real important and I'm frightened, but I'm sure you'll know what to do."

"Yeah...I might at that."

"You asked me to get you the videos that Leo made; well, I couldn't get them. I found them, but I couldn't get them out of the room without getting caught so I watched a few of them in Leo's study while he was showing you around the courtyard and zoo. They're terrible. Everyone gets murdered. We're *all* going to die." She was crying before she finished. Little Peter was strung out. Debbie looked serious.

"I saw them as well, fuckin' bad news if you ask me," joined in Peter. "I fucked two of the guys - one was Walsh, I can't remember the other guy's name. I fucked them in the wind tunnel the first night they came but they never chose me to make a film with them. I'm fuckin' glad they didn't, now that I've seen everyone getting cut up and blown to pieces with shotguns. It's fuckin' sickening. I never knew Leo was such a bastard."

"I fucked 'em as well," said Wendy. "They were both vicious, like animals. Where the fuck does Leo get these monsters from?"

232

"Yeah, snuff movies, that's what he's up to. I half suspected. We're in Shit Street, fucking boogaloo to that."

"What?" asked Wendy. She pulled her bathrobe over tightly, shivering with fear.

"Yeah, boogaloo."

"All I know is we gotta get outta here. It's only a matter of time before someone chooses us to make a film with them, then we all get blown away! Shit!" said Debbie.

Bishman had already chosen Debbie and Wendy to make a film on the Sunday morning but he wasn't too keen on making a film right now, so he kept shtumm.

"Bob, what ideas ya got?" Debbie went on; "This place is like a fucking fortress. I've never thought of escaping. Up until yesterday I quite liked the joint, but I've been here long enough to know we can't escape easily. Not only that, we are on a fuckin' island and Leo's got fifty guards."

"Maybe. But I know how to create mayhem."

"What?"

"Never mind, tell me more about the films - you know, the videos, how do people get blown away, who did it?"

"It was just all good fucking around to start with, you know, like we've been doing." Wendy looked at Bishman and then across to Debbie.

"Yeah, then what?"

"Well, suddenly, towards the end, after a lot of fucking and sucking, Walsh got hold of a huge knife from somewhere and started slashing with it. Anyone, everyone, it was awful. He kept looking up at the camera as though someone was cheering him on," said Debbie.

"Was Leo on the video?"

"No, Leo wasn't on any of the videos we saw, was he, Deb?"

"None, the bastard. I suppose he must have been behind the camera."

"So what happened next?"

"After Walsh had literally massacred both girls and the two little boys, he looked up at the cameras and screamed. It was sickening."

"Why, what was Walsh screaming at?"

"I don't know," replied Wendy, "but the next thing his head was blown clean off with a shotgun. You see it in vivid detail - in slow motion as well. It was sickening. There was nothing left, just his neck and sinew with blood spewing out, then the video ended. It was fucking awful, Bob. Awful!"

"Tell me about the other videos," Bishman said, cold as ice.

Wendy glanced at Bishman, who was getting a hard-on, and she knew it.

"They were all the same, awful, every one of them starts the same, just with romping about, plain sex, a lot of fun and at the end everyone was killed. Bob, these are not paint games, these are people getting killed for real. I've seen it, I knew those kids who got slashed. That's why none of them ever come back to the slave den once they've made a film - 'cause they're fuckin' dead, that's why."

"You got that right. I knew there was a payback time." Bishman lit a smoke and threw one across to Wendy, who reached over for a light and said, "What's payback time?"

"Leo picked me up, coming out of Manhattan on Friday afternoon. He's been treating me great ever since, like a long-lost brother. I knew there had to be a payback. But I've got news for him. He doesn't know me...yeah, boogaloo." The evil and coldness in Bishman's death eyes filled the room, making everyone more scared than they already were.

"Whadda we do now?" asked Wendy.

"Well, for a start you can get your laughing gear around this. After that I'll let you know." Bishman lay back on the furs, thinking, *gobble 'til ya wobble,* as Wendy halfheartedly went down on him. After a while Debbie eased her out the way and went at the job with lots more enthusiasm, bobbing her head up and down like a jack rabbit, stopping every few minutes to say, "You gotta get us outta here, Bob. We're counting on you, this guy's a fuckin' maniac, he'll get us all killed."

Wendy took over again and finished him off. He liked coming in Wendy's mouth, for some reason.

"This is the plan. We sleep for two hours. I'll wake you up. Mind you, when I say *'get up'* for fuck's sake get up. Don't fuck me around, I'll create a diversion. You two girls get everyone out, just the slaves. Fuck everyone else, it's everyone for themselves. I'm not stopping for anyone. This place won't know what's hit it.

235

Remember you're on an island, every which way you go will have boats. Get yourself a boat and paddle like fuck. Don't wait around for anything - these guys play for keeps. Boogaloo." He put a cigarette in his mouth and lit it off the last one. Don't trust anyone - all these motherfuckers are in this together. Once the diversion starts, scram."

"How will we know when the diversion has started?" Wendy asked.

"Yeah, you'll know it, trust me, Boogaloo." He bugged his eyes out at them. "Goodnight. You've got two hours, then it's mayhem time. Sweet dreams."

He looked at little Peter snoring and gently kissed Wendy goodnight. Debbie's eyes were closed but Bishman wasn't sure if she was really asleep. Before long though, all the sex slaves were. They looked rather angelic. Bishman couldn't keep his eyes from Debbies' huge tits, covered with freckles, and that huge bush of red pubes, so he jerked off and came all over her face. There wasn't too much jism left, but enough to trickle down her nose and chin.

Bishman set his internal biological clock for an alarm call in two hours and then started to visualize mayhem. He saw flames, guns, bodies, muck and bullets. A semi-plan started to come together. As it did, he fell asleep.

Harvey was listening to the Bishman tapes repetitively. Far more times than was necessary to make sensible scripts out of the disjointed and often disturbing revelations.

He started to have nightmares of his own and he wasn't enjoying his mind much, either. Something had to be done, and done soon. *Dangerous beings have to be neutralized!*

FOUR

Another time, another place, another session. Bishman's eyes swept with violence before he stepped into the regression, as though he'd never been away. Harvey was relieved, he'd listened to enough rantings and ravings to last a lifetime and wasn't sure how much more he could take. He looked inwardly at his own state of mind and breathed an exasperated sigh: *How much more of this bad shit can I take?*

Bishman woke up on the dot, five o'clock, ready for mayhem and aggro like you wouldn't believe humanly possibly. He was vicious and he was ready for action. God help anyone who was going to get in his way.

He woke the three sex slaves. They showered under the waterfall together, but didn't even talk and were sombre as they put their dressing-gowns on. Bishman sat them down.

"I need twelve minutes. This is what's going to happen next, and you gotta move on this.

I'm going down to my room to get changed into my street clothes. You kids do the same, you can get back to your slave quarters and get fixed up, right?" They nodded in agreement.

"You'll need heavy clothes - it'll be fucking freezing out there in the fog. When you hear the diversion, all run out in different directions, but make sure you go through the portcullis and straight out the main gate, then run any way you like to the shore to get a boat. Tell the other sex slaves exactly what to do. No messing now...I'm outta here! Boogaloo." He bugged his ice-blue eyes at them and was gone. They were scared.

Bishman crept over to the cave that Leo had gone into with the six young boys. He took with him a heavy boulder. He slipped into the cave. *Shit! They've all flown the nest in the middle of the night.* Bishman coolly walked out and headed to the elevator and went to the ground floor. As soon as he was there he quickly ran up the first flight of stairs and jumped into his clothes.

He ran back down the stairs, straight down into the armory. His adrenalin was pumping and he was moving incredibly quickly, his movements were precision. He loaded himself up with an armful of firearms, a World War Two bayonet and a shoulder bag full of grenades. He knew *exactly* the kind of mayhem he had in mind.

He carefully put his heavy pile of weapons in the corner of the courtyard. *A mini-arsenal!* Although he was in a hurry, he had a tremendous respect for them - a professional regard, even: he was keen to see how they performed in the field.

The time was 5:30. The fog hung low. It made everything look spooky and it was bone-chilling. Not a soul in sight, but Bishman *knew* the guards were around, he could *sense* them, and he was raring to go. He went into the motorcycle museum and slashed about twenty gas pipes with the bayonet. The smell of gasoline was overpowering. He then deliberately went over to the Brough Superior and flicked on the starter switch. He started running, and as he went he clicked another hundred switches. He was working to a time-frame. He knew the first machine would fire up in three minutes.

As an afterthought Bishman finally threw the master switch that would fire up all of the five thousand motorcycles.

Bishman snuck back in the castle and hit the organ button, first turning the volume up *loud*. Just as he was doing so, one of the guards appeared. Bishman caught him by surprise and let him have it with the Uzi. However, only one bullet came out when he squeezed the trigger: luckily it went between the guard's eyes. He switched the Uzi over from 'S', which was semi, to 'F', which was fully automatic. He had thirty-one 9mm bullets left.

The full-size organ started to belt out *Prelude and Fugue on the Name of B-A-C-H* by Franz Liszt - loud enough to shake the foundations of the castle. It was frightening. Bishman made sure no-one could shut it off, he smashed the switch with the butt of the guard's AK-47.

Bishman's plan was coming together quicker than he expected. He did his chameleon trick. He wrenched off the guard's black tracksuit bottoms and pulled them over his own corduroys. He then did the same with the black top and the balaclava, and added the guard's AK-47 to his armory. He was one of them. To all intents and purposes Bishman was invisible.

The motorcycles were firing up, the noise from the museum was deafening; joined with the organ it was thunderous. Bishman's mayhem plan was working. It was only a matter of time before the gasoline caught light, adding to the chaos. Bishman was on a roll.

Bishman took a Mag-10 Roadblocker, a monster 10-gauge shotgun, over to the dew-covered Sikorski helicopter and let rip. One blast and the helicopter actually lifted off its skids. The first thing Bishman noticed was the searing pain in his right shoulder. Despite the substantial rubber butt pad, this thing had a hell of kick, *Shiiiiit!*...all the helicopter's glass shattered, the rotor went limp and the whole helicopter blew apart in a spectacular fireball. Bishman had never experienced such power from a shotgun. *Jeeeezus! No wonder they call it a fuckin' Roadblocker, this thing could stop a MACK truck,* thought Bishman.

Five guards appeared in the courtyard behind Bishman and were reluctantly levelling their weapons at him, not really sure which side he was on. Bishman had no choice, he let rip again. The problem with Mag-10 is you only have three rounds. You have to use them judiciously. The five guards dropped to the ground in a fusillade of heavy steel pellets. They were blown apart, decimated, blood and guts everywhere. They didn't even know what had torn them apart.

What the hell? thought Bishman, as he opened the garage door where the stretch Cadillac was parked, next to the Chamber of Horrors. He let the Cadillac have it. *It's worth it, to see how this gun performs*. The windows shattered and the hood and trunk flew open simultaneously, and the Caddy burst into flames. The power of the Mag-10 was awesome. However, it was now spent. Bishman eyed the racing red Ferarri Testarossa, a silver gull-winged BMW and a midnight blue Lamborghini Countach that were garaged next to the Caddy and knew it wouldn't be long before *they'd* be ablaze as well. Bishman dumped the weapon, then rubbed his shoulder...*Jeeeezus!*

He went back to his haul of weapons, loaded the grenade launcher and levelled it at the portcullis. Just as he was about to fire he sensed someone at a window on the second floor of the castle. *Shit!* He swung the grenade launcher around at the window and fired. Whoever had been standing at the window didn't stand a chance; a billow of black smoke was coming out the window, the room was well and truly ablaze. *Anyone* in the room would have been killed instantly by the blast.

Bishman sensed someone in the courtyard, about twenty yards behind him. It was Leo, King of Snuff Movies, and he was furious. He was brandishing a lethal Skorpion submachine gun, the type of gun used to mow down Francesco Coco, the chief prosecutor of Genoa. Without hesitation Leo held the gun at his hip and opened fire: rat tat tat tat tat tat, a burst of thirty rounds in under two seconds. Bishman felt no pain. He couldn't believe his luck: the rounds had all been blanks. Leo was puffed-up, red in the face, with a look of rage, disbelief and frustration, screaming abuse.

Bishman, King of Serial Killers, whipped a Colt .45 automatic from the rear of his trouser belt. He *knew* his gun wasn't loaded with blanks because he had injected the clip himself. Further, he had selected teflon-coated shells that were slippery enough to go straight through even the toughest bulletproof vest. With deadly concentration he took careful aim at Leo's chest and squeezed the trigger. The gun jammed. *Shit! Fuck!* Bishman went white and felt his asshole pucker. There wasn't another weapon within easy reach.

The King of Snuff movies snarled at the King of Serial Killers, head to head, their eyes locked in open warfare, the Clash of the Titans.

Without warning, a frightening explosion rent the air and the front of the motorcycle museum blew out in a massive whirlwind of dust and a fireball of smoke and flame, practically lifting Leo off his feet. By the time the dust had settled Leo had disappeared; however, about half of the five thousand motorcycles were still roaring away, and the other half were ablaze.

Bishman turned his attention back to the portcullis, reloaded the grenade launcher and fired. When the brick and concrete dust cleared, a gaping hole emerged. By this time the courtyard was filling with sex slaves. Debbie and Wendy were there, telling the others what to do.

Nine guards were waiting on the drawbridge and they were opening fire with AK-16s and AK-47s. Fearsome weaponry. Bishman held the Uzi around the corner and let rip, holding the thing on fully automatic until the clip was spent. He then threw two M26 grenades for good measure. These grenades were used in Vietnam and took out more than their share of Vietcong. They were also used for "fragging" unpopular officers behind the lines. He poked his head around the wall: he'd taken them all out, blind. *Good one!*

The sex slaves were anxious to rush through the portcullis, but Bishman restrained them. They could hardly hear him over the noise of the motorcycles and the organ that were going wild. *Time to bring out the heavy artillery!* He picked up a Soviet RPG-7 rocket launcher and rushed through the obliterated portcullis and over the drawbridge. He dropped to one knee, put the launcher on his shoulder and fired right down the driveway. He couldn't see the front gates, there were too many swirls of greasy fog, but he knew that they were at the end of the driveway. The rocket went off with a tremendous *Whooooosh.* They heard a huge explosion a second later. They hoped the gates would be demolished when they got there. *This rocket can penetrate 12.6 inches of armour plating - two wrought-iron gates shouldn't pose a problem,* thought Bishman.

Bishman gave the order for everyone to run towards the gates, keeping off the drive. He told them over and over again to keep off the drive, and most of them did. Bishman scooped up the rest of his weapons.

They arrived at the gates only to find them still there. *Shit!* However, there was a gaping hole in the driveway some twenty feet before the gates, where the rocket had struck.

Six guards were gathered around the abyss in awe. Their firing was making a hell of a din, taking out a few of the sex slaves in the process, but they deliberately avoided shooting at Bishman a chameleon in his black tracksuit. Bishman took them out with a grenade. They fell in the hole with surprised looks on their faces as though it was a ready-made grave. *That's why they call it the graveyard shift*, thought Bishman.

Bishman fired three grenades at the gates and they still didn't budge. Not an inch. Solid wrought-iron gates, made to last. *Grenade-proof, obviously! Shit!* Bishman fired his last grenade, it bounced back at him and nearly blew him to smithereens - he just had the presence of mind to throw himself to the deck at the last moment. The blast killed two young sex slaves who weren't so fortunate...*Holy Shommolies!*

Just then, little Peter ran over to the guard house and threw a lever. As if by magic the two huge wrought-iron gates were swung open by their powerful motors, pushing bodies and debris out the way. The sex slaves ran like bunnies and Bishman followed, only glancing behind him momentarily: the fog had lifted enough for him to see the silhouette of the majestic castle with flames licking all around it and just at that instant he saw the driveway explode spectacularly and then collapse, leaving an ugly quarter-mile gash between the manicured lawns where the driveway had been. Bishman had set and timed some explosives in the armory on Friday night when he and Leo were there. He timed them to go off at 6:am, Sunday morning. *Intuition!* He knew the four-hundred-and-forty-yard firing range ran under the driveway. *Perfect timing!* The organ and motorcycles were now in competition with explosives and ammunition rending the air.

Bishman *saw* and *heard* the humor. *A sight from Hell.* He legged it off down the road. Wendy was waiting - possibly a big mistake. They ran hard. They got within a hundred yards of the beach. They lay in the grass, and looked up and over to reconnoitre the situation. Some small boats were moored and a couple of drunken fishermen were arguing in one of them.

Bishman had the hots. All the killing had got him excited. He ripped off Wendy's bubble-gum-pink panties. Her pussy looked like an axe wound - it glistened, she was soaking wet, he fingered her like crazy. *Here's to the wound that never heals, the more you stroke it, the better it feels!* thought Bishman. Wendy came in about three minutes flat. He licked his fingers then turned her over and came in from behind, fucking her doggy-fashion, baby seeds punching up inside of her. Wendy started having multiple orgasms that Bishman didn't have time for, so he pulled out. She whispered in his ear, "Bob, I love you, and I want to thank you." Wendy's eyes were wet, her mascara running.

Bishman replied, "I love you to death." What Wendy didn't notice was the look in his ice-blue eyes. The look of death. Bishman simply couldn't stop himself, even if he'd wanted to. And part of him did. He put his hands around her neck and wrung it like a Boise Idaho farmer strangling a chicken, until she was dead.

He picked himself up and ran the hundred yards over to the boat. He looked dishevelled...but harmless.

Harvey had made up his mind that it was *his duty* to free the State of this human trash. He decided to be the judge, jury and executioner. *Human garbage must be cleaned off the face of the Earth. Kill, kill, kill, the shithead!*

To Harvey's delight, Bishman carried right on with the story, although they hadn't seen each other for three days. It was as though he'd never been away, the memory was like a film rolling on, Bishman's brain combing out tangles of the past.

As he did, Harvey did some scheming of his own, all the time questioning the state of his *own* mental health:

"Hey, you guys! I gotta get over to Groton. Any chance of a ride?" Bishman knew he was going for a ride in their boat, one way or another. The way depended on *them*.

"You shittin' me fella. All this fuckin' fog and you wanna fuckin' ride to Groton. I suppose you're from Leo Prendegast's party - that's where all the noise sounded as though it was coming from, hic. I thought he'd finished with those firework parties of his years ago."

"No, he hasn't, and the reason why I've got to get to Groton is that I've got a couple of cases of Wild Turkey over there in the trunk of my Chevy. Give me a ride, you get one case."

"Now you're talking." The old drunk pulled the starter cord on the Evinrude. The little two-stroke burst into life, *nearly* drowning the noise of organ music, motorcycle engines and explosives that were vying for airwaves.

As Bishman looked back, all he could see was the eerie silhouette of the mighty castle with flames licking all around, lighting up the black night.

The drunks stopped arguing and they broke open a bottle of whiskey and passed it around.

"Have you gotta smoke?" Bishman nodded to the drunks.

"There ya go."

"What about a light?"

"Fuck me, the guy wants a light as well." He passed a book of matches to Bishman who was thinking, *button your lip, pelican head, or I'll cave your skull in.*

"I tell ya, fella, there had better be that Wild Turkey when we get to fuckin' Groton."

"You'll get your Wild Turkey." *That's if I don't stick a fucking knife in your neck before we get there...pal,* thought Bishman as he smiled.

Twenty-two miles in the fog on the Sound is a rough ride for a small craft, no matter how drunk you are. It can be quite scary. However, none of them looked worried. Bishman wanted to get the hell out of there; those two old drunks had their tongues hanging out for Wild Turkey...*Fair's fair, right?*

"Hey, why you dressed all in black, anyway, hic? You look like one of those fuckin' Ninjas - ha ha ha?" He steered the boat in a drunken manner. Luckily the craft knew its own way to Groton.

"Oh, just a bit of a gimmick, a bit of fun for the party."

"All sorts of things been going on up at Skybo Castle for years you know, so they reckon."

"Like what sorta things?" quizzed Bishman.

"I dunno. Things. All sorts of things - hey, pass that fuckin' bottle over. You a fuckin' gannet or what?"

It was rough and choppy and the little vessel bobbed and rode those waves like there was no tomorrow. Two drunks desperate for more booze and Bishman, anxious to put the miles in. He knew that miles were the key. The fog lay over the Sound, visibility was about fifty yards. Foghorns sounded, emphatically loud. The little outboard sung like a sewing machine. *Christ, I hope we don't run out of gas*, Bishman was thinking.

"Hey, you guys - when did you last fill this tug up with gas?"

"Don't worry about that, fella. We'll, hic, get ya there, about another forty minutes I reckon. Give me a smoke." The second drunk passed one over, and Bishman reached over and took one too. It felt good: a smoke, the bourbon, the cold air, the swirling fog, the cover of darkness. The outboard buzzing merrily. The foghorns blaring, deep and loud. Nothing but fog for three hundred and sixty degrees. They passed within twenty yards of a humungous submarine. Bishman nearly fell out of the boat, it came as such a surprise out of the fog.

"Jeeesus, what the fuckin' hell's that?" bellowed Bishman, his voice getting swallowed up by the fog.

"That's one of those multibillion dollar Tridents. They build them over at Groton, at the nuclear submarine base. They don't dive until they get another five miles out. Hairy, eh? Enough firepower to take out the whole of Russia!"

"Fuckin' sure it's hairy, I didn't realize how big they were until we got up close. Do you think they saw us?" *Enough nuclear firepower on board to blow another huge chunk off the Earth and send it spinning into orbit. That means we'll have two fucking moons and double the number of lunatics,* thought Bishman.

"I doubt they saw us. I shouldn't think they'd give a shit for us anyway. Why, who gives a fuck?" *I do,* thought Bishman, but then he changed his mind. *I don't give two fucks.*

"We'll soon be hitting the shore," said one of the drunks; "I hope we come in just about right. Where did you say you parked your car? That's where the booze is, right? See, I haven't forgotten, hic."

Bishman could vaguely see land. He knew that was enough. The drunks hadn't noticed him pick up an oar lying in the bottom of the craft. He deftly hit the first drunk across the head so hard the oar broke in half, knocking the drunk clean out of his seat into the sea, unconscious.

The second drunk got the broken end of the oar in his veined face and the next vicious blow across the back of his fat neck. Bishman nearly overturned the fragile little craft in the process. Bishman hauled him overboard. The drunk was already dead, they never stood a chance. Bishman rubbed his shoulder, which was still sore from firing the Mag-10 Roadblocker. Using the oar as a club had aggravated it. *Gee, that smarts!*

Bishman took hold of the rudder and eased down the revs. He slipped off the black tracksuit, both the top and bottom, and dropped them overboard. He felt the freezing air, his prick was so cold it tried to crawl up his ass to keep warm. He threw five gold coins and his personal back-up gun in the water. He collected them on the way. It hurt to part with the coins *and* the fully-working .44 Bulldog revolver that was neatly tucked into his belt at the rear. Bishman was full of self-protective habits. You don't survive long in the field without them. Slowly and quietly he drifted to shore.

He swiftly kicked a board in the bottom of the craft until the water began to seep through and turned the boat around, set it on half-throttle and jumped ashore. It would probably get out about a mile before it sank, but it would soon be stolen away by the fog. *Wild Turkey, my ass. Two Turkeys, more like it. Boogaloo,* thought Bishman as he started to hum the old negro spiritual, *Michael Row the Boat Ashore. Alleluia.*

Harvey switched off the tape recorder, Bishman immediately snapped out of his trance and Harvey quickly rammed the cold steel of his .38 revolver deep into his pocket. They went for a pizza and a de-briefing session. Harvey gave valuable feedback and was looking forward to seeing where and how it was all going to *end*.

After a four-hour drive into the countryside, Bishman started his narration within minutes of the induction, and Harvey was anxious to get into Bishman's mind for further discoveries. He hoped he'd continue his story and not spin off at a tangent, like he did so often, because time was running out for Bishman. Harvey planned to exterminate this *despicable vermin.* Harvey *owed* it to the State:

Bishman had a penchant for creating extreme havoc and violence and walking away scot free. What's more, he'd just done it again. He made a mental note to buy a sweatshirt next time he visited Manhattan that had the slogan, **PEACE THROUGH SUPERIOR FIREPOWER!** He smiled at the thought.

Up on the freeway, Bishman walked about two miles to a truck stop. He looked around. He saw what he was looking for: Dunkin' Donuts. He was cold and hungry, but he knew what would hit the spot: "Large coffee, extra sugars and four jelly donuts, no - make that five, yeah, to go."

There were lots of trucks around; the oily fumes of diesel fuel permeated the invigorating morning air. Bishman sat, ate and drank. He enjoyed the taste. The coffee was the best and it was hot. He rubbed his arms and wished he'd kept the tracksuit top. He went and bought a pack of cigarettes. He used the bathroom and treated himself to a disposable toothbrush that already had paste on it, to freshen his stale, boozy breath. Bishman strolled over to a truck that had a Pittsburgh address on it, as he finished his last donut.

"Hey buddy, you heading back to Pittsburgh," said Bishman, licking the sugar from the donut off his hand.

"I sure am, buckerroo."

"Want some company?"

"It's against company policy, but who gives a fuck, and in this fog maybe an extra pair of eyes is not a bad idea. Jump in."

The big diesel was already running; they pulled out slowly then gradually built up speed. As they moved further inland, the fog slowly began to lift. The sun was trying hard to get the better of it. 7:30, Sunday morning, 20th of October. It was good to be alive.

"What's your name, fella?" asked the truckie, who had a full beard and a ruddy complexion. He looked like a man peering through a hedge.

"Bishman, Bob Bishman, pleased to meet you." Bishman offered his hand and smiled.

"I'm Larry King, but my handle's 'Groper' - you know, for the CB. When I get those young chicks up in my bunk, they know all about it. I slip 'em twelve inches and make 'em bleed. Well, not quite, but I give 'em six inches twice and punch 'em on the nose." They both laughed. Larry gripped Bishman's hand in a powerful vicelike grip. Bishman got the smokes out, and they puffed away. They made small talk and cracked a lot of filthy jokes. It helped pass the time on a long trip.

"I've been trucking for fifteen years. What about you - on the road?"

"Sure am, about seven years now and thinking of doing something different."

The big diesel pulled its load effortlessly, the miles slowly but surely getting gobbled up, the weather improving with each mile.

Larry looked at Bishman's muscular body wedged into the black sweatshirt and smiled at the slogan and outline of the murder victim. He got out some white pills and bounced three of them, one at a time, off the windshield, and caught them deftly in his mouth. He handed three to Bishman.

"Bennies, uppers!"

"Thanks." Bishman bounced one of the pills off the windshield and failed to catch it in his mouth. He picked it up and swallowed it with the other two.

"Right," said Larry, "I'll crack you up. Let's have all the names you can think of for prick." He lit a joint.

"Dick, peepee, meat, monster, choking the chicken," shouted Bishman.

"How about pork sword, mutton dagger, pussy meat, willie, winkie, pounding the Pope..." screamed Larry.

Bishman cut him off: "Weapon, plonker, one-eyed-trouser-snake, winkle, cock..."

"Dork, peeper, willie, guided love muscle..." said Larry excitedly.

"Dong, peter, old man, pork pioneer, pecker, tube steak!" Bishman was getting into his stride."

"Meat Puppet, tool, dongler, John Thomas, dong, corie," called Larry.

"PENIS!" shouted Bishman, and the two of them roared so hard it ended the game. Tears were rolling down their cheeks. Bishman took a toke and handed the joint back. The distinctive smell of marijuana filled the cab.

Larry swerved hard to miss a Mercury Cougar with four yahoos in it, who pulled out just as he was about to overtake. He dropped a gear, wrestled with the big rig and got it under control.

He put his hand down toward his trouser fly and simulated that he was jerking off, then he spat a huge juicy groobly at the top of the windscreen, where it slowly dribbled down: it looked just like cum. They both laughed hysterically.

"Fucking jerk-off!" shouted Larry, but the drongo was half-way to Kansas.

Larry put on his sunglasses and said, "You look fuckin' tuckered out buckerroo, why don't you grab a few zzz's up in the bunk. I'll give you a shout when we pull into Pittsburgh, in time for dinner."

"You got that right, I think I'll take you up on the offer." Bishman slipped off his sneakers and climbed into the bunk. Before long he was running a film in his brain of air machines, young nubiles, gun collections and snuff movies, not necessarily in that order. Despite the Benzedrine, his consciousness soon clouded with sleep.

The trip to Pittsburgh was uneventful. Larry spent time on the CB catching up on a few tales and Bishman was in the land of sleeping serial killers.

"Hey buddy, you all right up there? You been snoring like a fuckin' cow for nearly six hours."

"Yeah, guess I'm OK, how we doing for Pittsburgh, I'm fucking hungry, I could eat a cow, ha ha ha." Bishman clambered out the bunk and back down into the cab. *Ouch!* He rubbed his right shoulder. *Fucking Roadblocker, they ought to call them Bonebreakers,* he thought. The scenery had changed and the sun was shining bright. Despite his shoulder, he felt good. Real good.

"We'll reach Pittsburgh in about twenty minutes, I wanted to see if you were still alive. Let's see what's on the news." Larry reached over and dialled in the radio; some pop music was coming to an end. It was Joni Mitchell singing *Big Yellow Taxi*.

"BZFN 108 brings you the latest news and weather update. Here's Michael Pizzinelli."

"Early this morning, drug-crazed hippies attacked and destroyed the multimillion dollar Skybo Castle at Fairfax Island belonging to billionaire publishing magnate. Mr. Leonard Prendegast, told us in an exclusive interview from his Monaco residence, that he hasn't been to Skybo Castle for some eighteen months now, but he had heard about the problems with the hippies on Fairfax Island. Some thirty people are feared dead. Damage is estimated at two hundred million dollars as fire and explosions ravaged the castle estate.

"The good news is that Mr. Prendegast is launching a new magazine, *Tycoon*, which will be hitting the news-stands in three weeks' time. *Tycoon* will be a skin magazine plus tips and features on making money. It will be in competition with *Playboy* and *Penthouse*. We have a full one-hour exclusive special report on the launch of *Tycoon* after the rest of the news and after these messages."

"Did you hear that?" growled the driver. "A fucking multibillionaire has an estate wiped out, thirty people killed and he's busy talking about launching a new magazine. Anyway it sounds all right, *Penthouse* and *Playboy* get a bit stale after a while and I've yet to meet anyone who actually reads them. This new magazine sounds as though it might be a good read as well - I mean, who isn't interested in pussy and money, ha ha ha." Larry passed Bishman a cigarette. Bishman took it and lit up. He made himself more comfortable, and yawned.

"Yep, it sure sounds OK," said Bishman as he massaged his shoulder, trying to appear not to be *too* interested.

"After lunch, where ya heading on to, buckerroo?"

"I've been thinking about that myself. I guess it'll be Los Angeles. I'm visualizing meeting a girl there. I'll probably stay there for quite a while."

"Good luck on getting a ride, buckerroo. I've enjoyed your company. You sure do tell the filthiest jokes I've ever heard, ha ha ha."

They pulled into Belinda's Truck Stop, where the waitresses all have big tits and where they serve the best fresh-brewed coffee, the most delicious roast beef and the tastiest apple pies in town, à la mode. No wonder all the truckies go there.

After the five-hour regression Bishman went from hypnotic state into deep sleep, too exhausted to move.

Saddened, sickened and enthralled, the time had finally come for Harvey to rid the earth of this *human garbage*. He whipped out his precision-made .38 Smith and Wesson, dexterously flicked open the chamber and removed five bullets. He spun the chamber, pointed it at Bishman's head and without hesitation or remorse pulled the trigger. *Click.*

Harvey unzipped his fly, got out his monstrous cock and started to jerk off. Again he spun the chamber and pointed at Bishman's face. He squeezed the trigger, *click,* he squeezed again, *click,* and again, *click.*

Although Harvey was hot and bothered, his face was red and he was nearly coming, he had a bead of cold sweat on his forehead. He kept pounding away with his giant prick. He spun the chamber again and fired point blank at Bishman's face. Again *click.* Harvey came, great gobs of steaming hot jism exploded all over Bishman's face and hair. Harvey pulled the trigger yet again, *click.*

Shit! Some people are just not meant to die!

FIVE

A yellow Rolls Royce pulled in to Buccaneer Street in Venice. The driver, Patrick Collinson, took out his small briefcase from the trunk, walked to the apartment door and rang the bell.

Julia Ablestein opened the door and let the stranger in. It was a big mistake; it could very well prove to be her last. As soon as Collinson was in he started feverishly ripping at her clothes. She giggled. He ripped harder as the flimsy material began to tear. She giggled some more.

Collinson slapped her hard around the face and dragged her into the bedroom. He threw her onto the bed and ripped her blouse clean off. She was red in the face but started to giggle again. For that she got slapped a lot harder this time. He ripped her skirt clean off. She fought and struggled and clawed.

He managed to rip her panties off, despite the fact she was bucking and humping and clawing like one possessed. She was unbelievably strong. Collinson fought, struggled and eventually overpowered and penetrated her. He pumped away and she still kept struggling. The more she fought the more excited he got and the more he pumped, but he was so excited he came quickly - but not before she had. She lay on the bed sobbing.

He went over to his briefcase and got out four police-issue handcuffs and before she knew it he had her handcuffed to the four-poster bed. Spread-eagled. He went down on her - she was soaking wet from both his come and hers. She came again, remarkably quickly, this time in violent spasms. Collinson fucked her again.

He went back to his briefcase and took out a roll of strong tape, the brown stuff used for sealing parcels. He took out a pair of scissors and cut a piece off, six inches in length. He sealed her mouth before she could say anything. She looked frightened as he pressed the tape down.

From the briefcase, he pulled out a video which he promptly inserted in the VCU. He then took out a vibrator, a stupendous one shaped like a huge dick. It was even *longer* and *bigger* than his own cock, which is saying something. He fitted new, heavy-duty batteries and inserted it into her vagina. He massaged it around and she was still dripping wet. He pushed it as far as it would go, then forced it another half an inch. Then he proceeded to tape it to her leg. He used two pieces of tape twelve inches long, and secured the cock-like vibrator firmly to both thighs, then he switched it on to maximum speed and taped the switch. It had an unusually powerful motor.

He then cut another piece of tape and sealed off one of her nostrils. She managed to keep breathing through the other nostril, although her breathing increased dramatically. The vibrator was making a humming noise, the batteries could probably last for hours. He played with her full breasts, licking, sucking and fondling them. Her breathing got deeper and deeper.

Collinson then cut another piece of tape and sealed her other nostril. Despite the fight she put up, writhing around on the bed with her arms and legs securely handcuffed and the weight of a fully-grown man laying naked on top of her, she couldn't protect herself, and he held her face and secured the tape. In no time at all she thought she would explode.

Her face grew crimson, and after about a minute and half she felt like passing out. He continued squeezing her breasts and viciously twisting her nipples, but she didn't have enough strength left to fight. Her eyes were wet and her makeup was running, but again she started thrashing around on the bed, the handcuffs tightening up on her wrists and ankles, the skin becoming raw in places. She was humming and squealing and 'mmmming' and squeaking, and making all sorts of frantic noises through her throat, intensely loud. Her chest was convulsing and she started throwing her head back and forth very quickly, thrashing and writhing, using up precious oxygen. Her face was now whiter than white and her chest and belly and pubic mound were heaving back and forth. Her eyes started to roll and move rapidly around in their sockets. The huge-cock shaped vibrator was humming away like a swarm of angry bees.

There was a sort of death rattle that comes when someone is dying: it is a gurgling sound that is caused by air passing through mucus in the lungs and air passages, and they both heard it. She started crying and 'mmmmmming' hysterically and gave a final heave, thrusting her orgasmic pussy in the air, shooting out white, creamy, sticky, steaming juices out, past the super-vibrator.

Collinson let her pass out. The phone rang once, then twice, then it stopped: not enough rings to activate the answering machine. Collinson was startled. *Whew!* He thought he heard a scratching noise at the front door. He cocked his ears. *I'm imagining things.* He pulled the tapes from her nose, and her lungs quickly filled with air, although her breathing was erratic to start with.

Her vaginal muscles were still twitching and slip-in-easy juices and creamy substances were literally jetting out of her, past the gigantic humming vibrator. Her eyes were still rolling in their sockets and her breathing was fast and furious as the color started to come back to her face.

He took from her crocodile-skin pocketbook the keys to the front door. Then he switched on the video, made sure that the pictures came on and the sound was working. Finally, he closed the door behind him without looking back.

Three hours and twenty minutes later the yellow Rolls Royce pulled back into the drive and Collinson unlocked the front door.

Julia Ablestein was still crying, her wrists and ankles were badly chafed, she was sweating profusely from all over her body and she'd lost weight. Her face was covered in runs of tears and mascara.

Collinson tugged at the tapes which had stuck firmly to her thighs, so he pulled them off really quickly. He knew that the slower you do it the greater the pain. He pulled out the vibrator. Her pussy was dripping wet and the bed was soaking. It looked like someone had spilled a gallon of wallpaper paste.

He switched the vibrator off and he stripped. He already had a mighty erection and he stuffed his huge pulsating cock into her and humped away for over an hour. She just lay there. He undid the two handcuffs that held her feet and she started to kick and buck with all her might; she started to fight like a wild cat, fiesty as hell. He viciously pounded and violently pumped her like a crazy man. Jism came flooding out of him in spasms. He lay on top of her for a while, absolutely exhausted.

The video came to an end. Collinson put it back in his briefcase along with the scissors, tape, the huge-dork shaped vibrator and the four pairs of handcuffs, and walked out.

"Bastard!" she wimpered, but he was gone.

Anita was doing a grand job filling in while Jai was on vacation. She knew intimately all the ins and outs of electronic transfers, various off-shore accounts, systems to check and how to organise the thousands of figures that Max had sent down for Harvey's information, from headquarters in Springfield.

On her fourth day in the office, she and Harvey were talking about the various electronic transfers and financial arrangements Anita was putting into place for him, having money whizzed all over the world into off-shore accounts - something he'd been meaning to do for years. All of a sudden he got a whiff of Anita's perfume, *Serendipity*, and felt the blood rush to his cock.

He had her sit on his lap and he started stroking her sheer stockinged thighs; he ran his hand over her pubic mound and he could feel the moisture seeping through her panties. He eased off her pantihose and they had a knee trembler, right there, standing in the middle of the floor of the conference room. It was heaven.

They were both startled at the same time. They heard someone in the reception room. With all the excitement of the quickie, they had forgotten that the outer office was unattended.

Anita pulled down her skirt and went out to see who it was. Harvey quickly grabbed her pantihose and stuffed it into his desk drawer, then quickly grabbed her panties from the floor and stuffed them into his pocket.

Just in the nick of time, too. Anita was already waltzing in two smart-looking guys who had come to talk to Harvey about word processors. Harvey had forgotten to look in the day-book. Quickies were more important.

The two salesmen sat themselves down. Typical salesmen, they wanted to talk. But they didn't want to listen to Harvey's particular and unique requirements. They blathered on and on and on. Between the two of them *they* nearly *hypnotized* Harvey.

Harvey got quite flustered and simultaneously had the urge to blow his nose and mop his forehead. You should have seen the look on the faces of those two salesmen when Harvey pulled out the frilliest, prettiest pair of black lace, crotchless panties that you ever did see. They didn't get the order, either.

During Bishman's hundreds of hours of hypnotic regressions he told Harvey literally thousands of stories - like when he was still a kid, Bishman's neighbor bought a brand new car. A lot of people in the neighborhood were envious. Young Bishman and company decided to teach him a lesson.

Every night Bishman and a few other drunken yahoos would syphon off gasoline from parked autos around the town and at about three in the morning they'd top the guy's tank up with gas.

For weeks he went around bragging that his new car was doing three or four hundred miles to the gallon, it nearly drove him nuts trying to puzzle it out.

Back in Bishman's early, heavy boozing, pill-popping days, he associated with all the town drunks. They'd regularly go on binges together.

One of the alkies, Doogie Helming, was a right asshole. He'd get drunk too quickly, he'd run out of money too quickly, he'd throw up too quickly, he'd attract the heat too quickly, he'd get everyone into trouble too quickly. He was a regular pain in the butt. He was plain bad news. Bishman and company decided to teach *him* a lesson.

Late one night, they were all as drunk as skunks, but as usual Helming was off the wall. They pulled up in their various cars at a coffee joint and started eating burgers and hotdogs.

Helming wanted to take a piss but was so far gone, he needed help. The gang saw their opportunity. Helming needed someone to unzip his fly and get his dick out. Bishman volunteered. Bishman fiddled around with Helming's zip, but he didn't undo it, instead he took a sausage from a hot dog and put Helming's hand around it. "OK big buddy, there ya' go, you can take your piss now," Bishman told him.

When Helming had finished pissing, he shrieked out: "Shit! Hey, you guys, my fuckin' cock's come off in my fuckin' hand and I can feel the warm blood trickling down the inside of my leg!" With that he passed out.

SIX

"**M**ax, it's Bill. I just had to talk someone. I'm at my wits' end, I really don't know what to do, ...I'm worried sick about Anita." Harvey's knuckles turned white as he gripped the telephone.

"You sound in a right panic, old buddy, slow down and tell me what the problem is," said Max in his most reassuring voice.

Harvey croaked: "It's Anita. She never turned up to work this week. She hasn't answered any of my calls. I've left hundreds of messages on her answering machine and I've driven over to Venice countless times - there's no sign of her or her Mercedes. I don't know whether I should call the police or what. She seems such a sensible girl, you know streetwise, that kind of thing, I can't imagine her getting into trouble. I'm sure she can take care of herself...but..."

"How long is it since you saw her last?" said Max, trying to coax and comfort at the same time.

"A week ago...I thought because you were old buddies she might have phoned you to say there was a problem between us, and she wanted time out from our relationship or something."

"Bill, she hasn't phoned here. The last time I spoke to her was way back when, at the party at Pinewood, and then it was only briefly. When you say she didn't turn up at work, is that your place or the bank?"

"No, the bank; she only had to do a week here, to fill in for Jai. She did a brilliant job, transferred money for me, set up off-shore accounts - you know, all the stuff I went over with you. That was her first week off from the bank in eight years. Then she went back to the bank, was there for one week and no-one's seen her since." Harvey paused, then continued: "And there's another strange thing. When I asked Anita to help me out in the office I was only half joking. I expected her to maybe help me in the evenings and at weekends, but she jumped at the chance when I mentioned Jai was taking a week off."

"In these cases it's always so hard to advise. She's a grown woman, quite entitled to take time out and piss off out of town for a few days, we've all done it. But then again there's so many whackos and wierdos in Los Angeles, I don't know what to think. You know what they say about L.A, don't you? When God made the world he shook it on the last day and all the loose bits fell into Los Angeles, ha ha ha." Max laughed. Harvey didn't.

"Well...I do have another problem. I've never really put two and two together until now, but Bishman has missed his last two appointments

269

as well. He's never done that before - he was going like clockwork."

"What!!..Shit!!...You don't suppose..."

Harvey cut him short. "Fuck me, mate, I hope not...I don't know, but I gotta tell you: on a number of occasions I've dropped Anita off in Venice, sometimes at three, four, five o'clock in the morning, gone for a walk along the beach on my own and who should appear? You got it in one...Bishman!...Outta' nowhere!"

It was hot and muggy and there had already been the usual smog warnings. Los Angeles was suffering one of its hottest summers for over a decade. It was stifling. LAPD Headquarters had already dealt with the usual suspicious persons, flashers, drunks, domestic disputes, muggings, murders, rapes, hit and runs, shootings, a freeway crash, and a SWAT team was just about to take out a guy who was holding three women hostage - and it wasn't quite eleven in the morning.

"Hernandez, you drive these two British police officers over to Pasadena, San Miguel Avenue. They have to ask a guy some questions. They know he always goes to this office address every Wednesday morning. They may bring him back for us to baby-sit, or if he doesn't object you can take them straight back to the airport. See what happens. And make sure all the paperwork is in order, no matter what you do." He handed Hernandez an untidy pile of documents.

"Yes, Sergeant." Hernandez took the Brits out to his car, a shabby Pontiac Bonneville. They were dressed in suits. They didn't really look like police officers - in a crowd, you'd never know.

One of the guys jumped in the front with Hernandez and the other clambered in the back, moving over some maps, magazines and empty soda and beer cans.

"San Miguel Avenue, Pasadena, right? We'll be there in under an hour, traffic permitting. Is this your first trip to the States?" The officers replied that it was, simultaneously, and they laughed. They introduced themselves and lit cigarettes.

"Who's this guy ya gotta pick up - pretty bad shit? I'm told. Anything exciting?" Hernandez looked in the rear mirror to draw Martinson into the conversation as well. It worked.

"Yeah, quite tasty. We reckon this fellow's been up to some pretty bad stuff. Right nasty bastard if you ask me. We've got to ask him some questions and tie up a few loose ends, but we're pretty sure it's him. If it is, we have an arrest warrant and we can take him back, providing he doesn't object. If he objects you guys get to retain him until we get an extradition order.

"We hope the bastard will come back with us. On the other hand if he doesn't, we get to spend some time in California, which isn't such a bad idea. Mind you, I don't know how you guys put up with this fuckin' heat." Martinson sat back and loosened his jacket. Then he took it off completely.

"Yeah, it's hot and the air conditioning in here's not working too good. If you roll your window up it may come on a bit better." Hernandez messed around with the control lever.

"Well, what kinda mess has this guy got himself into. Serial killer or something, isn't he? We've got plenty of those bastards here. I worked on the Charles Manson *and* the Hillside Strangler cases, way back when."

"Well, I reckon we're onto a winner. We've done our research pretty damn good and everything points to him being here every Wednesday morning. Killed a lot of people, by the looks of things. We've put together twelve cases that tie into his modus operandi and movements, and about another thirty possibles." Martinson stubbed out his cigarette and carried on.

"You've got your share of these guys over here, apparently - we've been reading up on them."

"You'd better believe it - some right crazies and weirdos," said Hernandez as he braked hard to avoid a dog.

"I think the heat does the dogs in too. That one didn't know whether he was coming or going, I bet he doesn't last the day if he carries on like that." Hernandez built up speed and fiddled with the air conditioning lever again.

"This guy we're after has been going for years and not left too many clues. The only way we tracked him down is because this little thirteen-year-old girl recently came out of a coma after eight years and gave us some clues.

"One of our chaps put two and two together, and dozens of unsolved murders have all started to fall into place. Came together like a cosmic jigsaw puzzle." Martinson brought both of his hands together and meshed the fingers like two cogs, as if to demonstrate the process. "Because of some of the nasty stuff this guy's been up to, the press has been calling him 'The Creep.' Been giving us a bad time for not bringing him in. Up until now we didn't have too much to go on.

"This little girl had his cock stuffed down her throat and it suffocated her. She passed out and he left her for dead. She went into a coma, which probably saved her life." Martinson sighed.

"Jeeeeez! The Creep. Sounds like a fucking weirdo." Hernandez took in a deep breath.

"Yeah the guy's been hard to track down because he's kept on the move all the time. He operated on a figure-of-eight circuit all over England," said Martinson wiping the sweat from his brow.

Hernandez swung into San Miguel Avenue and started to look out for numbers. "What number did you say? Oh here it is, I can see it on the left." He parked the Pontiac Bonneville.

There was a knock on the door of Harvey's office. He was meditating in a sort of funny way - he was glancing through *Tycoon* magazine, looking at some very seductive and voluptuous females in a number of extremely erotic poses. He quickly put the magazine under his desk.

"Yes, come in Jai."

"Bill, there are three gentlemen here to see you, they say they're from the police. They look rather official. Shall I show them in?" The three officers waited in the mock-Chippendale waiting room.

"Yes sure, take the rest of the day off and put the answering machine on - and lock the front door when you leave. I'm winding up here myself soon. Have a good one." No sooner had he finished speaking than Jai was showing in three suited gentlemen. They looked more like businessmen than police officers. One of them spoke:

"I'm Officer Hernandez from LAPD. These gentlemen are from England, I'll let them introduce themselves." The officer nodded to his two associates, who were holding out their identification.

"I'm Detective Sergeant Martinson; you are Bill Harvey also known as Dr. Bill, is that correct?" He offered Harvey his hand. Harvey shook it.

"Yes, I am," said Harvey.

"I'm Detective Sergeant Flashman, and we have to ask you some questions pertaining to your activities in the United Kingdom. Can we sit down? This will take quite bit of time."

"Yes, sure, why don't you draw up those three chairs from over there?" Harvey pointed to the chairs and the officers pulled them up in front of Harvey's husky walnut desk. They didn't notice the soft background music, it wasn't distracting at all. Baroque music, sixty beats a minute.

"Before we start, gentlemen, do I detect a Sunderland accent in you two gentlemen?" Harvey looked at the two Englishmen in a friendly, 'nice to hear another Brit' sort of way.

"Yes sir, you do, how did you pick that up? Most people get it muddled up with Newcastle or Liverpool."

"I've travelled all over England and America and studied phonetics." He nodded to the American cop, "I bet you're not from around here originally; I'd say that was a Boston accent." The cop nodded in agreement.

"There used to be a little pub we'd go to in Sunderland, the Jolly Wagoners. I bet it's still there. And when I used to live in Boston I used to go to Red Sox and Bruins games all the time." Harvey chose his words *carefully*. He paused briefly, to allow them to *assimilate* what they had just heard. He mentally whisked them from where they were to where he wanted them to be, then continued:

"Now look, before we start I'd like to make a statement." They hadn't noticed that Harvey had dropped his tonality and was speaking softly and quietly and deliberately, as he continued:

"You see, when I first came out to the States from England I had everything going very *comfortably*. Things were *easy*. I was extremely *relaxed*. The more *relaxed* I became the *easier* it was for me to be more *comfortable* and the more *comfortable* I became the more *relaxed* I became.

In actual fact I became so *relaxed* I felt *sleepy* most of the time, sometimes even *drowsy*."

He kept his tempo down, decidedly monotone, boring, almost hypnotic you might say; he never stopped the boring monologue but just kept going, very gently:

"Then I made myself *comfortable* by breathing *deeper,* and the *deeper* I breathed the more *relaxed* I became." The three guys just sat and gazed and listened and Harvey increased his breathing slowly but surely until he was breathing fairly heavily. His right hand wavered in front of him as though he had a slight tremor and the three cops were transfixed on this as they listened to his voice. Harvey turned up the music just slightly. He never stopped his boring monologue or his hand shaking, not for a single moment.

"Sometimes I even notice my eyes closing and I just let them. My eyes become *heavy* and I let my breathing get *deeper* and *deeper* and then my arms become *heavier* and *heavier*, and at the same time I notice my legs becoming *heavier* and *heavier*, and before I know where I am I've slipped into a wonderful deep state of *relaxation*. You can let yourself *relax* and you may drift off into a very pleasant state of *relaxation*."

Harvey increased the volume of the music. All the time just talking away, monotonic, and breathing heavily. He never altered his pitch, not once, not even for a few seconds; it was the most boring monologue he'd ever given in his entire life. And probably the most important.

"You can sit and look at the pictures in your mind, feel the emotions, hear the sounds and I'm just going to step out to the bathroom and..."

Very quietly he closed the door on the way out. He could hear them snoring through the closed door and half-way down the corridor. He didn't even look back.

The gnomes of Zurich supply discreet banking services and financial engineering for *all sorts* of interesting clients around the world, and up until recently they were pretty good at it.

The streets of Zurich are clean, not a candy wrapper in sight. Every building has its own bomb shelter fully equipped with six months rations of food, water and other necessities.

Today, like most days, the air was crisp and clean. You could see for miles.

Gerado Lererkramer walked into the main office on the fourth floor.

"I just got another fax through from the IRS in Los Angeles, sir. It's the second one we've had this week concerning a numbered account. Our client's name is Anita Broughton a.k.a. Rosie Future." The gnome slipped the fax onto his superior's desk, and stood back.

Grubach pushed his glasses up his nose. "Yes, I've already seen it. You can telephone Suzy in Los Angeles and give her the following information on that *confidential* numbered account." He almost sniggered when he said *confidential*, Lererkramer noticed, then he continued:

"During the period August 1982 to September 1990, we received total deposits of thirteen point seven million U.S dollars, which, at the customer's request, was converted to Japanese Yen and various other currencies. On the 19th of September 1990 we received a deposit of four point two million U.S. dollars. On 20th of September 1990 the account was closed and all funds were withdrawn. That is *all* you can tell her. Give her my regards and tell her she owes us one, and mention that everything worked out well for our mutual client, Mr. Joseph Goldstein." He handed some papers to Lererkramer.

Grubach puffed on his cigar, but it had gone out and it was leaving a stale taste in his mouth.

"For your information only, just out of interest, those funds were electronically transferred through Austria to Liechtenstein, then on to a numbered account in Jersey in the Channel Islands, the last four million dollars going to Moscow Narodny Bank, would you believe it or not?" He smiled and rubbed his hands together like a miser, and continued: "I'd also like to bet she hasn't had a day off in eight years. Most employees who embezzle are frightened someone will discover them the minute their back is turned and I bet that's what she's been up to, would you believe it or not?"

"Yes sir, I would believe it. One shrewd lady, that one. She made a good turn on her money, despite our astronomical charges and then disappeared without trace, just in the nick of time. Her alias...Rosie Future? Is that some kind of a joke, sir?"

The desk sergeant at LAPD headquarters was getting a little irritable. He'd had a particularly busy morning. The usual crap as far as he was concerned. Lots of 488s, a 261, a 415, three 11-54s, a 10-72 and some 10-57s. What had really been bugging him was the SWAT team and the hostage situation. It was still touch and go. Then there were phone calls, instructions, a veritable hive of activity best likened to a scene out of *Hill Street Blues*, only this was for real.

"Hey! Any of you guys seen or heard from Officer Hernandez? He's been gone for over three hours with those two English guys. He hasn't reported in to my knowledge, and even if he ran them to the Airport he'd be back by now."

"Perhaps he's showing them Hollywood Hills," wisecracked a rookie.

"OK smart ass, you can phone up the office in Pasadena and see if they've left and if not, why not," barked the desk Sergeant. "And move on it!"

"Yes, Sergeant. Consider it done." The rookie moved over to the phone and dialled.

"Sergeant, all I'm getting is an answering machine with some beautiful sounding dame telling me it's the International Organization of Hypnotherapy and for me to leave a message or contact I.O.H. headquarters, Springfield, Missouri."

"OK, I'll get one of our cars to drop in and take a look see. Why don't you go with Swartze?"

"Yes, Sergeant." The rookie looked around for Swartze, who was propping up a counter drinking coffee and stuffing his face with cinnamon-roll.

PRICKS is a leading tattoo parlour located on the fashionable Portobello Road in London. In the windows are cuttings of newspaper articles and stills from various television shows that Jacob Jacobson has appeared on. He doesn't make a fortune, but he sure makes a good living. He's achieved fame, and that was his main goal. Many famous people come here from all over the world, especially from New York City where tattooing has been illegal since 1961, banned on moral grounds.

Once inside the shop you cannot be anything other than impressed. The first thing you see is an impressive display of trophies, plaques and certificates of recognition, from all over the world. You know you have arrived in the emporium of an internationally recognized tattoo artist.

Neither can you help but be awe-struck by the three magnificent Harley Davidsons that are on display, beautifully decked out in chrome and polished aluminum, finished off with a specially designed, airbrushed paint job. On the middle Harley was sitting a skeleton flanked by two Hell's Angels in suits of armour.

Here is the man who can create an awful lot with a tiny needle and a few different colored inks. This is the man who offers psychedelic options, he will set you apart from the crowd.

A guy and a girl, both punk rockers, walked in. The girl had red hair, made up into about twenty twelve-inch-long spikes. She wore a low-cut top that showed ample boobs, covered in a mass of pretty freckles. The guy was completely bald and was immediately recognized by Jacobson.

"Hey Mungo, how ya doing? Outta nick, then. What's this - a new girl?"

"Yeah, been out nine mumfs now. This is Debbie. She's a Yank, I met her while hanging out on Chelsea Bridge."

"Good for you, mate. Are you just visiting or did you want a tattoo? You still do all that shit with the Road Rats?"

"Na, I'm frew with all that shit, we're punks now - fuck me, can't you tell?" He pointed at Debbie's hair, pulled on the ring in his nose and pointed to the rows of safety-pins in his ears.

"We want tattoos, right - and not the hunt scene with the fox disappearing up my arsehole." Debbie giggled, Mungo stubbed his cigarette on the floor.

Mungo looked at Debbie and grunted: "Gi'us a snout, or I'll chin ya!"

"There ya go, honey," said Debbie as she handed over a cigarette.

Jacobson couldn't help smiling, or for that matter staring at Debbie's boobs.

"Where are you from then, Debbie?" Jacobson sat back on his chair, trying to make conversation.

"I'm from America."

"I know *that*. Whereabouts?" Jacobson toyed with an electronic tattoo needle, playing variations on its unique buzzing noise.

"Oh, Brooklyn. You've heard of the Brooklyn Bridge right? Well I lived in Brooklyn. I got involved with some bad shit out at a place called Fairfax Island. I doubt you've heard of it. It's where all the rich people live. Anyway I wanted to get away from that shit so I came here. I got a 3,000 mile ride all the way from Groton to Liverpool in a Trident submarine. The crew were a lecherous lot, I've never been fucked so many times in all my life...I suppose that's what they call working your passage, ha ha ha...I met Mungo the first week I came down to London. Fuckin' good job too, ha ha ha."

"We know what we want, don't we luv? HIS and HERS right, got me?" Mungo laughed.

"His and hers what?" asked Jacobson.

"On 'er forehead you tattoo HIS and on my forehead you tattoo HERS. Got me?...HIS and HERS...got it? ha ha ha."

"Got it."

"No fuckin' pain, right, or I'll chin ya. Right?"

"Right," said Jacobson.

SEVEN

The Hotel Russell is not the best hotel in London, but it certainly has some great things going for it. It's got some seductively pleasant suites and its location is perfect for American tourists who want to see London: lots of handy restaurants, museums and galleries; within walking distance from the British Museum and the Holomart Exhibition of Holography and Tottenham Court Road. Only a subway ride to Madame Tussaud's, the Planetarium and the London Dungeon.

"What's that tune you've been humming all morning?" asked Anita as she started to undress.

Bishman lit a smoke and sipped his champagne. "Well, it's a bit screwed up. It started out as *The Night They Invented Champagne* and finished off as *I'm So in Love With You*."

They'd been for a short walk around the block thinking they might find a little restaurant that sold American-style breakfasts, but came back a little disappointed and decided to have a champagne breakfast of their own.

Anita took off her blouse and slipped off her skirt. She stood in her sexy black lace bra and panties - the ones that had made so much impact upon Harvey. There was a knock at the door. She covered herself up again with her bathrobe.

"Who is it?"

"Room service, ma'am."

"Come right in."

Anita got up and let the bellboy in. He was pushing a small chrome trolley, which he carefully unloaded.

"There you go, ma'am, flowers, chocolates and more champagne. I managed to get you *The Los Angeles Times*. It's yesterday's edition. I hope that's OK." He placed the champagne in an ice bucket, the bouquet flowers in a vase that he'd brought with him, and he laid the chocolates on the table.

"Fine, buddy." Bishman gave him a couple of pound coins. "There you go, honey, some presents for you," said Bishman, sucking on his cigarette as though it were oxygen.

"Thanks, hon, whatever made you get *The Los Angeles Times*?"

"I just wanted to see if Dr. Bill has missed his million bucks yet, and I wanted to catch up on what's happening back at home. Home away from home - I thought you'd like it. We'll look at that later...much later." Bishman sipped his champagne and unwrapped the large box of Milk Tray chocolates.

"I do like it. I like it lots and lots." Anita wrinkled her nose as champagne bubbles went up it. "Why did you pick this hotel, Bob? There's hundred of hotels in London, why this one? I mean there's nothing wrong with it, I quite like it, but I'm just curious."

"It was Dr. Bill. He talked about this place and I felt as though I knew it. I just wanted to check it out for myself. Nothing sinister, honest." He laughed, then Anita laughed.

"I knew the minute I met you we'd be soulmates." Anita squeezed his hand.

"Yeah, it's funny you know, the minute I met you, I knew you were a crook. A million bucks my ass, what are we going to do with a million bucks. Boogaloo!...Ha! Ha! Ha!" Bishman laughed heartily.

"All I want to do is have a blast, see the world, have a Rosie Future."

"Yeah, boogaloo, I'll drink to that." They clinked glasses.

"Whatever made you steal the million bucks in the first place, Anita? Dr. Bill must have done something pretty bad, huh?"

"The bastard nearly killed me. He went too far in one of our fantasies. Much too far, the bastard left a huge vibrator up me for about three hours, and left some video playing that was sickening. He really did some bad stuff. I truly believed I was about to die. I still wake up in cold sweats thinking about it. I thought I'd teach the bastard a lesson."

"Well, he wouldn't have killed you. Anyway, no matter what he *did* to you, it's not half as bad as what he *could* have done to you. Believe me."

"I believe you. What do you mean, he wouldn't have killed me. How do you know?"

"Let's just say you have a guardian angel looking out for you, who wouldn't have let any *real* harm come to you, and leave it at that!"

"Bob, two questions for you. Where do you want to go for the second leg of our honeymoon? And what do you want for your birthday?" She cuddled up to him and stroked him gently. Bishman put his head on her golden bush and caught the musky odor of her pussy and thought, *Aahh, the smell of success!*

Smiling, he replied: "Well, I was going to suggest Boise, Idaho but that's a private joke. I thought I'd leave our honeymoon up to you. We've got the money, we can go anywhere we want."

"You know what? I don't know why, but I always fancied taking a look at Scandinavia - you know, Norway, Sweden, Denmark. It's one place I've never been but they reckon it's good. Yourv sveng is borgen, ding a ding, inga ding." She giggled at her girlish attempt at Swedish.

"That's it then! Later today get the airline tickets. Let's go to Copenhagen, make reservations at the Hilton Hotel and let's live it up for a while. While you're doing that I think I'll go over to the Chelsea Bridge again. When we were strolling there the other day I'm sure I recognized someone, a blast from the past." Bishman hucked up a large grisly golly of brown phlegm, swallowed it and thought, *there's only one girl with huge boobs*

286

covered in freckles and if it is her...I have some unfinished business.

"Done! I'll get the flight tickets and book the hotel. What about the second question, your birthday?" said Anita, swallowing a large draft of bubbly at the same time.

"Well, I know what I want, but I don't know how you wrap it!" chuckled Bishman as he caressed her ample breasts and stroked her short, wavy, jet-black hair.

Anita sipped her champagne and paused before she spoke. "Here's a question for you. Do you think Bill ever suspected us? Do you think he knew we were lovers before he even came out to Los Angeles, or do you think he was totally oblivious to the whole affair."

"There's more to Dr. Bill than meets the eye," mused Bishman, "so you can never tell. If he knew, he never let on to me. I don't think he did. He always talked about you and had to leave messages for you, wherever we were. I think he genuinely loved you - in his own way. He was always making me jealous, but he never knew that.

"I decided I could afford to wait. I wanted you to get him out of your system properly and completely. And let's face it, it's more than served our purpose; he screwed you - but you more than screwed him! But I still say there's more to him than meets the eye. I can almost sense something familiar about him, like how we got on so well...even though he knew exactly all the bad shit I'd done. But I can't quite put my finger on what it is."

"So I don't suppose he even knows that I was the one who gave you all the cuttings from the business magazines in the first place and recommended that you seek him out for help, or the fact that you had keys to my apartment and used to come in for showers," said Anita.

"Well, if you didn't tell him, I certainly didn't tell him. He never helped me, anyway. He sure took me into hypnosis a lot, fed me a crock of shit sometimes and sure as hell got me to do some incredibly weird and wonderful things. We talked a lot. But as it happens, in the end, I sorted myself out. No more headaches or nightmares, no more depressions. And I got the girl!"

"Bill always said you'd say hypnosis hadn't helped. He was brilliant, you know, and I think he did help you. Let's face it, you were well screwed up and paranoid when we first met, a real chocolate mess. You're a lot more together than you were before he arrived - and no less sexy! Give him credit."

"All right, I concede...I used to be well fucked up, but I'm all right now." Bishman laughed...he could afford to!

Bishman went down on Anita and she on him, and he thought: *To hell with breakfast, fuck coffee and donuts, 69 is the breakfast of champions!*

"Leo, I have a call for you from Switzerland. Will you take it? The gentleman insists it's extremely important." Madelaine was in the office at the rear of the penthouse suite.

"Madelaine, I told you no calls. No calls!" Leo Prendegast was deep in thought, looking out of the fifth-floor apartment window overlooking the race track at Monaco. The Formula One cars were doing about a 160 mph, they were just a blur. He slid back one of the triple-glazed windows and for a brief moment took in the roar of the race cars.

In the harbor were the luxurious yachts of the rich and famous and the smaller sailboats of the not so rich and famous. Red and blue sails, white ones too, their owners eating caviar, drinking champagne, smoking cigars and watching the road action, all there to catch the rays and soak in the atmosphere.

Leo's apartment had thirty rooms, all with high ceilings, its own pool and completely white throughout: white walls, white carpet, white furniture, white soft furnishings tastefully outlined in gold leaf where appropriate. Everywhere there stood lavish crystal vases of red roses.

Leo let rip a raucous fart, as was his way. *Well at least that bit's still working*, he thought.

Marlene Friedeman, the interior designer from Manhattan, no less, had been called in to refurbish Leo Prendegast's Monaco apartment, now that he was spending more time there. She'd been responsible for the one hundred and thirty million dollar re-fit of the Aristotle Onassis yacht, the *JACKIE-O*. That was her claim to fame. Incidentally, the *JACKIE-O* used to be docked regularly in the number one berth in Monaco harbour when Ari was alive; Leo was a regular guest when they threw their extravagant parties - but that's another story.

Marlene Friedeman's budget for the Prendegast apartment was just a tad over eighty-five million dollars and she had done a stunning job. She had taken special care to get the lighting right, spending just under two million dollars on a selection of chandeliers and precisely-placed spotlights to highlight stunning paintings, sculptures, artefacts and other valuable antiques that she had especially imported from all over Europe.

Leo wasn't thinking about the decor. He was too busy contemplating the evening's entertainment: *What has the night in store for me?*

"Leo, I'm ever so sorry, this guy is quite insistent. He said to say his name was Dr. Bill."

"Put him on immediately, Madelaine. Why didn't you say it was Dr. Bill in the first place?" Leo picked up the phone and pressed a button.

"Hi, buddy! Good to hear you, a blast from the past."

"Hi, Leo, I take it you still have the anti-bugging device on this line? It's a safe line, Leo, right?"

"Sure it is, nothing changes around here, buddy. Just got the latest technology installed about three weeks ago, British stuff you know. Good to hear that voice, I saw your escapade in the press. Hypnotized three policemen for three hours.

My arse!" said Leo mimicking a British accent for the last sentence, just for fun.

"Yeah, I saw yours too, what a blast. By the way, I'm not Bill anymore, it's John."

"John, I like it! What's happening, John?" pressured Leo excitedly.

"Well, as you can imagine, I've changed my name and fingerprints, got that done in Brazil together with a little cosmetic face work, nose job, ears tucked. Those guys have a complete price list, it's like the menu in your Cadillac, fully comprehensive. Just painful for six weeks, that's all. Looks good and I feel good. Better than ever. Raring to go. Looking for some action. *Action, Leo!*"

"Look, there's so much happening it's unreal. I'm having lots of fun in Monaco, but in three days time I'm off to Denmark to shoot some movies, and some stills for the new magazine. My man over there, I think you may even know him, is a fellow countryman of yours, Jon Golding. I'm involved with him on the *Tycoon* magazine, which - as you've probably gathered - has gone through the roof."

"I'll say, how could anyone not notice with all the press and publicity? What a splash! The Skybo Castle affair must have been worth a fortune to you. Sounds to me your narrow escape from Skybo Castle was as close as mine from the Pasadena office," said John.

Leo broke in: "Yeah, I've always told you about back doors and escape plans. Well, I guess you must have taken some of it on board, you always were a bit slippery."

"I think you needed the action at Skybo to get *Tycoon* off the ground and probably stimulate other areas of your life at the same time."

"Yeah, we couldn't have had a better stunt if we'd planned it ourselves, and there are still some people who think I was behind the whole thing. But as you know, the actual facts are nothing further from the truth. The other thing, of course, it's got me out of the rut of going there every weekend. I'm even seeing a bit of the world these days. You still drive like a maniac? Do you still smoke the figure-of-eight in your Trans-Am, you crazy bastard?"

"Yes, I sure try to, as often as I can."

"Whaddaya doing in Switzerland, as if I can't guess already?" Leo prodded a huge cracked lobster that was on a white table full of other snacks and delicacies. There was an Uzi submachine gun on the table too, that looked quite out of place.

"I came to visit my money. There's plenty here, but I'm one point five million down, I know who got it, though I can't for the life of me figure out how she did it. She's one smart girl. She did a brilliant job of covering her tracks. I only discovered it accidentally."

"Still, buddy, no matter what she *did* to you, remember it's not half as bad as what she *could* have done to you. You'd better believe it."

"I believe it."

"You know what, old buddy, I've never forgotten what you did for me. I don't know if I ever told you all those years back, but those doctors had given me eighteen months to live, crazy bastards. They'd given me up for dead. I've had an extra twenty years because of you. There are no spots on my lungs at all. I have regular check-ups and I still smoke like a darn trooper. You're right you know. It's all in the mind. People have to be taught how to *visualize* themselves healed."

"You got that right. Our people who own the franchises know that and they do a damn good job. Now it's my turn to relax."

Leo suppressed a burp. "You know what. My fuckin' Gene Vincent tape got mangled up the other day, that's about the tenth one I've been through since you put me onto it. I must see if I can get *Be-Bop-a-Lula* on compact disc," said Leo, dunking a lobster tail into hot garlic butter sauce.

"You probably can, but I've got another one for you. It's called *Sweet Dreams Are Made of This* by a British group called the Eurythmics. It drives me wild, probably because it's got a special message. I suppose *Be-Bop-a-Lula* did, come to think of it."

"I'll get it. What about Denmark? You up for that?"

"You bet, when d'you say you'll be there?"

"This Thursday. I'll be staying in the Hilton in Copenhagen. Jon organized the complete top floor so there's plenty of room for us. Why don't you meet me there on Thursday?"

"Why don't I?"

"Good and don't forget..."

"I know...I know...it's my shout for dinner, right!"

"You got that right!" At that moment Leo Prendegast let rip a thundering fart; he covered the telephone mouthpiece and under his breath, said "It's still working." It was a wet one, so he wished it wasn't.

"What was that, Leo, I think the line's going funny on us. I didn't quite hear what you said?"

Leo chuckled, "It's the line, John, I didn't say anything." Leo changed track: "Did you here about the politician they recently found dead. He had a whole load of cornflakes wedged up his ass, - they're looking for a cereal killer! ha ha ha! - By the way, do you know how a syphon works?"

"What?" said John, unable to pick up the train of thought.

"Never mind, I'll tell you when I see you Thursday. You can fill me in on what on earth you did for six weeks recuperating, you must have been bored out of that tiny skull of yours?"

"I wasn't bored at all, Leo. In actual fact, I wrote a book. Pieced together some of my own experiences, some of other people's. All true, but the *really* gruesome bits will probably get edited by the publishers. *You* know what it's like. Still it kept me busy - I could manage to use a word processor despite having bandages on my fingers, which are still rather sore. I used thimbles, it made life interesting."

"All true my ass, I suppose you're still a world class liar!"

"I am Leo, you know I can't help myself. In writing the book, I found it even more difficult than usual to separate truth from fantasy, it all mingles into one, and I guess a few of my readers will have a problem with it too. The joke is, the chunks they think are flights of fancy and imagination running wild are probably true, and the sections that are realistic are probably fantasy. Life's like that."

Leo laughed, "I know it! By the way, how will I recognize you?"

"Don't worry about it, Leo. *I'll find you.* See you Thursday, Hilton, Copenhagen."

"What name are you booking in under, John?" enquired Leo.

"John Foster."

"I like it, John Foster, my ass!" chuckled Leo.

"Yes, John T. Foster."

Click. They hung up simultaneously.